P9-DNW-581

FIFTY STORIES
for 7
YEAR OLDS

This edition published in 1990 by Gallery Books,
an imprint of W.H. Smith Publishers, Inc.,
112 Madison Avenue, New York 10016.

Some of the material in this book is taken from
A Treasury of Animal Stories (1982), *My Favorite Goodnight Stories* (1986), and *The Hare and the Tortoise* (1986).

ISBN 0-8317-3277-6

Printed in Yugoslavia

Gallery Books are available for bulk purchase
for sales promotions use. For details write or
telephone the Manager of Special Sales,
W.H. Smith Publishers, Inc., 112 Madison Avenue,
New York, New York 10016. (212) 532-6600.

Edited by
Marie Greenwood

Illustrated by
Annabel Spenceley

GALLERY BOOKS
An Imprint of W. H. Smith Publishers Inc.
112 Madison Avenue
New York City 10016

ACKNOWLEDGMENTS

Stories retold from traditional sources that in this version are
© Grisewood & Dempsey Ltd are as follows:

The Little Mermaid; The Two Frogs; Sinbad and the Island-That-Never-Was; The Sun and the Wind; The King who Wanted to Touch the Moon; Old Sultan; Robin Hood Meets Friar Tuck; The Seven Foals; Golden Hairs and Golden Stars; Joseph and his Coat of Many Colours; The Coming of King Arthur; The Boy Who Cried Wolf; Clumsy Hans; The Necklace of Princess Fiorimonde; The Water of Life; Goat's Ears; Wuli Dad the Simple-Hearted; The Giant's Clever Wife; The Queen Bee; The Frog Princess; Jorinda and Joringel; are retold by Nora Clarke

Snow White and the Seven Dwarfs; Aladdin and the Wonderful Lamp; Puss-in-Boots; Brer Rabbit Gets Himself a House; The Black Bull of Norroway; The Dragon and the Monkey; Sleeping Beauty; The Fox and the Crow; The Little Jackal and the Crocodile; are retold by Linda Yeatman

The Giant with Three Golden Hairs and Kate Crackernuts
are retold by Marie Greenwood

Pygmalion's Statue is retold by Pamela Oldfield

The Publishers would like to thank Nora Clarke for her kind assistance
in the making of this book

For permission to include copyright material,
acknowledgment and thanks are due to the following:

Curtis Brown Associates, Ltd and the Canadian Publishers, McClelland and Stewart, Toronto,
for *The Rabbit Makes a Match* from
"More Glooscap Stories" © 1970 Kay Hill

The Beast with a Thousand Teeth and *Jack One-Step* is from "Fairy Tales" by Terry Jones. Copyright © 1982 by Terry Jones. Reprinted by permission of Schocken Books, published by Pantheon Books, a Division of Random House, Inc.

Aaron Judah for *Whose Shadow?* from "Tales of Teddy Bear"

The Pear Tree is from "The Kingdom Under the Sea and Other Stories" by Joan Aiken. Text Copyright © Joan Aiken, 1971. All rights reserved. Reprinted by permission of Viking Penguin, a division of Penguin Books U.S.A., Inc. and Brandt and Brandt Literary Agency, Canada

Blackie and Son Ltd for *The Clever Peasant Girl* from
"Salt and Gold" by Marie Burg

Judy Corbalis and Andre Deutsch Ltd for *The Wrestling Princess* from
"The Wrestling Princess and Other Stories," 1987 edition

Richard Hughes and Chatto & Windus for *The Elephant's Picnic* from
"Don't Blame Me and Other Stories"

Katharine Briggs and the University of Chicago for
The Tortoises' Picnic from "Folktales of England"

Century Hutchinson Ltd for *Little Old Mrs. Pepperpot* by Alf Prøysen
from "Little Old Mrs Pepperpot"

The Bodley Head for *Arion and the Dolphin* from
"To Read and to Tell" edited by Norah Montgomerie

Faber and Faber Ltd for *The Riddlemaster* from
"The Adventures of Polly and the Wolf" by Catherine Storr

CONTENTS

THE LITTLE MERMAID

Hans Andersen

Deep under the sea, colourful fishes glide among strange plants which wave gently to and fro in the crystal-clear water. In the deepest part which no human has ever visited, the mer-people live. The mer-king's palace has coral walls and a roof of oyster shells which open and close gently with the waves, each one hiding a gleaming pearl. Now the mer-king had six beautiful daughters but the youngest mermaid was the loveliest of all. Her eyes were deepest sea-blue, her skin like a rose petal and the scales on her mermaid tail shone like precious jewels.

The mermaids loved hearing about the world above the sea and their grandmother often told them about great ships, countries and people who lived there. The youngest mermaid time and time again asked her grandmother about trees, flowers and birds, which she called feathered fish.

"When you are fifteen," grandmother said, "you may swim to the top of the ocean and see these wonderful things for yourself."

The older mermaids came back and described what they had seen to her. How impatiently she waited for her fifteenth birthday.

At last the day arrived. She combed her long golden hair, she polished the scales on her tail, then waving to her sisters she put her arms together and glided, silently and gracefully, up, up through the waves.

When she lifted her head above the water, the clouds were rosy from the setting sun and the first stars twinkled in the sky. She saw a big sailing ship with a large anchor and chain holding it firmly in place. She noticed sailors lighting pretty lanterns along the deck. The mermaid swam swiftly to a porthole in the captain's cabin and when the waves lifted her up, she peeped inside. There were many fine gentlemen but the finest of all was a prince. He was laughing and shaking hands with everyone while soft music played. She had never seen anyone like him before. She could not keep her eyes away from him.

The sky darkened and the ship started to roll. The sailors heaved up the anchor and unfurled the sails to get away, for they saw now that a fierce storm was coming. They were too late. The waves grew mountainous, thunder rolled around and the ship was tossed up and then plunged down into the stormy seas. The mermaid loved this excitement for storms do not worry merpeople. Suddenly she heard a fearful crack. The ship's mast snapped and the ship rolled right over. The mermaid swam around broken planks when, in a flash of lightning, she saw that the ship was sinking. At first she felt happy for now the prince would sink to her father's palace.

"But humans can't live under the sea," she remembered. "I must save his life somehow." And she swam through the wreckage until she spied the prince, just as he was slipping beneath the waves. His eyes were closed for he had no strength left. He was drowning. Quickly, the mermaid seized his head and held it above water. Then she rested on a huge wave and let it carry her and the prince safely away from the wrecked ship.

When morning came the storm died away and the warm sun

appeared. The mermaid still held the prince but he did not move. She touched his face gently and kissed his cold lips. His eyes did not open. "Wake up, please don't die," she whispered.

Now she could see dry land ahead and, still clutching the prince, she swam into a pretty bay with calm clear water. There were flowers and trees growing everywhere and she saw feathered fish flying in the trees. Tenderly she laid the prince on the warm golden sand away from the waves. At that moment she saw some girls walking along the sands. Quickly she swam away. She covered herself with seaweed and hid behind some rocks and watched the prince anxiously. "Please wake up," she begged.

Soon one girl noticed him and called for help. He opened his eyes and smiled at the girl who had found him. As the prince was carried away the mermaid dived sadly into the waves and swam back to the mer-king's palace.

"What did you see? Did you enjoy yourself?" her sisters asked. She told them nothing but all day long she dreamed quietly by herself. At night she often swam to Prince Bay as she called it. She smelled the flowers and watched the birds but she never saw the prince there. She became sadder each time she swam back home.

The mermaid now had only one wish – to be a human. The world above the sea looked so interesting. She started to ask her grandmother many questions: "Do humans live for ever? Do they die like us?"

"They die," came the reply, "only human lives are shorter than ours. We live for three hundred years then we turn into foam upon the waves. Humans have souls that live for ever in the skies."

"Why can't I be like that?" sighed the mermaid. "I'd like to exchange my three hundred years for one day of human life. I'd rather live in the sky for ever than change into foam!"

"That's no way to speak," said her grandmother crossly.

"Can't I ever get this human immortal soul?" the mermaid asked over and over again until in the end her grandmother said: "There is only one way. If a man loved you more than anyone or anything else then his soul could run into you and you would be immortal. But this won't happen because humans say that our tails are ugly. They only like something they call 'legs'."

She glided away and the little mermaid looked sadly at her lovely tail. She couldn't forget the prince. Somehow she must become human. "I'll ask the sea-witch to help," she exclaimed. Off she swam to the whirlpool where the evil witch lived. The waters bubbled and hissed but she dived bravely through. There was dirty grey sand everywhere and a hut made from the bones of shipwrecked sailors. Grey slugs crawled around and in the middle sat a fearsome creature.

"So, mermaid," she cackled, "first, you want to lose your beautiful tail. Then you want the prince to love you and give you an immortal soul." She laughed so horribly that even the slugs scuttled away. "I'll mix something for you to drink when you've reached the shore. Your tail will shrink and divide into two funny things called legs. You will have a terrible pain like a knife cutting through you and this pain will never leave you. You will always be beautiful and you'll be the best dancer in the world but every step you take will be painful. I can only help you if you are willing to bear this fearful pain."

"I'll bear anything for the prince," the mermaid said bravely.

"There's something else," warned the witch, "once you've become a human you can never be a mermaid again. You can't return to your father's palace. If the prince doesn't love you, you cannot be immortal. You will turn into foam the day after he marries someone else."

The mermaid trembled. "I'll do it," she whispered.

"I haven't finished," the witch said. "In return for this drink I demand that you give me your voice, for it is the sweetest of all the mermaids. That shall be my payment."

"But how will I speak and charm the prince?" she asked.

"You're beautiful, you'll dance, you'll smile. Come, put out your tongue."

The little mermaid shivered but her mind was made up, so from that moment she could neither speak nor sing.

The witch scratched a few drops of blood from her scrawny arm, added snails and worms and poured everything into a pot. Groans, strange shapes and a horrible smell rose from the pot, then, when the liquid inside was clear, the witch handed it to her. She took it carefully and swam through the whirlpool. Behind her, she left the mer-king's palace, her beloved sisters and grandmother. Her heart was breaking but she blew kisses to them as she went up through the waves to the world.

She found the shore nearest to the prince's palace and as the sun was rising she drank the magic liquid. A pain worse than a thousand sharp cuts went through her and she fainted on the sand. She woke with a jump and the terrible pain came back. She groaned inside herself then she saw the prince of her dreams gazing down at her, greatly astonished. She looked away and at once she saw that her shimmering tail had gone. Her golden hair was now covering two long and graceful legs.

"Who are you? Where did you come from?" asked the prince, but she could only smile in reply. He took her by the hand towards his palace – but exactly as the witch had said, every step was like touching red-hot metal. She could not cry out, yet she walked so gracefully that everyone gazed at her as she passed by.

The prince ordered his servants to bring rich satin and silk dresses for her. Even though she could not speak, everyone thought her the loveliest girl in the palace. She heard many girls singing sweet songs to the prince who thanked them kindly. She felt sad because she used to sing far far better than any of these girls. Some other girls started to dance. The little mermaid shook out her long hair and moved across the floor. Her steps were perfect and her hands and arms moved gracefully to the music. The prince clapped and she danced on and on though terrible pains shot through her feet.

The prince loved the mermaid but he did not think of marrying her. "You are the sweetest girl I know," he often said. "You remind me of a maiden who saved my life when my ship was wrecked. I only saw her but once yet I cannot forget her. She is the only one I can truly love."

"He little knows that I carried him through the waves to the shore, that I saved his life," she sighed to herself.

One day the king ordered the prince to visit the faraway kingdom of an old friend who had one daughter.

"I must obey my father," he told the little mermaid, "but nobody can make me marry this princess. You are more like my lost love so if I must get married, I'll marry you." He kissed her gently and she was filled with happiness.

They sailed away with many courtiers to the distant land and when they had landed they were led towards the royal palace. Each day there were games and feasts but the princess did not appear. At last she walked shyly into the ballroom.

"What lovely dark eyes! What long eyelashes! Such beautiful hair," everyone gasped. So did the little mermaid.

"It is my true love," exclaimed the prince. "You're the one who saved my life, let us be married at once!" He kissed her hand.

"How happy I am," he said to the mermaid. "I know you will share my joy for I know that you love me truly."

The little mermaid's heart broke then. She smiled bravely but she wanted to die there and then even before the wedding day dawned. But the very next day church bells rang, trumpets sounded and fireworks went off as the prince and princess were married. The little mermaid held the bridal veil but she could not think of anything except her own death.

That night everyone went on board the prince's ship and soon there was dancing and soft music. The little mermaid danced more beautifully than ever. She forgot her fearful pain for she knew this was the last night she would see the prince. "I've borne all this terrible pain," she thought, "my voice was taken away, I've lost my dearest family, yet the prince will never know."

At midnight, the music stopped and the prince led his bride to a beautiful purple velvet tent on the top deck. All was silent yet the little mermaid stayed awake, waiting for the dawn. Suddenly she saw her sisters. They rose from the sea but why were they so pale? Where was their long golden hair?

"We gave our hair to the witch," they whispered, "to make her help you. We don't want you to die so this is what she says you must do. Take this dagger and before the sun rises you must plunge it deep into the prince's heart. When his blood pours out, your fishtail will return and you will turn into a mermaid again. You'll live for three hundred years! Remember, it is your life or his. Hurry! Kill him quickly. Do not see the sun or it will be too late." With this they sank beneath the waves.

The little mermaid crept inside the purple tent where the happy couple were sleeping peacefully. As she kissed the prince she held the dagger over his heart – then she hurled it far away into the sea. Flames spurted up where it landed. She looked once more at the prince then she dived into the sea where her body turned into white sparkling foam. She heard sweet music. She saw a thousand delicate shapes floating and singing around her. She saw that she was floating above the waves.

"Where am I going? Who are you?" she asked.

"We are daughters of the air," they sang. "Mermaids are given souls if a human loves them but we can only have one if we do good deeds for three hundred years. We are sorry for you, little mermaid, so we'll help you to get your soul."

She saw the prince searching for her. He gazed sadly over the sea as if he knew what had happened. Unseen, she kissed him and smiling sweetly, she rose into the golden clouds with the daughters of the air and she whispered joyfully: "In three hundred years, I shall join my prince again in Heaven."

THE TWO FROGS

Japanese Traditional

Many years ago there were two frogs who lived in faraway Japan. A cosy ditch in a seaside town called Osaka was home for one while the other lived in a stream which trickled through Kyoto. They were happy frogs. Then, curiously, at the same time they had the same idea. They decided to travel and look at the rest of the world.

"I'd like to see the Mikado's wonderful palace in Kyoto," croaked one.

"I've never seen the sea at Osaka," honked the other.

So early one morning both frogs set off. They travelled along the same road but one started from Osaka and the other from Kyoto. The road was long and dusty. Their legs grew tired and they had to leap into deep grass many times to rest and cool off. About halfway, each noticed a high mountain which they had to climb. Hop, hop they went, getting slower and slower until they reached the top. Croaking happily, both jumped into a cooling pond and almost crashed head on!

"I'm sorry," the first frog said politely, "I wasn't expecting company."

"Neither was I," said the other. "This is a pleasant surprise." Both washed off the dust then they hopped over to some cool damp shade under a stone and stretched out their weary legs.

"I've heard Kyoto has many wonderful palaces," began the first frog, "I'd like to see them and the rest of Japan too."

"I've never seen a ship and I'd love to see the beach and a whale and perhaps a shark," replied the second one.

"I don't care for whales or sharks," the first frog shuddered. "They're rather big, you see. Have you ever seen the Mikado?"

"No–o–o, not exactly," was the reply, "but I've seen his soldiers." They chatted about their homes and agreed that it was difficult to keep cool in the summer in either Osaka or Kyoto.

"This mountain is halfway between both towns," said the

Osaka frog thoughtfully. "It's so high that if we were taller we could see both places at once. Then we could decide whether we wanted to go on." His legs still ached from all that hopping up the mountain!

"What a good idea," replied the Kyoto frog. "I'll tell you what we'll do. We'll stand on our back legs and hold each other up, then we'll get a good view at the same time."

Both frogs jumped up. They stretched as high as they could on their back legs and clutched each other very tightly. The Kyoto frog looked over his new friend's shoulder towards Osaka. The Osaka frog looked over his friend's shoulder to Kyoto. But those silly frogs forgot that when they were standing up, their eyes were at the back of their head. You can check this for yourself!

"Dear, dear, Kyoto is exactly like Osaka," cried one. "What a waste of time my journey has been!"

"Osaka is the same as Kyoto," exclaimed the other. "I may as well have stayed at home!"

They dropped their front legs and down they fell, *ker-plop*. Both frogs bowed politely to each other and hopped back home.

The towns of Osaka and Kyoto are as different as chalk and cheese, but for the rest of their lives those frogs believed they were exactly the same. They never wanted to leave their comfortable damp little homes again – ever!

SINBAD AND THE ISLAND-THAT-NEVER-WAS

Arabian Nights

Sinbad's father was one of the richest merchants in Baghdad and when he died he left all his fortune to his son. However, Sinbad wasted most of the money and finally, realizing his stupidity, he bought with the money that was left silks and fine carpets. He went to sea with some merchants, hoping to sell the goods for profit in some far and distant land – and so his adventures on the sea began.

Sinbad sailed with the merchants from port to port. They sold their goods and then bought more things to sell later on.

One day the wind dropped so they could not sail. The ship rested near a small island which looked smooth and pleasant. Sinbad and the merchants decided to stretch their legs and take a walk. Some sailors began washing their clothes and some lit big fires while Sinbad walked along to the end of the island.

Suddenly the ground seemed to quiver and shake. The men left behind on the ship shouted loudly: "All aboard! Run for your lives. You're standing on a gigantic fish!"

That smooth island was not an island at all but was indeed a fish that had lived in peace and quiet for hundreds of years until sand had covered it and even some trees had grown on its back.

Well, some sailors swam to the ship, others raced up the landing planks because the poor fish had felt the heat from the fires and had dived suddenly to cool off. Sinbad was still standing there when everything moved under his feet and he fell into the sea. He grabbed a piece of firewood and struggled to stay above the waves.

The captain rescued everybody he could see then as a little breeze sprang up, the sails were hoisted and the ship sailed away.

Poor Sinbad was left all alone. He found a wooden washtub floating nearby which he managed to hold on to and he paddled furiously all night. Just as his arms were feeling really tired the waves carried him along to another land and threw him onto the

shore. He lay there thankful to be alive. Then he was so tired that he fell sound asleep.

The warm sunshine woke him up. He felt much better so he went to look for food and fresh water. He was very pleased to find a clear spring and some fruit trees so when he had washed, he picked some fruit and had a long cool drink.

A little later, he walked along the shore to see if he could find anyone. In the distance, he saw an animal and he was worried in case it was wild and savage. Carefully he crept closer and to his surprise, he saw a beautiful mare. It was quietly eating the grass and did not seem to see him. Then his foot hit a stone. The mare was startled and gave a loud neigh. Sinbad was startled too, especially when he heard a voice calling to him out of the ground. Then a man scrambled out of a cave and said:

"Who are you? Where have you come from?"

"I was washed overboard, from a fish's back."

Sinbad told him about the ship and the fish and when his story ended the man took him into the cave and gave him a good meal. Sinbad was grateful but puzzled. "Why are you living in this cave? Does that beautiful horse outside belong to you?" he asked.

"No, I am only the groom," was the reply. "I work for King Mahrajan and every year many grooms bring the king's best horses here because the grass is so good. Tomorrow we are going back to the city and we'll take you with us."

That night Sinbad slept in the groom's cave and next day the other grooms arrived with their horses. One of them lent him a fine horse for the trip back to the city where King Mahrajan lived. They took Sinbad to visit the king who listened carefully to his story. "I'm sorry now that I wasted my father's money but at least I'm alive and I will work hard for you," Sinbad promised the king. And he worked so well that he was put in charge of the docks, for this city was on the sea and many ships sailed in and out each day.

Sinbad longed to see his own city of Baghdad and one day he was standing on the dock when a ship arrived. Some merchants began to carry large boxes and bundles ashore and Sinbad was astonished to see his own name written on some of them.

He went to find the captain. He knew his face at once but the captain just looked at him and went on with his work.

"Captain," said Sinbad, "please tell me who owns these boxes."

"It's a sad tale," replied the captain, "they belong to a merchant called Sinbad. Alas, he was drowned on my last voyage and I'm hoping to sell these goods here and take the money back to his family."

"These bales and boxes belong to me," Sinbad said. "My named is indeed Sinbad and I sailed with you from Baghdad."

"What nonsense," the captain cried, "I saw Sinbad sink under the waves with my own eyes! You're just trying to get hold of this valuable cargo without paying. What a mean trick!" The captain was so angry and shouted so loudly that a crowd of sailors and merchants gathered and muttered angrily too.

"Please listen to me," begged Sinbad. And when he described the island-that-never-was everybody nodded. He could not have made that up, they thought.

At last the captain and sailors believed his story. "I know you now!" the captain said. "These are your goods. Please take them and do whatever you wish with them."

Sinbad looked carefully at his boxes and he found that not a single one was broken or missing. He opened one box and picked out two of the most valuable presents.

"Captain," he said, "please take this gift as a reward for your honesty and for looking after these things so well for me." He offered the second present to King Mahrajan.

"I am grateful for all your kindness, Sire," Sinbad said, "but I long to see my family again. Please allow me to return to Baghdad when the captain sets sail once more."

The king was pleased at this happy ending to a strange story and he gave Sinbad a much bigger present before he left.

Sinbad sold the rest of his goods in the market for plenty of gold and at last, he set sail for home in his old ship.

His family were overjoyed to see him again and Sinbad told them he wanted to buy a house with his money and settle down. He did not guess that there were many more adventures to come!

LITTLE OLD MRS PEPPERPOT

Alf Prøysen

There was once an old woman who went to bed at night as old women usually do, and in the morning she woke up as old women usually do. But on this particular morning she found herself shrunk to the size of a pepperpot, and old women don't usually do that. The odd thing was, her name really was Mrs Pepperpot.

"Well, as I'm now the size of a pepperpot, I shall have to make the best of it," she said to herself, for she had no one else to talk to; her husband was out in the fields and all her children were grown up and gone away.

Now she happened to have a great deal to do that day. First of all she had to clean the house, then there was all the washing which was lying in soak and waiting to be done, and lastly she had to make pancakes for supper.

"I must get out of bed somehow," she thought, and, taking hold of a corner of the eiderdown, she started rolling herself up in it. She rolled and rolled until the eiderdown was like a huge sausage, which fell softly on the floor. Mrs Pepperpot crawled out and she hadn't hurt herself a bit.

The first job was to clean the house, but that was quite easy;

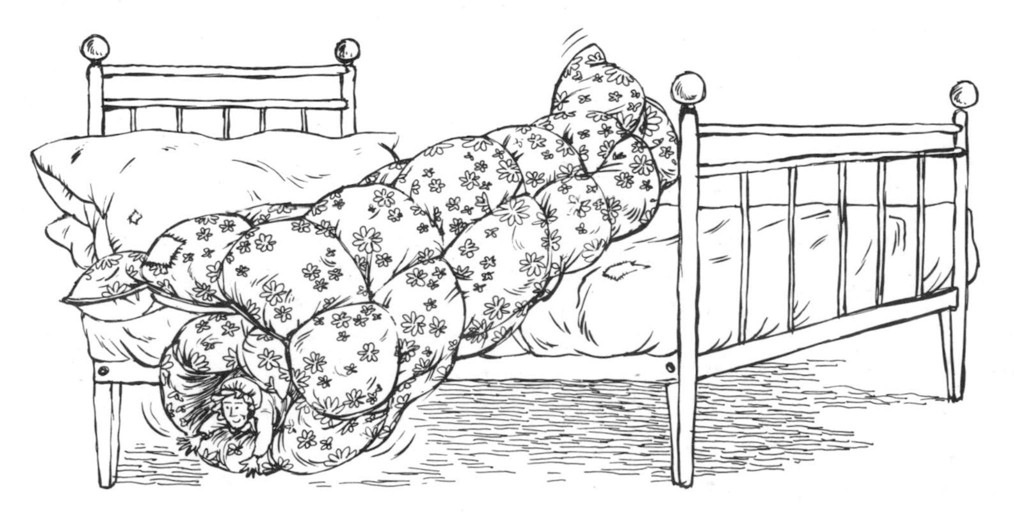

she just sat down in front of a mouse-hole and squeaked till the mouse came out.

"Clean the house from top to bottom," she said, "or I'll tell the cat about you." So the mouse cleaned the house from top to bottom.

Mrs Pepperpot called the cat: "Puss! Puss! Lick out all the plates and dishes or I'll tell the dog about you." And the cat licked all the plates and dishes clean.

Then the old woman called the dog. "Listen, dog; you make the bed and open the window and I'll give you a bone as a reward." So the dog did as he was told, and when he had finished he sat down on the front doorstep and waved his tail so hard he made the step shine like a mirror.

"You'll have to get the bone yourself," said Mrs Pepperpot, "I haven't time to wait on people." She pointed to the window-sill where a large bone lay.

After this she wanted to start her washing. She had put it to soak in the brook, but the brook was almost dry. So she sat down and started muttering in a discontented sort of way:

"I have lived a long time, but in all my born days I never saw the brook so dry. If we don't have a shower soon, I expect everyone will die of thirst." Over and over again she said it, all the time looking up at the sky.

At last the raincloud in the sky got so angry that it decided to drown the old woman altogether. But she crawled under a monk's-hood flower, where she stayed snug and warm while the rain

poured down and rinsed her clothes clean in the brook.

Now the old woman started muttering again: "I have lived a long time, but in all my born days I have never known such a feeble South Wind as we have had lately. I'm sure if the South Wind started blowing this minute it couldn't lift me off the ground, even though I am no bigger than a pepperpot."

The South Wind heard this and instantly came tearing along, but Mrs Pepperpot hid in an empty badger set, and from there she watched the South Wind blow all the clothes right up on to her clothes-line.

Again she started muttering: "I have lived a long time, but in all my born days I have never seen the sun give so little heat in the middle of the summer. It seems to have lost all its power, that's a fact."

When the sun heard this it turned scarlet with rage and sent down fiery rays to give the old woman sunstroke. But by this time she was safely back in her house, and was sailing about the sink in a saucer. Meanwhile the furious sun dried all the clothes on the line.

"Now for cooking the supper," said Mrs Pepperpot; "my husband will be back in an hour and, by hook or by crook, thirty pancakes must be ready on the table."

She had mixed the dough for the pancakes in a bowl the day before. Now she sat down beside the bowl and said: "I have always been fond of you, bowl, and I've told all the neighbours that there's not a bowl like you anywhere. I am sure, if you really wanted to, you could walk straight over to the cooking-stove and turn it on."

And the bowl went straight over to the stove and turned it on.

Then Mrs Pepperpot said: "I'll never forget the day I bought my frying-pan. There were lots of pans in the shop, but I said: 'If I can't have that pan hanging right over the shop assistant's head, I won't buy any pan at all. For that is the best pan in the whole world, and I'm sure if I were ever in trouble that pan could jump on to the stove by itself.'"

And there and then the frying-pan jumped on to the stove. And when it was hot enough, the bowl tilted itself to let the dough run on to the pan.

Then the old woman said: "I once read a fairy tale about a pancake which could roll along the road. It was the stupidest story that ever I read. But I'm sure the pancake on the pan could easily turn a somersault in the air if it really wanted to."

At this the pancake took a great leap from sheer pride and turned a somersault as Mrs Pepperpot had said. Not only one pancake, but *all* the pancakes did this, and the bowl went on tilting and the pan went on frying until, before the hour was up, there were thirty pancakes on the dish.

Then Mr Pepperpot came home. And, just as he opened the door, Mrs Pepperpot turned back to her usual size. So they sat down and ate their supper.

And the old woman said nothing about having been as small as a pepperpot, because old women don't usually talk about such things.

JACK ONE-STEP

Terry Jones

A boy named Jack was on his way to school, when he heard a tapping noise coming from an old log. He bent down and put his ear to the log. Sure enough, it sounded as if there was something inside it. And then he heard a tiny voice calling out: "Help! Please help!"

"Who's that?" asked Jack.

"Please," said the voice, "my name is Fairy One-Step, and I was sleeping in this old hollow log when it rolled over and trapped me inside."

"If you're a fairy," said Jack, "why don't you just do some magic and escape?"

There was a slight pause, and then Jack heard a little sigh and the voice said: "I wish I could, but I'm only a very small fairy and I can only do one spell."

So Jack turned the log over and, sure enough, a little creature the size of his big toe hopped out and gave him a bow.

"Thank you," said the fairy. "I would like to do something for you in return."

"Well," said Jack, "since you *are* a fairy, how about granting me three wishes?"

The fairy hung his head and replied: "I'm afraid I haven't the magic to do that – I'm only a very small fairy, you see, and I only have one spell."

"What is that?" asked Jack.

"I can grant you one step that will take you wherever you want to go," said the fairy.

"Would I be able to take one step from here to that tree over there?" asked Jack.

"Oh – farther than that!" said the fairy.

"Would I be able to take one step all the way home?" asked Jack.

"Farther, if you wanted," said the fairy.

"You mean I could take one step and get as far as London?" gasped Jack.

"You could take your one step right across the ocean, if you wanted – or even to the moon. Would you like that?"

"Yes, *please!*" said Jack.

So Fairy One-Step did the spell and Jack felt a sort of tingle go down his legs.

Then the fairy said: "Now *do* think carefully where you want to go."

"I will," said Jack. Then he thought for a bit, and asked: "If I have only one step, how do I get back again?"

Fairy One-Step went a little red and hung his head again and replied: "That's the snag. If *only* I wasn't such a small fairy." And with that he flew off, and Jack went on his way to school.

All that day he hardly listened to what his teacher said, he was so busy thinking of where he would like to step to.

"I'd like to go to Africa," he thought, "but how would I get back? I'd like to go to the North Pole, but I'd be stuck there . . ." And try as he might, he *couldn't* think of anywhere that he wouldn't want to get back from.

That night, he couldn't sleep for thinking but, the next morning, he leapt out of bed and said: "I know where I'll go!"

He went out of the house and said aloud: "I'll take my step to where the King of the Fairies lives." As soon as he'd said it, he felt a tingle down his legs, and he took a step and found himself rising into the air. Up and up he went, above the trees, higher and higher, and, when he looked back, his home was like a doll's house on the earth below, and he could see his mother waving frantically up at him. Jack waved back, but he felt his step taking him on and on, over hills and valleys and forests, and soon he found himself over the ocean, going so fast that the wind whistled past his ears. On and on he went, until in the distance he could see a land with high mountains that sparkled as if they were made of cut-glass. And he found himself coming down from the clouds . . . and down . . . until he landed in a green valley at the foot of the cut-glass mountains. And there on a hill up above him was a white castle with towers and turrets that reached up into the sky. From it he could hear strange music, and he knew that this must be the castle where the King of the Fairies lived.

There was a path leading up the hill to the castle, so he set off along it. Well, he hadn't gone more than a couple of steps when a cloud of smoke appeared in front of him. When it cleared away, he

found himself staring straight into the eyes of a huge dragon that was breathing fire out of its nostrils.

"Where do you think you're going?" asked the dragon.

"To see the King of the Fairies," replied Jack.

"Huh!" replied the dragon, and breathed a long jet of flame that set fire to a tree. "Go back where you came from."

"I can't," replied Jack. "I came by one magic step and I haven't got another."

"In that case," said the dragon, "I shall have to burn you up."

But Jack was too quick for him. He sprang behind the dragon's back, and the dragon span round so fast that it set fire to its own tail, and Jack left it trying to put out the flames by rolling in the grass.

Jack ran as hard as he could, right up to the door of the castle, and rang the great bell. Immediately the door flew open and an ogre with hair all over his face looked out and said: "You'd better go back where you came from or I'll cut you up into pieces and feed them to my dog."

"Please," said Jack, "I can't go back. I came by one magic step and I haven't got another. I've come to see the King of the Fairies."

"The King of the Fairies is too busy," said the ogre, and pulled out his sword that was six times as long as Jack himself. And the ogre held it over his head and was just about to bring it down, when Jack jumped up and pushed the ogre's beard up his nose. And the ogre gave a terrible sneeze and brought down his sword and cut off his own leg.

Jack dashed inside, and shut the door. The castle was very dark, but in the distance Jack could still hear the fairy music that he had heard before. So he crept through corridors and down passageways, expecting at any moment to meet another monster. He found himself walking past deep black holes in the wall, from which he could hear horrible grunts and the chink of chains, and he could smell brimstone and the stench of scaly animals. Sometimes he would come to deep chasms in the floor of the castle, and find himself looking down thousands of feet into seething waters below, and the only way across was a narrow bridge of brick no wider than his shoe. But he kept on towards the fairy music, and at length he saw a light at the end of the passage.

When he reached the door, he found himself standing in the great hall of the Fairy King. There were lights everywhere, and the walls were mirrors so that a thousand reflections greeted his gaze and he could not tell how large the hall really was. The fairies were all in the middle of a dance, but they stopped as soon as they saw him. The music ceased, and at the end of the hall sat the King of the Fairies himself. He was huge and had great bulging eyes and a fierce beard and a ring in his ear.

"Who is this?" he cried. "Who dares to interrupt our celebration?"

Jack felt very frightened, for he could feel the power of magic hovering in the air, and all those fairy eyes, wide and cold, staring at him.

"Please," said Jack, "I've come to complain."

"Complain!" roared the King of the Fairies, turning first blue and then green with rage. "*No one* dares to complain to the King of the Fairies!"

"Well," said Jack, as bravely as he could, trying to ignore all those glittering fairy eyes, "I think it's most unfair to leave Fairy

One-Step with only one spell – and that not a very good one."

"Fairy One-Step's only a very small fairy!" bellowed the King of the Fairies, and he stood up and he towered above all the other fairies. Then he held his hands in the air, and everything went deathly silent.

Jack felt even more frightened, but he stood there bravely and said: "You ought to be ashamed of yourself. Just because you're the biggest of the fairies, that's no reason to treat the small ones badly."

Well, the King of the Fairies went first green then purple then black with anger. But just then a little voice at Jack's elbow said: "He's right!" and Jack looked down and found Fairy One-Step standing by him.

Then another voice at the other end of the hall said: "That's true! Why should small fairies be worse off than big fairies?"

And suddenly another fairy said: "Why?" and soon all the fairies were shouting out: "Yes! *Why?*"

The King of the Fairies drew himself up, and looked fearfully angry and roared: "Because I'm more powerful than *any* of you!" and he raised his hands to cast a spell.

But the fairies called out: "But you're not more powerful than *all* of us!" and do you know what happened then? In a flash, all the other fairies disappeared and, before he could stop himself, the King of the Fairies had cast his spell right at his own reflection in one of the mirrors. The King of the Fairies shook and trembled, and first his beard fell off, then he shrank to half his size and fell on all fours and turned into a wild boar and went charging about the hall of mirrors.

Then the other fairies reappeared, and threw him out of the castle. And they made Fairy One-Step their king, and granted Jack one more magic step to take him home.

And that's just where he went.

SNOW WHITE AND THE SEVEN DWARFS

Grimm Brothers

One winter's day, when the snow was falling, a beautiful queen sat sewing by a window. As she looked out on to the white garden she saw a black raven, and while she looked at it she accidentally pricked her finger with the needle. When she saw the drop of blood she thought to herself, "How wonderful it would be if I could have a little girl whose skin was as white as the snow out there, her hair as black as the raven and her lips as red as this drop of blood."

Not long afterwards the queen had a baby daughter, and when she saw her jet black hair, snowy white skin and red red lips she remembered her wish and called her Snow White.

Snow White grew up to be a pretty child, but sadly, after a few years, her mother died and her father married again. The new queen, Snow White's stepmother, was a beautiful woman too, but she was very vain. More than anything else she wanted to be certain that she was the most beautiful woman in the world. She had a magic mirror, and she used to look at herself in it each day and say:

"Mirror, mirror on the wall,
Who is the fairest one of all?"

and the mirror would always reply,

"You, oh Queen, are the fairest one of all."

The queen would smile when she heard this for she knew the mirror never failed to speak the truth.

The years passed. Each year Snow White grew prettier and prettier, until one day, her stepmother looked in the magic mirror and said,

"Mirror, mirror on the wall,
Who is the fairest one of all?"

and the mirror replied,

"You, oh Queen, are fair, 'tis true,
But Snow White is fairer now than you."

The queen was angry and jealous. In a terrible rage she decided that Snow White should be killed.

She called for a hunter and told him to take Snow White far into the forest and to kill her there. In order to prove that Snow White was indeed dead, she commanded him to cut out Snow White's heart and bring it back to her. The hunter was very sad. Like everyone in the king's household he loved Snow White, but he knew he must obey his orders. He took her deep into the forest and, as he drew his knife, Snow White fell to her knees.

"Please spare my life," she begged. "Leave me here. I'll never return to the palace, I promise." The hunter agreed gladly. He was sure the queen would never know he had disobeyed her. He killed a young deer and cut out its heart and took this to the queen, pretending it was Snow White's heart.

Poor Snow White was tired, lonely and hungry in the forest. She wandered through the trees, hoping she would find enough berries and nuts to keep herself alive. Then she came to a clearing and found a little house. She thought it must be a woodman's cottage where she might be able to stay, so she knocked at the door. When there was no answer, she opened it and went inside.

There she saw a room all spick and span with a long table laid with seven places – seven knives and forks, seven wooden plates and drinking cups, and on the plates and in the cups were food and drink. Snow White was so hungry she could not bear to leave the food untouched so she took a little from each plate and each cup. She did not want to empty one person's plate and cup only.

Beyond the table were seven little beds all neatly made. She tried out some of them, and when she found one that was comfortable, she fell into a deep sleep, for she was exhausted by her long journey through the forest.

The cottage was the home of seven dwarfs. All day long they worked in a nearby mine digging diamonds from deep inside the mountain. When they returned home that evening, they were amazed to see that someone had been into their cottage and had taken some food and drink from each place at their table. They were also surprised to find their beds disturbed, until one dwarf called out that he had found a lovely girl asleep on his bed. The Seven Dwarfs gathered round her, holding their candles high, as

they marvelled at her beauty. But they decided to leave her sleeping for they were kind men.

The next morning Snow White awoke and met the dwarfs, and she told them her story. When she explained how she now had no home, the dwarfs immediately asked her whether she would like to stay with them.

"With all my heart, I'd love to do that," Snow White replied, happy that she now had a home, and she hoped she could be of help to these kind little people.

The dwarfs suspected that Snow White's stepmother, the wicked queen, had magic powers and they were worried that she would find out that Snow White had not been killed by the hunter. They warned Snow White that when she was alone all day she should be wary of strangers who might come to the cottage.

Back at the palace the queen welcomed the hunter when he returned with the deer's heart. She was happy that now she was once more the most beautiful woman in the world. As soon as she was alone, she looked in her magic mirror and said, confidently,

"Mirror, mirror on the wall,
Who is the fairest one of all?"

To her horror, the mirror replied,

"You, oh Queen, are fair, 'tis true,
But Snow White is fairer still than you."

The queen trembled with anger as she realized that the hunter had tricked her. She decided that she would now find Snow White and kill her herself.

The queen disguised herself as an old pedlar woman with a tray of ribbons and pretty things to sell and she set out into the forest. When she came to the dwarfs' cottage in the clearing, she knocked and smiled a wicked smile when she saw Snow White come to the door.

"Why, pretty maid," she said pleasantly, "won't you buy some of the wares I have to sell? Would you like some ribbons or buttons, some buckles, a new lacing for your dress perhaps?"

Snow White looked eagerly at the tray.

The queen could see that she was tempted by the pretty lacing and so she asked if she could help to tie it on for her. Then she pulled the lacing so tight that Snow White could not breathe, and fell to the floor, as if she were dead. The queen hurried back to her palace, sure that this time Snow White was really dead.

When the dwarfs came home that evening, they found Snow White lying on the floor, deathly pale and still. Horrified, they gathered around her. Then one of them spotted that she had a new lacing on her dress, and that it was tied very tightly. Quickly they cut it. Immediately Snow White began to breathe again and colour came back to her cheeks. All seven dwarfs heaved a tremendous sigh of relief as by now they loved her dearly. After this they begged Snow White to allow no strangers into the cottage while she was alone, and Snow White promised she would do as they said.

Once again in the palace the queen asked the mirror,

"Mirror, mirror on the wall,
Who is the fairest one of all?"

And the mirror replied,

"You, oh Queen, are fair, 'tis true,
But Snow White is fairer still than you."

The queen was speechless with rage. She realized that once more her plans to kill Snow White had failed. She made up her mind to try again, and this time she was determined to succeed.

She chose an apple with one rosy-red side and one yellow side. Carefully she inserted poison into the red part of the apple. Then, disguised as a peasant woman, she set out once more into the forest.

When she knocked at the cottage door, the queen was quick to explain she had not come to sell anything. She guessed that Snow White would have been warned not to buy from anybody who came by. She simply chatted to Snow White and as Snow White became more at ease she offered her an apple as a present. Snow White was tempted as the rosy apple looked delicious. But she refused, saying she had been told not to accept anything from strangers.

"Let me show you how harmless it is," said the disguised queen. "I will take a bite, and if I come to no harm, you will see it is safe for you too."

She knew the yellow side was not poisoned and took a bite from there. Thinking it harmless, Snow White stretched out her

hand for the apple and also took a bite, but from the rosy-red side.

At once Snow White was affected by the poison and fell down as though dead. That evening when the dwarfs returned they were quite unable to revive her. They turned her over to see if her dress had been laced too tightly. But they could find nothing different about her. They watched over her through the night, but when morning came she still lay without any sign of life, and they decided she must be dead. Weeping bitterly, they laid her in a coffin and placed a glass lid over the top so that all could admire her beauty, even though she was dead. Then they carried the coffin to the top of a hill where they took turns to stand guard over their beautiful Snow White.

The queen was delighted that day when she looked in her mirror and asked,

"Mirror, mirror on the wall,
Who is the fairest one of all?"

and the mirror replied,

"You, oh Queen, are the fairest one of all."

How cruelly she laughed when she heard those words.

Not long after this a prince came riding through the forest and came to the hill where Snow White lay in her glass-topped coffin. She looked so beautiful that he loved her at once and he asked the dwarfs if he might have the coffin and take it to his castle. The dwarfs would not allow him to do this, for they too loved Snow White. But they did agree to let the prince kiss her.

As the prince kissed Snow White gently, he moved her head. The piece of poisoned apple fell from her lips. She stirred and then she stretched a little. Slowly she came back to life. Snow White saw the handsome prince kneeling on the ground beside her, and fell in love with him straight away. The Seven Dwarfs were overjoyed to see her alive once more and in love with a prince, and they wished them a long and happy life together.

When the queen far away in the palace heard from the mirror,

"You, oh Queen, are fair, 'tis true,
But Snow White is fairer still than you."

she was furious that Snow White had escaped death once more. And now the king discovered what mischief she had been up to, and banished her from his land. No one ever saw her or her mirror again.

As for Snow White, she said farewell to her kind friends the dwarfs, and rode away on the back of the prince's horse. At his castle they were married and they both lived happily for ever afterwards.

THE SUN AND THE WIND

Aesop's Fables

One day long ago, the Sun and the North Wind were having a big argument.

"I'm much stronger than you are," puffed the Wind.

"Oh no you are not. I am far stronger," said the Sun.

This quarrel went on for months. In the end they made a bargain. The one who could make a man take off all his clothes must be the stronger and would be the winner. The North Wind tried first. It spotted a man walking along the road so it blew quite hard around him. The man buttoned up his coat so the wind blew harder still. This made the man put on his gloves, pull down his hat and hug his coat tightly around him. The wind blew until it was out of puff and could blow no more.

Now it was the Sun's turn. First it shone gently and the man took off his gloves and his hat. Next the Sun shone more brightly and the man removed his coat. The Sun went on shining and off came the man's sweater. There was not a cloud in the sky for the North Wind had blown them away and the Sun shone and shone.

The man's face turned bright red from the Sun's heat and with a sigh of relief he spotted a river across the fields. He rushed over, stripped off his clothes and plunged into the cooling water.

"Ha, ha. I've won," said the Sun. "My gentle rays were better and stronger than all your fierce huffing and puffing."

THE KING WHO WANTED TO TOUCH THE MOON

Caribbean Traditional

There was once a king who had only one idea in his head. He wanted to reach up and touch the moon. But how could he do this? He thought and he thought until he gave himself a headache. He stopped doing any of his royal work but spent all his time making plans. The palace looked most untidy and his crown stopped shining because the king could not bother with anything except his plans.

One day he sent for the royal carpenter and said: "I've thought of a good plan. I want you to build a tower right up into the sky. Make it really tall for me."

The carpenter was worried. A tower would need far more wood than he kept in the royal workshop but he did not dare to disobey the king's command. So he bustled about carrying his ruler, pencils and a drawing-board. He measured the ground and pretended he was making lots of plans.

Weeks went by. Nothing happened! The king became annoyed. "You have three days," he roared at the head carpenter, "if my tower isn't ready by then, I'll have your head chopped off."

The carpenter scurried around again. He carried his hammer and wondered what he could do. One day went by, then another and on the third day he went to the king with this idea.

"Your Majesty," he said, "I have thought about your tower. I've even dreamt about it and now I know what to do. Will you kindly order all your subjects to bring every wooden box or crate they have to the palace gardens. Then I'll have enough wood."

So the king sent his soldiers to collect every box in the kingdom. Some poor people had to empty their goods out on the floor! When they arrived, the head carpenter stood there busily giving his orders. "Pile them up, one atop the other," he shouted.

"That's not high enough," the king moaned. "We need more boxes. Chop down every tree, saw them into planks and make bigger boxes!"

Workmen banged and hammered until every plank had been made into a box and every box had been piled on the top of the tower.

It was a very tall tower indeed.

"I'd better climb up and test it, Your Majesty," the carpenter said.

"Certainly not!" the king spluttered, "I must take first place. Whoever heard of a carpenter climbing so high in the world!"

Then the king jumped on the first box and started his climb. He climbed and he climbed. He puffed and he panted until at last he reached the top box. He stretched out his hand to touch the moon but he could not quite get there.

"I only need to stretch a few more inches," he thought. So he shouted to the head carpenter far below: "Bring me one more box. And bring it quickly. I'm freezing here."

The carpenter made everyone search in their cupboards once again. There was not a single box or crate to be found. Even worse, there wasn't any wood to make any more boxes for every tree in every part of the country had been cut down already.

The king jumped up and down in his rage when the carpenter gave him this news.

"Send up the flagpoles from the palace roof, all the fishing-rods and soldiers' spears. If I tie them firmly together, I can climb them," the king bellowed.

The people looked doubtfully at

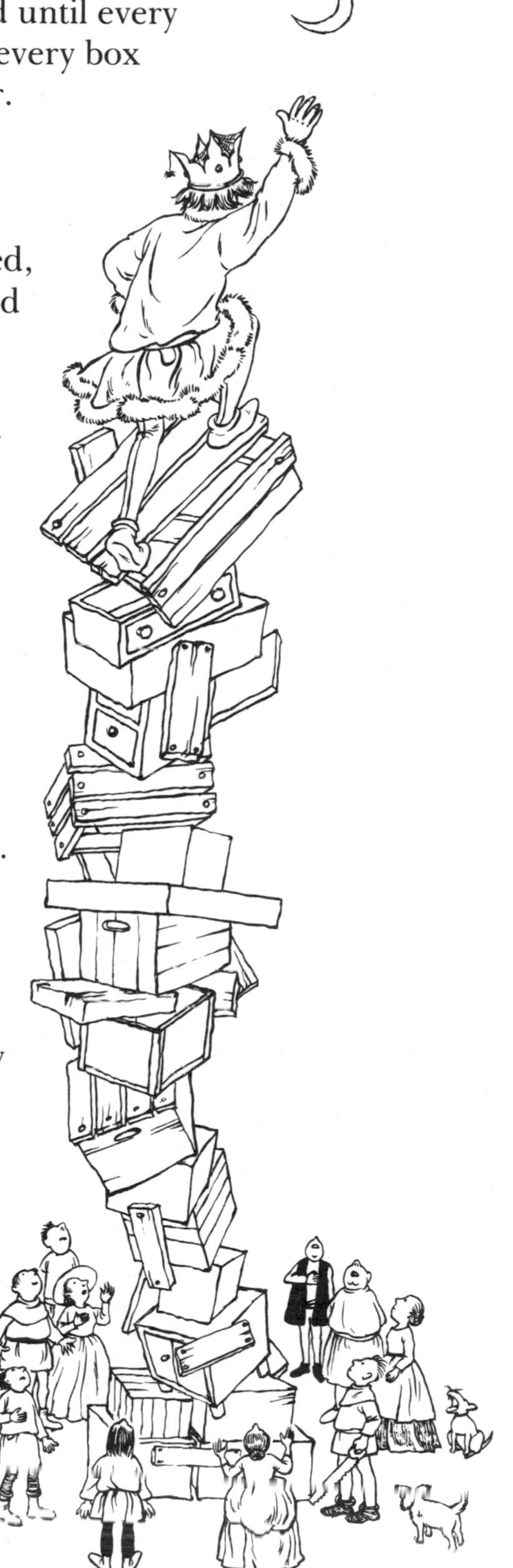

each other but they obeyed the king's orders. They collected a heap of poles and sticks and the carpenter tied them in bundles. But when he tried to hoist them aloft they slithered and slipped and the bundles all fell apart.

"I will not give up now," the king sighed, "so near and yet so far away. I must, I WILL touch the moon!"

Then a brilliant idea struck him.

"Bring me the large box from the bottom of the tower up here to me," he ordered.

"The first one?" everybody gasped in amazement. "You cannot mean the box on which all the other boxes are piled." They forgot to say 'Your Majesty' so upset were they.

"What other box can I mean, dolts," roared the king. "And if you don't hurry, I'll have your heads chopped off."

The head carpenter was very upset because he wanted to obey the king's orders. The soldiers, the workmen and the townspeople looked unhappy because they were willing to help the king to touch the moon if that was what he wanted but was this the right way? They muttered uneasily until another roar from the king made them look up.

"How many more times must I order you to bring that box up here. Hurry up, I say!" and he shook his royal fist.

His loyal subjects waited no longer. They pushed, they pulled and they tugged at the bottom box as the king had ordered.

First there was a creak, then a crack. The box popped out. Then with a mighty roar, the tower tumbled down and somewhere inside the thousands of boxes was the king! Was he ever found? Nobody knows, but everybody knows that he never ever did touch the moon.

A MAD TEA-PARTY

Lewis Carroll (from *Alice's Adventures in Wonderland*)

There was a table set out under a tree in front of the house, and the March Hare and the Hatter were having tea at it: a Dormouse was sitting between them, fast asleep, and the other two were using it as a cushion, resting their elbows on it, and talking over its head. "Very uncomfortable for the Dormouse," thought Alice; "only as it's asleep, I suppose it doesn't mind."

The table was a large one, but the three were all crowded together at one corner of it. "No room! No room!" they cried out when they saw Alice coming. "There's *plenty* of room!" said Alice indignantly, and she sat down in a large armchair at one end of the table.

"Have some wine," the March Hare said in an encouraging tone.

Alice looked all round the table, but there was nothing on it but tea. "I don't see any wine," she remarked.

"There isn't any," said the March Hare.

"Then it wasn't very civil of you to offer it," said Alice angrily.

"It wasn't very civil of you to sit down without being invited," said the March Hare.

"I didn't know it was *your* table," said Alice: "it's laid for a great many more than three."

"Your hair wants cutting," said the Hatter. He had been looking at Alice for some time with great curiosity, and this was his first speech.

"You should learn not to make personal remarks," Alice said with some severity: "it's very rude."

The Hatter opened his eyes very wide on hearing this; but all he *said* was "Why is a raven like a writing-desk?"

"Come, we shall have some fun now!" thought Alice. "I'm glad they've begun asking riddles – I believe I can guess that," she added aloud.

"Do you mean that you think you can find out the answer to it," said the March Hare.

"Exactly so," said Alice.

"Then you should say what you mean," the March Hare went on.

"I do," Alice hastily replied; "at least – at least I mean what I say – that's the same thing, you know."

"Not the same thing a bit!" said the Hatter. "Why, you might just as well say that 'I see what I eat' is the same thing as 'I eat what I see'!"

"You might just as well say," added the March Hare, "that 'I like what I get' is the same thing as 'I get what I like'!"

"You might just as well say," added the Dormouse, which seemed to be talking in its sleep, "that 'I breathe when I sleep' is the same thing as 'I sleep when I breathe'!"

"It *is* the same thing with you," said the Hatter, and here the conversation dropped, and the party sat silent for a minute, while Alice thought over all she could remember about ravens and writing-desks, which wasn't much.

The Hatter was the first to break the silence. "What day of the

month is it?" he said, turning to Alice: he had taken his watch out of his pocket, and was looking at it uneasily, shaking it every now and then, and holding it to his ear.

Alice considered a little, and then said, "The fourth."

"Two days wrong!" sighed the Hatter. "I told you butter wouldn't suit the works!" he added, looking angrily at the March Hare.

"It was the *best* butter," the March Hare meekly replied.

"Yes, but some crumbs must have got in as well," the Hatter grumbled: "you shouldn't have put it in with the bread knife."

The March Hare took the watch and looked at it gloomily; then he dipped it into his cup of tea, and looked at it again: but he could think of nothing better to say than his first remark, "It was the *best* butter, you know."

Alice had been looking over his shoulder with some curiosity. "What a funny watch!" she remarked. "It tells the day of the month, and doesn't tell what o'clock it is!"

"Why should it?" muttered the Hatter. "Does *your* watch tell you what year it is?"

"Of course not," Alice replied very readily: "but that's because

it stays the same year for such a long time together."

"Which is just the case with *mine*," said the Hatter.

Alice felt dreadfully puzzled. The Hatter's remark seemed to her to have no sort of meaning in it, and yet it was certainly English. "I don't quite understand you," she said, as politely as she could.

"The Dormouse is asleep again," said the Hatter, and he poured a little hot tea upon its nose.

The Dormouse shook its head impatiently, and said, without opening its eyes, "Of course, of course: just what I was going to remark myself."

"Have you guessed the riddle yet?" the Hatter said, turning to Alice again.

"No, I give it up," Alice replied. "What's the answer?"

"I haven't the slightest idea," said the Hatter.

"Nor I," said the March Hare.

Alice sighed wearily. "I think you might do something better with the time," she said, "than wasting it in asking riddles that have no answers."

"If you knew Time as well as I do," said the Hatter, "you wouldn't talk about wasting *it*. It's *him*."

"I don't know what you mean," said Alice.

"Of course you don't," the Hatter said, tossing his head contemptuously. "I dare say you never spoke to Time!"

"Perhaps not," Alice cautiously replied, "but I know I have to beat time when I learn music."

"Ah! That accounts for it," said the Hatter. "He won't stand beating. Now, if you only kept on good terms with him, he'd do almost anything you liked with the clock. For instance, suppose it were nine o'clock in the morning, just time to begin lessons: you'd only have to whisper a hint to Time, and round goes the clock in a twinkling! Half past one, time for dinner!"

("I only wish it was," the March Hare said to itself in a whisper.)

"That would be grand, certainly," said Alice thoughtfully; "but then – I shouldn't be hungry for it, you know."

"Not at first, perhaps," said the Hatter: "but you could keep it to half past one as long as you liked."

"Is that the way *you* manage?" Alice asked.

The Hatter shook his head mournfully. "Not I!" he replied. "We quarrelled last March – just before *he* went mad, you know – " (pointing with his teaspoon at the March Hare), " – it was at the great concert given by the Queen of Hearts, and I had to sing:

Twinkle, twinkle, little bat!
How I wonder what you're at!

You know the song, perhaps?"

"I've heard something like it," said Alice.

"It goes on, you know," the Hatter continued, "in this way:

Up above the world you fly,
Like a tea-tray in the sky
Twinkle, twinkle – "

Here the Dormouse shook itself and began singing in its sleep "*Twinkle, twinkle, twinkle, twinkle –* " and went on so long that they had to pinch it to make it stop.

"Well, I'd hardly finished the first verse," said the Hatter, "when the Queen bawled out, 'He's murdering the time! Off with his head!'"

"How dreadfully savage!" exclaimed Alice.

"And ever since that," the Hatter went on in a mournful tone, "he won't do a thing I ask! It's always six o'clock now."

A bright idea came into Alice's head. "Is that the reason so many tea-things are put out here?" she asked.

"Yes, that's it," said the Hatter with a sigh: "it's always tea-time, and we've no time to wash the things between whiles."

"Then you keep moving round, I suppose?" said Alice.

"Exactly so," said the Hatter: "as the things get used up."

"But what happens when you come to the beginning again?" Alice ventured to ask.

"Suppose we change the subject," the March Hare interrupted, yawning. "I'm getting tired of this. I vote the young lady tells us a story."

"I'm afraid I don't know one," said Alice, rather alarmed at the proposal.

"Then the Dormouse shall!" they both cried. "Wake up, Dormouse!" And they pinched it on both sides at once.

The Dormouse slowly opened its eyes. "I wasn't asleep," it said in a hoarse, feeble voice, "I heard every word you fellows were saying."

"Tell us a story!" said the March Hare.

"Yes, please do!" pleaded Alice.

"And be quick about it," added the Hatter, "or you'll be asleep again before it's done."

"Once upon a time there were three little sisters," the Dormouse began in a great hurry; "and their names were Elsie, Lacie, and Tillie; and they lived at the bottom of a well – "

"What did they live on?" said Alice, who always took a great interest in questions of eating and drinking.

"They lived on treacle," said the Dormouse, after thinking a minute or two.

"They couldn't have done that, you know," Alice gently remarked. "They'd have been ill."

"So they were," said the Dormouse; "*very* ill."

Alice tried a little to fancy to herself what such an extraordinary way of living would be like, but it puzzled her too much, so she went on: "But why did they live at the bottom of a well?"

"Take some more tea," the March Hare said to Alice, earnestly.

"I've had nothing yet," Alice replied in an offended tone: "so I can't take more."

"You mean you can't take *less*," said the Hatter: "it's very easy to take *more* than nothing."

"Nobody asked *your* opinion," said Alice.

"Who's making personal remarks now?" the Hatter asked triumphantly.

Alice did not quite know what to say to this: so she helped herself to some tea and bread-and-butter, and then turned to the Dormouse, and repeated her question. "Why did they live at the bottom of a well?"

The Dormouse again took a minute or two to think about it, and then said "It was a treacle-well."

"There's no such thing!" Alice was beginning very angrily, but the Hatter and the March Hare went "Sh! Sh!" and the Dormouse sulkily remarked "If you can't be civil, you'd better finish the story for yourself."

"No, please go on!" Alice said very humbly. "I won't interrupt you again. I dare say there may be *one*."

"One, indeed!" said the Dormouse indignantly. However, he consented to go on. "And so these three little sisters – they were learning to draw, you know – "

"What did they draw?" said Alice, quite forgetting her promise.

"Treacle," said the Dormouse, without considering at all, this time.

"I want a clean cup," interrupted the Hatter: "let's all move one place on."

He moved on as he spoke, and the Dormouse followed him: the March Hare moved into the Dormouse's place, and Alice rather unwillingly took the place of the March Hare. The Hatter was the only one who got any advantage from the change; and Alice was a good deal worse off than before, as the March Hare had just upset the milk jug into his plate.

Alice did not wish to offend the Dormouse again, so she began very cautiously: "But I don't understand. Where did they draw the treacle from?"

"You can draw water out of a water-well," said the Hatter; "so I should think you could draw treacle out of a treacle-well – eh, stupid?"

"But they were *in* the well," Alice said to the Dormouse, not choosing to notice this last remark.

"Of course they were," said the Dormouse: "well in."

This answer so confused poor Alice, that she let the Dormouse go on for some time without interrupting it.

"They were learning to draw," the Dormouse went on, yawning and rubbing its eyes, for it was getting very sleepy; "and they drew all manner of things – everything that begins with an M – "

"Why with an M?" said Alice.

"Why not?" said the March Hare.

Alice was silent.

The Dormouse had closed its eyes by this time, and was going off into a doze; but, on being pinched by the Hatter, it woke up again with a little shriek, and went on: " – that begins with an M, such as mousetraps, and the moon, and memory, and muchness – you know you say things are 'much of a muchness' – did you ever see such a thing as a drawing of a muchness?"

"Really, now you ask me," said Alice, very much confused, "I don't think – "

"Then you shouldn't talk," said the Hatter.

This piece of rudeness was more than Alice could bear: she got up in great disgust, and walked off: the Dormouse fell asleep instantly, and neither of the others took the least notice of her going, though she looked back once or twice, half hoping that they would call after her: the last time she saw them, they were trying to put the Dormouse into the teapot.

"At any rate I'll never go *there* again!" said Alice, as she picked her way through the wood. "It's the stupidest tea-party I ever was at in all my life!"

OLD SULTAN

Grimm Brothers

There was once a faithful sheepdog called Sultan who had grown old and lost all his teeth. One day Sultan's master stood outside his cottage with his wife and shook his head sadly.

"I'll have to shoot Old Sultan. He isn't any use anymore."

"Please don't shoot him, husband. He's been a good friend all these years. He can't live much longer so let's look after him."

"He's useless," said the shepherd crossly. He can't even round up the sheep. No, tomorrow he must go." Poor Sultan was lying on the step and overheard every word. He was terrified. To think he had only one day left to live! That evening he crept off to visit his friend the wolf in the nearby wood. "Unhappy me," he barked. "My master plans to shoot me tomorrow."

"Don't worry," growled the wolf, "this is what we must do. Your shepherd and his wife always take their little boy with them when they go up to the field. They leave him by the shady hedge while they get on with their work. I'll run out of this wood, snatch him up and run away with him. You must chase after me just as fast as you can. When I drop him, you must pick him up. After that, you gently carry him back and his parents will be certain you've rescued their child from a wicked wolf – me!"

"What a clever idea," Sultan woofed, "thank you, old friend."

Well, everything went as they had planned. The wolf ran away with the boy and while the shepherd and his wife screamed Sultan raced along and caught up with the wolf then carried the poor child back.

"You've saved my son's life," the shepherd said, patting Sultan's head. "Your life must be spared. Go home, dear wife, and prepare a good dinner for this faithful friend and give him my soft blanket too." From that day, Sultan lived very comfortably indeed.

Soon afterwards, the wolf visited Sultan. "I have a favour to ask. I'd like you to turn your head the other way whenever I want to enjoy eating one of the shepherd's fine lambs."

"I couldn't do that," replied Sultan, "my master trusts me." The wolf didn't believe Sultan but when he sneaked in to steal a lamb, the shepherd was waiting with a heavy stick to chase him away. Sultan had told him about the wolf's plans in good time.

The wolf was furious. He promised to be revenged so he sent a huge boar to challenge Sultan to a fight. Sultan asked the shepherd's three-legged cat to go with him but the poor creature walked so awkwardly that her tail stuck straight up into the air.

When the wolf and the boar saw their enemy approaching through the grass, they saw the cat's tail sticking straight up and they were sure it was a mighty sword for Sultan to use. Then when the poor cat bobbed unevenly on her three legs, they thought she was picking up stones to hurl at them.

"Swords, stones. We can't fight like that," they whispered, so the wolf leapt up a tree and the boar hid behind a bush.

"Where have they gone?" asked Sultan.

"I don't know," replied the cat, "but I think I have spotted a mouse." And she pounced! Oh dear, the boar's ears were sticking up above his hiding place. When he twitched one of them, the cat scratched and tried to drag it out. The boar grunted in pain and sprang up. "There's the one you should be biting," he roared. They looked up and sure enough, they spotted the wolf.

"Scared of an old dog and a three-legged cat, are you?" they laughed. Shamefaced, the wolf crept down. He shook Sultan's paw and promised to be his good friend from then on.

THE GIANT WITH THREE GOLDEN HAIRS

Grimm Brothers

There was once a poor man whose only son was born under a lucky star – people said that the child would be blessed with good fortune and that he would grow up to be a wealthy man and would marry the sweetest, gentlest girl in the whole land.

Now the king of this land had a daughter who was not only beautiful but was also good and kind. Years passed, and the time came for the princess to be married. The king gave out a proclamation that said: "Any man who can descend into the wonderful cave and bring me three golden hairs from the head of the giant who lives there shall have my daughter's hand in marriage."

Princes and noblemen came from all over to try to win her hand, but they had little success.

Meanwhile the poor man's son had grown into a fine young man. One day, he happened to see the sweet princess as she passed by in her carriage and fell instantly in love with her. He decided to try for her hand and went at once to the king's palace.

The king was alarmed when he saw such a poor lad trying to win his daughter, but he said reluctantly: "Well, no one else has been successful, so you may as well try." Though he secretly hoped that the boy would fail.

So the young man set off on his journey to the wonderful cave. At the first city he came to, the guard of the gates into the city stopped him and asked: "Be so good as to tell us why our fountain in the market-place is dry and will give no water, and we will reward you with gold." The young man promised he would on his return from the wonderful cave.

He came to a great kingdom and there the guard asked him: "Tell us why a tree which used to bear us golden apples, does not even produce a leaf and we will reward you with silver." The youth promised he would on his return.

The young man walked on until he came to a great lake which

he knew he must cross. A ferryman agreed to take him and said: "Please tell me why I am bound forever to ferry people over this water and can never have my liberty, and I will reward you well." Again, the boy promised that he would on his return.

When he had crossed the lake he came at last to the wonderful cave, which looked dark and gloomy and full of foreboding. The brave lad was not to be deterred, however, and went boldly towards the cave. An old woman was sitting in a rocking chair at the entrance.

"What do you seek?" she said.

"Three golden hairs from the giant's head," came the quick reply.

"It will be difficult, but I can see you are a man blessed with a lucky star. I am the giant's grandmother and I will help you."

"I also need to know why the city fountain is dry, why the tree that bore golden apples is now without leaves, and why the ferryman cannot leave his position," the young man added hurriedly.

"These are puzzling questions, but listen to what the giant says when he returns to the cave." With that the old woman swiftly changed him into an ant and hid him in the folds of her dress.

Nightfall came and the giant returned home.

"I can smell man's flesh," he boomed. He searched around the cave in vain. Finally, he laid his head on his grandmother's lap and fell asleep. The old woman waited until he began to snore deeply, then she seized one of his golden hairs and pulled it out. Instantly, the giant woke up and cried out: "Good grief! What are you doing woman?"

"I'm sorry," the grandmother replied, "I had a strange dream: I dreamed that the fountain in the market-place of a city had dried up and would give no water. What could cause this?"

"That's easy," snorted the giant, "under a stone in the fountain sits a toad; if he is killed, the water will flow again." With that the giant promptly fell asleep.

The grandmother pulled out another golden hair. "Ouch!" screeched the giant.

"Oh, I'm sorry dear, but I had another strange dream," said the crafty old lady. "This time I was in a great kingdom and there

was a beautiful tree that used to bear golden apples that now could not even produce a leaf. What could cause this?"

"Must you keep bothering me? At the root of the tree a mouse is gnawing. If this mouse is killed, the tree will bear golden apples again. Now, let me sleep."

The grandmother waited until he was snoring loudly again, then quickly pulled out the third golden hair. At this the giant jumped up and bellowed at the old woman.

"Sorry, sorry!" she cried. "But I had such a strange dream – I saw a ferryman who was fated to go back and forth over a lake and could never be given his liberty. How can he escape?"

To this the giant replied crossly, "If he were to give the rudder to another passenger, he would be free, and the passenger would have to take his place." With this, the giant fell asleep.

The giant went out again early next morning. His grandmother turned the ant back into the young man and gave to him the three golden hairs and told him to be on his way. The young lad joyfully thanked the lady for all her help and ran quickly away.

He soon came to the ferryman who agreed to take him across the lake. As the young man got out of the boat he said: "Give your rudder to any passenger and then run away and you will be free." The ferryman thanked him and the young man went on his way.

He came next to the great kingdom with the barren tree. He said to the guard: "Kill the mouse that gnaws the root of the tree and the golden apples will grow again." The guard thanked him and rewarded him with silver.

The young man then came to the city with the dried-up fountain. He said to the guard there: "Kill the toad that sits under a stone in the fountain, and water will flow." The guard thanked him happily and the boy was rewarded with gold.

At last this child of fortune reached the king's palace and presented the three golden hairs on a velvet cushion to the king. The king was dismayed to see that the youth had fulfilled the task. "This is all very well," he said, "but I'm afraid you are not good enough for my daughter – you are too poor. You cannot marry her."

The young man cried out in anger at the king and then showed him all the gold and silver he had earned on his journey. "See, Sir, I am not as poor as you may think, and after all, you did give your word."

At the sight of all these riches the greedy king demanded to know where he had found them.

"On the side of a great lake, Sir," said the youth quickly. "If you ask the ferryman to take you across, you will see mountains of gold and silver on the other side."

The king didn't wait to hear any more, he rushed off to the great lake and got into the boat with the ferryman, who quickly gave him the rudder and sprang ashore, leaving the king to ferry back and forth for evermore.

Meanwhile, the sweet princess readily agreed to marry the young man and they lived in peace and happiness for the rest of their lives.

THE SEVEN FAMILIES OF LAKE PIPPLE-POPPLE

Edward Lear

In former days – that is to say, once upon a time, there lived in the Land of Gramblamble, Seven Families. They lived by the side of the great Lake Pipple-Popple (one of the Seven Families, indeed, lived *in* the Lake), and on the outskirts of the City of Tosh, which, excepting when it was quite dark, they could see plainly. The names of all these places you have probably heard of, and you have only not to look in your Geography books to find out all about them.

Now the Seven Families who lived on the borders of the great Lake Pipple-Popple were as follows. There was a family of Two old Parrots and Seven young Parrots. There was a Family of Two old Storks and Seven young Storks. There was a Family of Two old Geese and Seven young Geese. There was a Family of Two old Owls and Seven young Owls. There was a Family of Two old Guinea Pigs and Seven young Guinea Pigs. There was a Family of Two old Cats and Seven young Cats. And there was a Family of Two old Fishes and Seven young Fishes.

The Parrots lived upon the Soffsky-Poffsky trees – which were beautiful to behold, and covered with blue leaves – and they fed upon fruit, artichokes, and striped beetles.

The Storks walked in and out of the Lake Pipple-Popple and ate frogs for breakfast and buttered toast for tea; but on account of the extreme length of their legs, they could not sit down, so they walked about continually.

The Geese, having webs to their feet, caught quantities of flies, which they ate for dinner.

The Owls anxiously looked after mice, which they caught and made into sago puddings.

The Guinea Pigs toddled about the gardens, and ate lettuces and Cheshire cheese.

The Cats sat still in the sunshine, and fed upon sponge biscuits.

The Fishes lived in the Lake, and fed on periwinkles.

And all these Seven Families lived together in the utmost fun and felicity.

One day all the Seven Fathers and the Seven Mothers of the Seven Families agreed that they would send their children out to see the world.

So they called them all together, and gave them each eight shillings and some good advice, some chocolate drops, and a small green morocco pocket-book to set down their expenses in. They then particularly entreated them not to quarrel, and all the parents sent off their children with a parting injunction.

"If," said the old Parrots, "you find a Cherry, do not fight about who shall have it."

"And," said the old Storks, "if you find a Frog, divide it carefully into seven bits, and on no account quarrel about it."

And the old Geese said to the Seven young Geese, "Whatever you do, be sure you do not touch a Plum-pudding Flea."

And the old Owls said, "If you find a Mouse, tear him up into seven slices, and eat him cheerfully, but without quarrelling."

And the old Guinea Pigs said, "Have a care that you eat your Lettuces, should you find any, not greedily but calmly."

And the old Cats said, "Be particularly careful not to meddle with a Clangle-Wangle, if you should see one."

And the old Fishes said, "Above all things avoid eating a blue Boss-Woss, for they do not agree with fishes, and give them a pain in their toes."

So all the Children of each Family thanked their parents, and making forty-nine polite bows, they went into the wide world.

The Seven young Parrots had not gone far, when they saw a tree with a single Cherry on it, which the oldest Parrot picked instantly, but the other six being extremely hungry, tried to get it also. On which all the Seven began to fight, and they scuffled, and huffled, and ruffled, and shuffled, and puffled, and muffled, and buffled, and duffled, and fluffled, and guffled, and bruffled, and screamed, and shrieked, and squealed and squeaked, and clawed, and snapped, and bit, and bumped, and thumped, and dumped, and flumped each other, till they were all torn into little bits, and at last there was nothing left to record this painful

incident, except the Cherry and seven small green feathers.

And that was the vicious and voluble end of the Seven young Parrots.

When the Seven young Storks set out, they walked or flew for fourteen weeks in a straight line, and for six weeks more in a crooked one; and after that they ran as hard as they could for one hundred and eight miles; and after that they stood still and made a himmeltanious chatter-clatter-blattery noise with their bills.

About the same time they perceived a large Frog, spotted with green, and with a sky-blue stripe under each ear. So being hungry, they immediately flew at him and were going to divide him into seven pieces, when they began to quarrel as to which of his legs should be taken off first. One said this, and another said that, and while they were all quarrelling the Frog hopped away. And when they saw that he was gone, they began to chatter-clatter, blatter-platter, patter-blatter, matter-clatter, flatter-quatter, more violently than ever.

And after they had fought for a week they pecked each other

to little pieces, so that at last nothing was left of any of them except their bills.

And that was the end of the Seven young Storks.

When the Seven young Geese began to travel, they went over a large plain, on which there was but one tree, and that was a very bad one. So four of them went up to the top of it, and looked about them, while the other three waddled up and down, and repeated poetry, and their last six lessons in Arithmetic, Geography and Cookery.

Presently they perceived, a long way off, an object of the most interesting and obese appearance, having a perfectly round body, exactly resembling a plum-pudding, with two little wings and a beak, three feathers growing out of his head and only one leg.

So after a time all the Seven young Geese said to each other,

"Beyond all doubt this beast must be a Plum-pudding Flea!" And no sooner had they said this than the Plum-pudding Flea began to hop and skip on his one leg with the most dreadful velocity, and came straight to the tree, where he stopped and looked about him in a vacant and voluminous manner.

On which the Seven young Geese were greatly alarmed, and all of a tremble-bemble: so one of them put out his long neck and just touched him with the tip of his bill – but no sooner had he done this than the Plum-pudding Flea skipped and hopped about more and more and higher and higher, after which he opened his mouth, and to the great surprise and indignation of the Seven Geese, began to bark so loudly and furiously and terribly that they were totally unable to bear the noise, and by degrees every one of them suddenly tumbled down quite dead.

So that was the end of the Seven young Geese.

When the Seven young Owls set out, they sat every now and then on the branches of old trees, and never went far at one time. One night when it was quite dark, they thought they heard a mouse, but as the gas lamps were not lighted, they could not see him. So they called out,

"Is that a mouse?"

On which a Mouse answered, "Squeaky-peeky-weeky, yes it is."

And immediately all the young Owls threw themselves off the

tree, meaning to alight on the ground; but they did not perceive that there was a large well below them, into which they all fell superficially, and were every one of them drowned in less than half a minute.

So that was the end of the Seven young Owls.

The Seven young Guinea Pigs went into a garden full of Gooseberry-bushes and Tiggory-trees, under one of which they fell asleep. When they awoke they saw a large Lettuce which had grown out of the ground while they had been sleeping, and which had an immense number of green leaves. At which they all exclaimed,

"Lettuce! O Lettuce!
Let us, O Let us,
O Lettuce leaves,
O let us leave this tree and eat
Lettuce, O let us, Lettuce leaves!"

And instantly the Seven young Guinea Pigs rushed with such extreme force against the Lettuce-plant, and hit their heads so vividly against its stalk, that the concussion brought on directly an incipient transitional inflammation of their noses, which grew worse and worse and worse and worse till it incidentally killed them all Seven.

And that was the end of the Seven young Guinea Pigs.

The Seven young Cats set off on their travels with great delight and rapacity. But, on coming to the top of a high hill, they perceived at a long distance off a Clangle-Wangle, and in spite of the warning they had had, they ran straight up to it. (Now the Clangle-Wangle is a most dangerous and elusive beast, and by no means commonly to be met with. They live in the water as well as on land, using their long tail as a sail when in the former element. Their speed is extreme, but their habits of life are domestic and superfluous, and their general demeanour pensive and pellucid.)

The moment the Clangle-Wangle saw the Seven young Cats approach, he ran away; and he ran straight on for four months, and the Cats, though they continued to run, could never overtake him – they all gradually died of fatigue and exhaustion.

And this was the end of the Seven young Cats.

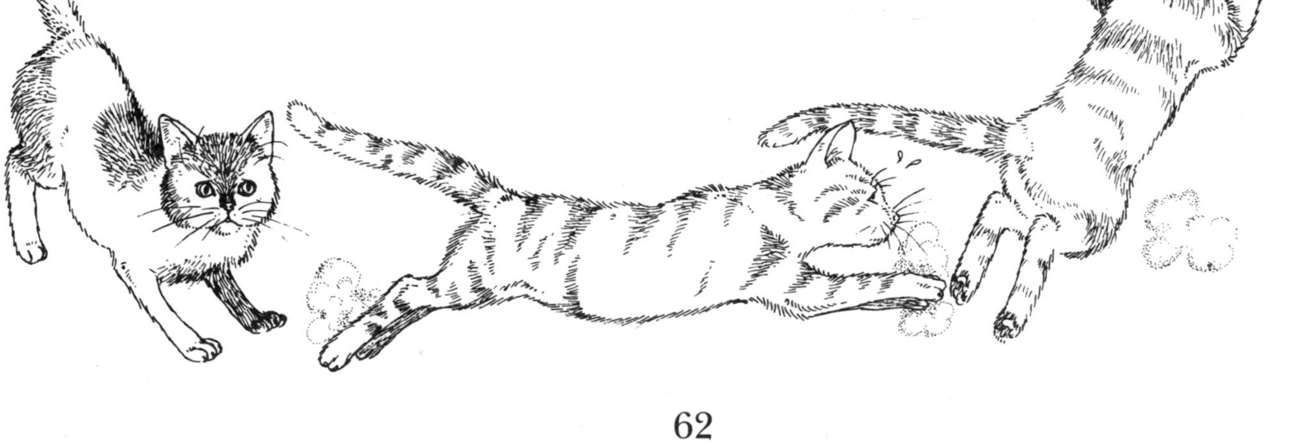

The Seven young Fishes swam across Lake Pipple-Popple and into the river, and into the ocean, where most unhappily for them, they saw, on the fifteenth day of their travels, a bright-blue Boss-Woss, and instantly swam after him. But the Blue Boss-Woss plunged into a perpendicular, spicular, orbicular, quadrangular, circular depth of soft mud, where in fact his house was.

And the Seven young Fishes, swimming with great and uncomfortable velocity, plunged also into the mud, quite against their will, and not being accustomed to it, were all suffocated.

And that was the end of the Seven young Fishes.

After it was known that the Seven young Parrots, and the Seven young Storks, and the Seven young Geese, and the Seven young Owls, and the Seven young Guinea Pigs, and the Seven young Cats, and the Seven young Fishes were all dead, then the Frog, and the Plum-pudding Flea, and the Mouse, and the Clangle-Wangle, and the Blue Boss-Woss, all met to rejoice over their good fortune.

And they collected the Seven Feathers of the Seven young Parrots, and the Seven Bills of the Seven young Storks, and the Lettuce, and the Cherry, and having placed the latter on the Lettuce, and the other objects in a circular arrangement at their base, they danced a horn-pipe round all these memorials until they were quite tired; then returned to their respective homes full of joy and respect, sympathy, satisfaction, and disgust.

ALADDIN AND THE WONDERFUL LAMP

Arabian Nights

Far off in a beautiful city in China a ragged urchin called Aladdin used to play in the street. His father, a poor tailor, tried to make him work, but Aladdin was lazy and disobedient, and refused even to help in his father's shop. Even after his father died Aladdin still preferred to roam in the streets with his friends, and did not feel ashamed to eat the food his mother bought with the money she earned by spinning cotton.

One day a wealthy stranger came to the city. He noticed Aladdin in the street and thought, "That lad looks as though he has no purpose in life. It will not matter if I use him, then kill him."

The stranger quickly found out that Aladdin's father, Mustapha, was now dead. He called Aladdin over to him.

"Greetings, nephew," he said, "I am your father's brother. I have returned to China only to find my dear brother, Mustapha, is dead. Take this money and tell your mother I shall visit her."

Aladdin's mother was puzzled when Aladdin told her the stranger's message. "You have no uncle," she said. "I don't understand why this man should give us money."

The next day the stranger came to their house and talked about how he had loved his brother and offered to buy a fine shop where Aladdin could sell beautiful things to the rich people in the city. He gave Aladdin some new clothes and in a short while Aladdin's mother began to believe this man was a relation.

The stranger now invited Aladdin to go with him to the rich part of the city. Together they walked through beautiful gardens and parks where Aladdin had never been before, until he found himself far from home. At last the stranger showed Aladdin a flat stone with an iron ring set into it.

"Lift this stone for me, nephew," he said, "and go into the cavern below. Walk through three caves where you will see gold and silver stored. Do not touch it. You will then pass through a garden full of wonderful fruit and beyond the trees you will find a

lamp. Pour out the oil and bring the lamp to me. Pick some of the fruit on your return if you wish."

Aladdin lifted the stone and saw some steps leading down into a cave. He was frightened to go down but the stranger placed a gold ring with a great green emerald on his finger.

"Take this ring as a gift," he said, "but you must go or I shall not buy you a shop."

Now the stranger was in fact a magician. He had read about a lamp with magical powers and he had travelled far to find it. He knew the magic would not work for him unless the lamp was fetched from the cavern and handed to him by someone else. After Aladdin had brought him the lamp the magician planned to shut him in the cave to die.

Down in the cavern Aladdin found all as he had been told. He hurried through the rooms filled with silver and gold, and passed through the garden where the trees were hung with shimmering fruit of all colours. At the far end stood an old lamp. Aladdin took it, poured out the oil, and then picked some of the dazzling fruit from the trees as the magician had suggested. To his surprise they were all made from stones. Aladdin took as many as he could carry and returned to the steps.

"Give me the lamp," demanded the magician as soon as Aladdin came into sight.

"Help me out first," replied Aladdin who could not hand him the lamp because his arms were so full. They argued fiercely until *crash,* the stone slab fell back into place. The magician could not move the stone from the outside, nor Aladdin from within. He was trapped. The magician knew he had failed in his quest and decided to leave the country at once.

For two days Aladdin tried to get out of the cave. He became weak with hunger and thirst and finally as he sat in despair he rubbed his hands together. By chance he rubbed the gold ring that the stranger had given him. There was a blinding flash and a genie appeared. "I am the genie of the ring. What can I do for you, master?" it said.

"Get me out of here," Aladdin gasped. He was terrified of the

great burning spirit of the genie glowing in the cavern. Before he knew what had happened he was standing on the ground above the entrance to the cavern. Of the stone slab there was no sign. Aladdin set off for home and collapsed with hunger as he entered the house.

His mother was overjoyed to see him. She gave him all the scraps of food she had and when she said she had no more Aladdin suggested selling the lamp to buy some food.

"I'll get a better price for it, if it's clean," she thought, and she rubbed the lamp with a cloth. In a flash the genie appeared. Aladdin's mother fainted in horror but Aladdin seized the lamp. When the genie saw him with the lamp it said:

"I am the genie of the lamp. What can I do for you, master?"

"Get me some food," ordered Aladdin.

By the time his mother had recovered there were twelve silver dishes of food and twelve silver cups on the table. Aladdin and his mother ate as they had never eaten before. They had enough for several days, and then Aladdin began to sell the silver dishes and cups. He and his mother lived comfortably in this way for some time.

Then it happened that Aladdin saw the sultan's daughter, Princess Badroulboudoir. Aladdin loved her at first sight and sent his mother to the sultan's court to ask the sultan permission for the princess to marry him. He told her to take as a gift the stone fruits he had brought from the cave.

It was several days before Aladdin's mother could speak with the sultan, but at last she was able to give him the stone fruits. The sultan was truly amazed.

"Your son has such fine jewels he would make a good husband for my daughter, I am sure," he told Aladdin's mother.

But the sultan's chief courtier was jealous. He wanted his son to marry the princess. Quickly, he advised the sultan to say he would decide on the marriage in three months' time. Aladdin was happy when he heard the news. He felt sure he would marry the princess in three months' time.

But at the palace, the chief courtier spoke against Aladdin and when Aladdin's mother returned in three months, the sultan asked her: "Can your son send me forty golden bowls full of jewels like the ones he sent before only this time carried by forty servants?"

Aladdin rubbed the lamp once more and before long forty servants each carrying a gold bowl filled with sparkling jewels were assembled in the courtyard of their little house.

When the sultan saw them, he said:

"I am sure now that the owner of these riches will make a fine husband for my daughter."

But the chief courtier suggested yet another test. "Ask the woman," he said, "if her son has a palace fit for your daughter to live in."

"I'll give him the land and he can build a new palace," declared the sultan, and he presented Aladdin with land in front of his own palace.

Aladdin summoned the genie of the lamp once more. Overnight the most amazing palace appeared with walls of gold and silver, huge windows, beautiful halls and courtyards and rooms filled with treasures. A carpet of red velvet was laid from the old palace to the new, for the princess to walk on to her new home. Aladdin then asked the genie for some fine clothes for himself and his mother, and a glorious wedding took place with a splendid banquet eaten off golden dishes.

Aladdin took care always to keep the wonderful lamp safe. One day the princess gave it to an old beggar who was the magician in disguise, but that story, and the story of how Aladdin got it back again, will have to keep for another time.

ROBIN HOOD MEETS FRIAR TUCK

A Robin Hood Story

Robin Hood and his band of Merry Men lived in Sherwood Forest many years ago. They liked to take money from the rich to give to the poor. When they had nothing else to do, they practised wrestling, archery and sword fighting. Naturally each outlaw thought he was the best!

"Why do you argue?" Robin Hood asked one day. "For nobody within a hundred miles can beat Little John, Will Scarlett or Much."

"Not true," Will Scarlett shook his head. "I know someone who could beat the lot of us in everything –including you!"

Robin was astounded. "Who can this wonder-man be?" he demanded.

"He was a friar but he left his abbey and now he lives all alone. His nickname is Tuck because he tucks up his habit so that he can more easily wield a sword or stick. He is as well known for a soldier as a priest!"

"I'll neither eat nor drink until I've met this battling friar," Robin declared. "Who can show me where he lives?"

"I can," said Will, "we can be there and back before nightfall."

First Robin put on his light armour then his Lincoln-green jacket. He buckled on his sword and his bow and arrows and wearing his jaunty green cap and feather, he set off with four trusty friends. They walked through the forest until they reached a wide stream.

"Round that bend is a ford," Will said. "It isn't deeper than your thigh so it's easy to cross. Somewhere on the other side lives Friar Tuck. Shall we cross over the ford with you?"

"No," said Robin. "I want to beat this friar myself. But if I sound my horn, then come quickly."

Robin strolled away and soon reached the ford. As he prepared to wade across he heard the sound of two men arguing about a meat pie and a chicken pie. He peered through a thick bush and there on the opposite bank sat the fattest man Robin had ever seen. His head was shaven over the crown; his neck was as thick as a bull's; his shoulders and legs were like young trees. His friar's robe was tucked up and on each huge knee he was balancing an enormous pie!

"Which is the better pie to eat first?" he had been asking each of them. Then, while Robin watched, he thrust a large hand inside the meat pie and pulled out juicy hunks of meat. Robin's mouth watered. He'd like some pie himself but first he had to cross the river. He seized his bow and arrow, stood up and pointed them at the friar.

"I want to cross over here without getting my feet wet. You will carry me safely across, won't you?"

The friar reached for his sword then he saw Robin's arrow aimed straight at him. "Put your bow down," he shouted. "I can see it is my duty to help you across." He put down his pies and waded over. Robin climbed on his back and the friar returned carrying Robin safely across.

"Thank you, worthy friar," said Robin, "my feet are completely dry."

"Dry, are they?" said the friar, grabbing his sword. "Strange to say, I need to cross back again and my poor wet feet are aching. I beg you to carry me over the stream."

Robin was too busy looking at the delicious pies and before he knew what was happening, the friar had his sword out and was pointing it at him. The friar's sword waved and Robin wondered how he could possibly lift up this man-mountain!

"I'm not very strong," he said, "you'd better take off your sword so that you'll be lighter to carry over."

"All right," agreed the friar, so Robin heaved him up and staggered across. He was bent double and sweat poured off him when he threw his heavy burden on the far bank. Before the friar could stand up, Robin stood over him with his sword in his hand.

"Ho, Master Friar! Your turn to carry me back, I think."

"You win this time, my son. Get on my back."

They were halfway across the ford when the friar suddenly tipped him over his shoulders into the water, with a great *splash!* He calmly waded to the side while Robin choked and spluttered. "I'll turn you into mincemeat!" Robin roared, slithering to dry land.

The friar tucked up his robe and Robin saw he was wearing chain-mail. Both of them drew their swords and the fiercest battle began. Back and forth they moved, swords flashing and clashing. Robin suddenly slipped. The friar politely helped him up.

"I'm ready for a rest," he said, puffing and blowing.

"Me too!" said Robin. "You could have killed me just now." They threw themselves down to get their breath back. At once Robin blew on his silver horn. His four friends ran to the river. Each one held a quivering arrow in his bow.

"These are my friends," said Robin, smiling grimly.

"And here are my friends," said the friar. Fingers in his mouth, he whistled and four big shaggy dogs leapt to his side. The dogs snapped and snarled so fiercely that Robin dropped his sword and swarmed up the nearest tree.

"Get his friends, now!" The friar shook with laughter.

The dogs raced to the river and the outlaws fired off their

arrows but the dogs simply caught them in their mouths and carried them back to the friar. Then the dogs plunged into the water and started to swim across. The outlaws were terrified, except for Will Scarlett. He stood there calmly and when the first dog scrambled up the bank he shouted: "Down, Sirrah. What are you doing? Get down, I say." The dog looked uncertain as he crept forward. His tail wagged gently then he licked Will's hand. The other dogs did the same.

"I know these rascals," Will grinned. "Their bark is worse than their bite."

"I'm glad they are not as fierce as they look," said Little John. "We'd better cross the river ourselves and sort things out."

"You can climb down, master! There's no more danger," called Will as they splashed their way over. Robin was feeling rather foolish while the friar was staring hard at Will Scarlett.

"I used to know a young fellow who could tame savage dogs. His name was Will Scarlett."

"It still is, good friar. Don't you know me?" Will laughed happily.

"You've changed." The friar slapped Will playfully on his back which sent him flying. "I didn't recognize you but the dogs knew you. Who are these rough fellows, may I ask?"

"Robin Hood's men," they replied very proudly.

"Oh dear," he gasped, "have I been fighting the famous Robin Hood?"

"Yes, and you've beaten me in a fair fight," said Robin. "I'm happy to meet you, Friar Tuck, but I'm happier still that Will knew your dogs! I confess they scared me greatly."

"I'm glad Will has joined your band," Friar Tuck spoke wistfully. "He will never be lonely. I confess I am lonely sometimes."

"We need a priest to care for our souls," said Robin thoughtfully, "and you would be useful in a fight. Friar Tuck, I'd be honoured to welcome you as one of my merry men."

"I can cook," said Friar Tuck. "In fact, I enjoy good food. Perhaps you'd like some of my meat and my chicken pies now?"

Robin laughed. "Don't you know that's why I wanted to cross the river!"

THE RABBIT MAKES A MATCH

Canadian Indian Traditional

Ableegumooch the rabbit is a sociable creature, a little boastful perhaps, but kind-hearted. So, when he saw his friend Keoonik the otter looking miserable, he wanted to know at once what was the matter and was there anything he could do. Well, it turned out that what the otter wanted was to get married. He wanted to marry Nesoowa, the daughter of Pipsolk; and the girl-otter was willing, but her father was not.

"Why not?" asked the rabbit, eyeing his friend. "You may not be the handsomest fellow in the world, Keoonik (otters can't compare with rabbits in looks), or the smartest (the rabbits are that), but you're honest and good-tempered and I daresay you'd provide quite a good living for a wife. Did you try anointing Pipsolk's head with bear grease?" This was the Indian way of asking if Keoonik had tried flattery on the girl's father.

"It wasn't any good," said Keoonik. "He thinks so well of himself already, nothing I could say would please him."

"How about a gift to sweeten his opinion?"

"No good. It isn't meat or presents he cares for – it's breeding and ancestors, and I haven't got any according to him." Keoonik added glumly – "I'm just an ordinary everyday kind of otter, not good enough for his daughter."

"Ah, Keoonik," sighed the rabbit, "there are many like Pipsolk, full of silly pride. (Pride – that's the one thing rabbits haven't.) Look my friend, since I am known everywhere as the wittiest and most persuasive Wabanaki in Glooscap's world,* wouldn't you like me to have a talk with Pipsolk?"

"What sort of talk?" asked Keoonik.

"I could tell him what a good fellow you really are and how much better it would be to have a decent son-in-law with no relatives than a bad one with too many!"

*The Wabanaki were Indians living in what is now eastern Canada, and Glooscap was their creator.

"Tell him I'm very fond of Nesoowa, and would try to make her happy."

"I'll tell him," said the rabbit, and off he went.

Ableegumooch found Pipsolk and his numerous family sliding happily down a muddy slope near their home on the lake. This is a favourite pastime of otters.

"Step over here, will you, Pipsolk," called the rabbit from a drier spot up the bank. "I'd like to talk with you about Nesoowa."

Pipsolk excused himself from his family and stepped over. "What about Nesoowa?"

"Isn't it time she was married?" queried Ableegumooch, "to a kind and hard-working husband? I don't know if it's occurred to you, but a good husband doesn't grow on blueberry bushes. And remember, with Nesoowa off your hands, you will have fewer mouths to feed."

"Very true," agreed Pipsolk, "but a man must do the best he can for his daughter. What kind of father would I be if I passed her over to the first common sort who came along? Tell me, Ableegumooch, who were your people?"

"Eh?"

"Your ancestors. Were they important? Were they well-bred?"

The rabbit stuck out his chest.

"Pipsolk," he said complacently, "my family is one of the best. I have a long and noble ancestry, with notables on every branch of the family tree since the days before the light of the sun."

"H'mm," Pipsolk nodded thoughtfully. "Can you show proof of your aristocratic background?"

"Certainly. Haven't you noticed how I always wear white in the winter time? That's the fashion of the aristocracy."

"Really? I didn't know that. But what about your split lip, Ableegumooch? It doesn't indicate anything common, does it?"

"On the contrary, it's a sign of breeding. In my circles we always eat with knives, which is the polite way of feeding. One day my knife slipped, which is how my lip was damaged."

"But why is it your mouth and your whiskers always keep moving even when you're still? Is that high style too?"

"Of course. You see, it's because I'm always meditating and planning great affairs. I talk to myself rather than to anyone of

lesser quality. That's the way we gentlemen are!"

"I see. One more question. Why do you always hop? Why don't you walk like other people?"

"All my aristocratic forebears had a gait of their own," the rabbit explained loftily. "We gentle folk don't run like the vulgar."

"I'd no idea you were so well-bred, Ableegumooch," said Pipsolk. "Very well. You may have her."

The rabbit had opened his mouth to say something more about his aristocratic forebears, but now he closed it.

"I don't as a rule approve of marrying outside the tribe, but circumstances alter cases. Welcome, son-in-law."

Ableegumooch felt as though he had accidentally walked under an icy waterfall. He – to be married – and to an otter-girl! The rabbit had never even thought of getting married. He opened his lips to say so, and hesitated, his whiskers twitching. Pipsolk was a man one didn't offend if one could help it. Many of his kind had a short way with rabbits! Moreover, the thought of marriage was rather pleasant, once one began to think about it. A pretty girl adds a nice touch to a wigwam. Besides, his grandmother was getting old and would be glad of help in the lodge.

He thought briefly of Keoonik, and worded an explanation silently in his mind. "I'm sorry, friend, but I didn't plan it this way, you know. I don't see how I can get out of it. Can I help it if Nesoowa's father wants the best for his daughter? You'll understand, I'm sure."

That night, Pipsolk invited all his relatives and friends to a feast and announced the engagement of Nesoowa to the well-known and aristocratic Ableegumooch, the marriage to take place at the end of the usual probationary period. It was customary among the Wabanaki of that time for a young man to provide for the family of his future bride for one year to show that he was capable of getting food and necessities for a wife and family. Keoonik was of course among the guests and hearing the dreadful news, he could hardly believe his ears. He gave his faithless friend a long bitter look as he left the party, and it quite shrivelled Ableegumooch for the moment.

The rabbit tried to find excuses for himself. "It wasn't my fault. It's too late now, anyway, to back down."

So he set up a lodge near Pipsolk's and brought over his grandmother, who complained bitterly at having to move to such a damp place near all those noisy otters, but the rabbit paid no attention. His mind was wholly occupied with the problem of feeding those otters. He knew it would be different from feeding himself and his grandmother. Rabbits live in meadows and forest undergrowth and are satisfied with herbs and grasses and tender twigs. Otters, on the other hand, live in or near water and like fish and frogs and salamanders for dinner. If Ableegumooch was to keep those otters fed, he must learn to be at home in the water, and a rabbit is not the best in the world when it comes to swimming. In fact, to be plain about it, of all swimmers and divers the rabbit is the very worst.

"Can you swim?" asked the young otters with interest.

"Well – not yet," said Ableegumooch, adding cheerfully, "but I can learn." Ableegumooch was always willing to try.

He put his nose to the water. It smelled dank and weedy, not at all nice. He dipped one toe in the water to test its temperature – ugh, cold! He pulled his toe out again. After a good deal of sighing

and dipping in and dipping out, the rabbit finally got himself into the water chest-deep and began to move his front paws in an awkward swimming motion. The watching otters nudged each other and chuckled. Then the rabbit tried to let go with his back feet, but sank at once and had to scramble in a panic to find solid ground again.

Nevertheless he kept trying, and after a whole day of failing and trying again, he managed to move a few strokes from the shore, and all the otters applauded. Ableegumooch felt quite proud of himself, though he couldn't understand why the otters laughed even as they cheered.

Next he must learn to fish, they said.

"Fish? Well, I can try."

Pipsolk was already fretting about the fact that it was long past his usual dinner time.

"Patience," said the rabbit, trying to recall how otters fished. They dived first. Yes, that was the hard part. It meant ducking one's head right under the water. Never mind, if an otter could do it, so could a rabbit. And he ducked his head in the manner of otters and muskrats, hoisting his other end high up in the air so that the little round tail would follow him down under the waves. Once upside down, with water in his nose and his ears and his eyes, the rabbit thought only of getting up to the surface again. He came up choking and spluttering, and oh didn't the air taste good!

"This way of fishing," he decided, "is not for me. Now, let me see, how do the bears go about it? I think they catch fish by just scooping them out of the water. I can do that, surely." So, standing in the water up to his chin, Ableegumooch reached for a leaping frog, made a swipe at a devil's-darning-needle, grabbed a trout flashing by – and missed all three, to the vast merriment of the otter family. Still the rabbit kept trying. He saw a fat insect alight on the branch of an Indian Pear Tree and at the same time a salmon swam into view. Trying to grab both at the same time, Ableegumooch stepped off into the deep water and sank. Down he went and at the very bottom his long hind foot caught in a pile of brush. There he was held fast. In a dreadful panic, he kicked and twisted, trying to get free. As he fought, a brown shape flashed past him under water, turned and came back. It was Keoonik!

Seeing his guilt clearly for the first time, Ableegumooch was sure the otter had come to take his revenge. Well, thought the rabbit, I suppose I deserve to die, but I'm not going to if I can help it – certainly not to please Keoonik! So he braced himself for one last effort, and at the same time his foot was miraculously freed. He shot up to the surface, more than half-drowned, where

Keoonik grabbed him and pushed him in no gentle fashion to the shore.

"False friend! Traitor!" growled the otter. "I ought to have left you there to perish!"

"Why didn't you?" gasped the rabbit, still coughing up water.

"Because drowning's too good for you," Keoonik grinned. "I'm waiting to see what Pipsolk does when he finds out he and his family must go hungry to bed tonight! Ah well – you'll make a good substitute, Ableegumooch. We otters are very fond of rabbit stew."

"I'm sorry I spoiled things for you with Nesoowa."

"You didn't," laughed the otter. "Nesoowa says she will run away with me rather than marry you." Keoonik glanced hurriedly over his shoulder. "Here comes Pipsolk now, and he looks hungry! You'd better start running!"

After one look at Pipsolk's face, Ableegumooch would have been glad to take Keoonik's advice, but he couldn't. He was still too weak and breathless to run anywhere – and in such a strait, as usual, he thought of the Great Chief and whispered a plea for help.

Suddenly Glooscap – who comes as the wind comes and no man knows how – stood between Ableegumooch and the wrathful otter.

"Boasting again, Ableegumooch," said the Great Chief, who probably loved the rabbit best of all his creatures, "and see where it's got you!"

"I'm sorry to bother you, Master," the rabbit apologized. "It was sink or swim – and I've already tried swimming!"

Glooscap shook his head in despair, trying not to smile. He turned to the otter, who was now looking innocent, as if rabbit stew had never entered his mind.

"Pipsolk, I want you to forget all about breeding and background and such nonsense and just tell Ableegumooch frankly what you think of him as a son-in-law."

Pipsolk turned to the rabbit.

"The fact is, Ableegumooch, you may be good enough in your way, but your breeding and ancestors won't fill my children's mouths. You'll never do as a husband for my daughter. She would soon starve. Indeed, after experiencing your kind of son-in-law, I can see more virtue in Keoonik's sort. I believe if Nesoowa is willing, I shall give him a trial after all."

"There!" cried Ableegumooch. "I told you I'd help you, Keoonik." But the otter had rushed away to find Nesoowa and tell her the good news.

Glooscap gave his rabbit a severe look. "I hope you have learned something from all this, Ableegumooch."

"Oh, I have," cried the rabbit. "I know now I'm not cut out for swimming and fishing. From now on, I shall be satisfied just to be what I am, the handsomest, the cleverest, and best-bred rabbit in the world! And" – as an afterthought – "the best matchmaker!"

Whereupon to the rabbit's surprise Glooscap began to laugh, and he laughed so hard that all the trees bent with the gust of his laughter, and Ableegumooch had to cling to the Master's leg to keep from being blown away.

And there, *kespeadooksit*,* our tale ends.

*This means 'the story ends'.

THE SEVEN FOALS

Norwegian Traditional

Most boys and girls have heard the story of Cinderella but not so many know about a boy called Cinders. He was the youngest of three boys and they lived with their mother and father in a tumble-down hut in the forest. They were often cold and hungry.

One morning the eldest son said he wanted to see the world and earn some money. His mother packed his bag and he set off. All day he walked and when it was getting dark he came to a palace. By chance the king was standing outside on the marble steps and he spoke to the youth:

"Where are you going at this time of night?"

"I'm looking for work," was the reply.

"I can give you work," said the king. "Will you look after my seven foals? If you watch them all day and can remember by the evening what they've eaten and drunk, you may marry the princess, my daughter. If you can't, then you will be given three strokes with a whip. That is fair enough, isn't it?"

The young man agreed. "An easy job," he thought to himself.

Early next morning, the grooms let out the seven young horses. They scampered away over the hills, across rivers, ditches and fields with the youth chasing after them. After some time he was tired of watching those foals! They galloped into a green valley where an old woman was spinning. "Rest awhile here," she called, "let me cool your head." His face was indeed streaming with sweat by this time, so he was glad to stop and while he lay on the ground, the old woman combed his hair until the sun began to set.

"I can't return to the palace," he decided. "I'd better go home."

"Don't do that," said the old hag, "the foals will gallop past when it's dark. You can run back too and no one will know that you've been lazing about here instead of guarding them."

When the foals came, she handed him a bottle of water and

some moss to show the king what his foals had been eating and drinking.

"Well, my boy?" asked the king that night. "Did you watch my fine young foals carefully all day?"

"Most carefully I did," replied the eldest son.

"What did they eat and drink then?"

"This moss and this water," and the youth held them out.

"What nonsense," the king roared, "you haven't watched my foals at all. Groom, give him three lashes and send him home."

Next day the second son told his father and mother that he would go now to seek his fortune.

He set off and walked all day until he also reached the palace. On the steps he met the king who called out:

"Where are you going at this time of night?"

The youth said he was looking for work. At once the king asked if he would work for him and look after his seven foals. He promised to reward him with the princess or punish him with the whip. "A simple task," the youth thought.

Early next morning, the grooms let out the seven foals and off they galloped over hill and dale. Off chased the boy after them. Like his brother he grew tired so when he reached the cool deep valley where the old woman sat spinning he was glad when she called out: "Rest awhile, my bonnie boy, and let me cool your head." The foals galloped on while he stretched out and the old woman combed his hair until the sun was setting. She gave him water and moss but when he returned to the palace, the king was enraged to hear the same answer to his question. "Give him three lashes and pack him off home," he thundered.

On the third morning, Cinders thought he would try his luck.

"Don't be stupid," his brothers said scornfully, "how can you know what to do? You only know about sitting among the ashes!"

"Well, I can at least try," he said. So off he went.

At sunset he met the king on the palace steps and asked for work just as his brothers had done. The king asked him if he would look after his seven foals, and Cinders readily agreed.

As usual, the seven foals were let out the next morning. They galloped wildly across moors and meadows with Cinders running hard to keep near them. They reached the valley where the old woman sat spinning. "Stop, brave Cinders. Let me comb your handsome hair."

"No time," gasped Cinders breathlessly as he caught hold of the youngest foal's mane. To his astonishment the foal said kindly: "You'd better ride on my back. We've many miles to go yet." They galloped on and on. "Can you see anything?" the foal asked.

"Nothing," said Cinders, so on they rode.

"Can you see anything now?" the foal asked again.

"Yes, I see something white, like a huge beech tree."

"Good. We're almost there," said the foal happily.

When they reached the tree, the eldest foal pushed it over. There was a door in the ground which the foal opened. Inside was a small room without any furniture. A rusty old sword and a jug were standing on the floor near the door.

"Can you wield this sword?" the eldest foal demanded. Cinders could not even lift up one end! The foals made him take drink after drink from the jug until suddenly the sword gleamed and he could whirl it round his head like a feather in a breeze.

"Excellent," the foals cried. "Take this sword and on your wedding day we beg you to cut off our heads. When you give the correct answers to the king about our food and drink he will give you the princess as your bride. We are her brothers but a troll cast a wicked spell on us. When you've cut off our heads you must be careful to lay each head on the body to which it belongs. Then the spell will be broken at last."

Gladly Cinders promised and away they galloped. The youngest foal asked if Cinders could see anything but he shook his head. On they travelled. Many times the foal asked the same question until at last Cinders said: "I see something that looks like a blue ribbon."

"That's the river we must cross," laughed the foal. When they reached the far bank he asked Cinders what he could see now.

"A church with a tall tower," he replied and when they rode into the churchyard, the foals turned into princes wearing magnificent robes covered with gold and silver. They went inside the church and a priest blessed them. Then he gave Cinders a tiny bottle of holy wine and some holy bread. When they went outside, the princes changed into horses again. They went across the river, through the valley where the old woman screeched angrily at them. Swifter than eagles, they galloped until they reached the palace where the king awaited them.

"Have you watched my foals all day?" he demanded. "Can you tell me what they have eaten and drunk?"

Cinders pulled out the holy bread and wine. "Here is their meat and here is their drink," he said quietly.

"At last I've heard the truth," said the king happily. "You shall marry my daughter with half my kingdom as your wedding gift."

He ordered a wonderful feast. Then, as they were sitting down, Cinders slipped away pretending that he'd forgotten something. He rushed to the stables. Drawing his sword, he cut off the foals' heads. Carefully he put each head by its proper body. Instantly the seven princes reappeared.

The king and the princess cried with joy when they saw them for the wicked spell had been broken at last. The Seven Foals were Seven Princes again. Cinders became a great king when the old king died and everyone was very happy indeed.

PUSS-IN-BOOTS

Charles Perrault

A miller once died, leaving his three sons all that he possessed – his mill, his donkey and his cat. They quickly arranged between them that the eldest son should keep the mill, the middle son the donkey, while the youngest should take the cat.

"It is very hard on me," grumbled the youngest son. "My brothers can earn their living with the mill and the donkey, whereas after I have eaten the cat, I will have nothing."

"Don't talk like that, master," said the cat. "Give me some boots and a sack with a string to tie it at the top and you shall see that it was a lucky day for you when you became my master."

The cat quickly went to catch some mice and rats to prove how useful he was, and the miller's son found him the boots and the sack which tied at the top. The cat was as pleased as punch with the boots and strutted around proudly. Then, taking the sack, he filled it with bran and tempting green leaves and set out for a nearby field where he knew there were many rabbits. There he lay down with the sack open beside him and pretended to be asleep.

Before long some curious rabbits came to investigate the sleeping cat and the sack, and when they smelt the delicious food they hopped into the sack. In a flash Puss-in-Boots jumped up, pulled the string tight, and caught the rabbits.

Now he strode off to the king's palace and demanded to see the king. "I have a gift for him from my master, the Marquis of Carabas," he announced. This was a name he had made up for the miller's son to impress the king. The king accepted the sack of rabbits graciously and sent a message to the cat's master thanking him for his kindness.

Some time later Puss-in-Boots set out again with his sack. This time he put a handful of corn in the sack and caught some partridge, and once more he took them to the king's palace, and presented them to the king from the Marquis of Carabas.

Not long afterwards Puss-in-Boots heard that the king was

going to drive by the river, and that his lovely young daughter was going to follow on in her carriage. He told the miller's son to follow him and do whatever he said. By now the lad realized that Puss was no ordinary cat, and he promised to do everything he was told.

Puss then asked the miller's son to take off his clothes and swim in the river. When the king's carriage came past he called out, "Help, help! My master, the Marquis of Carabas, is drowning!" The king recognized the Marquis's name, stopped his carriage, and ordered his guards to save the young man. While they were dragging him out, the cat told the king, "He was attacked by thieves who have taken all his clothes." The truth was that Puss had hidden the clothes under a stone.

The king sent one of his servants to fetch some fine clothes, for the Marquis of Carabas had been very generous to him in the past. When the servants returned and the miller's son put on the new clothes he looked very handsome indeed. By this time the king's daughter had arrived and she immediately fell in love with him. The king graciously agreed to him joining the princess in her carriage.

Puss ran on ahead, and found some men working in a field. "The king is about to drive past," he told them. "If he asks you who owns this field, you must answer 'The Marquis of Carabas'. If you don't," he added ferociously, "I shall make sure you are killed and chopped into little pieces."

A few moments later the king's carriage came along and the king asked the men who owned the land. They remembered the fierce threats from Puss-in-Boots and answered, "The Marquis of Carabas, Sire."

The king was impressed. Again the cat ran ahead and found some harvesters cutting corn. He told them to say all the fields they were working in belonged to the Marquis of Carabas. If they did not, he said he would make sure they were killed. When the king heard that the Marquis of Carabas owned this land too he was even more impressed.

Meanwhile Puss hurried on to a big castle where a wicked magician lived. The magician was the real owner of the land through which the king and his companions were driving.

The cat knocked at the door and asked to see the magician, and when he met him he bowed very low. "Is it true that you can change yourself into any animal – a lion, a tiger, even an elephant?" he asked with great respect.

"It is true," replied the magician and instantly turned into a great lion, and chased the cat. Puss-in-Boots was terrified and only just managed to scramble to safety on a roof – not easy for a cat wearing big boots. There he huddled until the lion changed back into the magician.

"That was truly remarkable," he said to the magician most politely. "But I don't suppose you can also turn yourself into a tiny animal like a mouse or a rat?"

"That's even easier," said the magician, and in a flash he became a tiny mouse, scampering on the floor. With a leap Puss pounced on him and that was the end of the magician.

Just then Puss-in-Boots heard the king's carriage arriving at the castle, so he went to the entrance and bowed low.

"Welcome to the house of my master, the Marquis of Carabas," he announced.

The king entered with his daughter and the miller's son and

looked round at the fine castle. Knowing that his daughter already loved the young man, he said, "Tell me, Marquis, what would you say to marrying my daughter?"

The miller's son, who had fallen deeply in love with the princess, replied, "With all my heart I would like to."

The young man and his princess lived happily in the castle for many years, and you may be sure Puss-in-Boots was always well fed and well looked after for the rest of his life.

PYGMALION'S STATUE

Greek Legend

Many years ago, on the island of Cyprus, lived a king called Pygmalion. Although he was king, Pygmalion was a quiet man. He was unmarried and had few friends. Pygmalion felt no need for friends because he spent all his time making statues. People came from miles around to see the beautiful statues he made, but Pygmalion never sold them. He was so rich that he did not need to earn his living like ordinary men and women. Instead he gave the statues to Aphrodite, the goddess of love, and they were used to decorate her temples.

Pygmalion's old nurse worried about him.

"I wish you would find yourself a wife," she told him. "I shall not live for ever, and who will look after you when I am gone? It's not natural for a king to live on his own. You must marry and have a son. Otherwise, who is to rule after you?"

Pygmalion smiled at her.

"When I find a woman as beautiful as one of my statues I shall marry her," he promised. The old nurse sighed. She suggested various women who might make a good wife for him, but Pygmalion rejected them all, saying "They are all greedy and cruel. I pity the men who have such women for their wives."

The old nurse gave up in despair. She had looked after Pygmalion since he was a boy and knew how stubborn he could be.

Several days later Pygmalion decided to make a new statue. He would create a beautiful woman out of the finest marble he could buy. As soon as he started it he knew that it would be the best statue he had ever made. Day and night he worked feverishly, unable to think of anything else.

"You must eat," begged his old nurse.

"Later," said Pygmalion

"You must sleep," she insisted.

The king took no notice at all.

He worked for nearly a month and then it was finished. As

Pygmalion gazed at the white marble statue, the beautiful face seemed to smile back at him. She was so lifelike that even Pygmalion was astounded.

"How did I create such beauty?" he whispered to himself. "Aphrodite must have inspired me." The old nurse came into the workroom and she, too, was astonished by Pygmalion's creation.

"It looks so real," she gasped. "I can't help thinking she will speak to us at any moment. It's certainly your finest work, and will look very good in Aphrodite's temple."

Slowly Pygmalion turned to her. "No," he said. "This statue will not go to the temple. I shall keep it here with me for ever."

As the days went by Pygmalion grew very fond of his statue. He began to talk to it as though it were alive and began to think of it as his wife. He even gave the statue a name – he called it Galatea.

He realized that he was falling in love with his own creation but still he would not give it up.

"I shall go to Aphrodite," he told himself. "I shall tell her about Galatea and ask her to help me. I have served Aphrodite well all my life. I know she will not fail me."

He went straight to the temple and knelt down.

"Take pity on me, goddess," he begged. "I truly love Galatea and if I cannot have her for my wife I shall go to my grave a lonely man, for I shall never love anyone else."

After a moment he became strangely weary and fell asleep. He had a dream in which he heard the sweet voice of Aphrodite.

"You are a good man, Pygmalion," she told him. "Go home and claim your bride." Pygmalion opened his eyes and looked around him, but he was alone in the temple.

"Did I dream all that?" he wondered. "Or did Aphrodite herself really speak to me?"

Full of hope he left the temple and hurried back to the palace. He went straight to his workroom and stood before the statue.

"Galatea," he said, "I claim you as my bride." He put his arms around the marble body and kissed the cold, beautiful lips. At once the cold marble grew warm and colour flowed over it. He saw that her hair was the colour of ripe corn and her eyes were as blue as the deepest ocean. Then she spoke to him.

"Dear Pygmalion, I shall be a good and faithful wife to you," she promised, "and I shall give you a son to rule after you."

The people of Cyprus were overjoyed at the news of their king's marriage. There were celebrations all over the island in honour of their wedding. True to her words, the following year Galatea had a baby son, whom they called Paphos. As the old nurse took the baby in her arms, there were tears of joy in her eyes.

"Now I can die in peace," she said. "Pygmalion is a happy man."

GOLDEN HAIRS AND GOLDEN STARS

Lithuanian Traditional

Many years ago a rich king married the most beautiful girl in the world. Everybody loved her except the king's evil mother who lived with them in the palace. She was jealous of the new queen and every day she tried out new ways to hurt her.

About a year later, the queen gave birth to a lovely baby boy who was born with three golden hairs behind one ear. Before anyone saw him, the wicked old queen pretended to lay him in his cradle. Instead, she bundled him into a shawl and put him in a wooden box. Then she scurried away to the river and dropped this box into the water where it floated away downstream. Rushing back to the palace she wrapped a stray cat in a shawl and put it into the baby boy's cradle.

When the king and his courtiers came to visit the baby they were horrified to see his hairy black face. The queen was so upset she could not say a word but the wicked mother clutched the king's arm and hissed softly: "She may be beautiful but your wife is a witch. Only witches can give birth to cats!"

The king did not believe his mother and after some time the young queen gave birth to a little daughter as beautiful as her mother, with three golden stars behind her tiny ear. Once more the old queen hid the baby and plunged it into the river. Then she wrapped a shawl around another cat and pushed it into the cradle. The king did not know what to think when he saw another hairy monster. "This proves your wife is a witch," his mother muttered. Everyone believed her except the king who never stopped loving his wife. She, poor lady, wept miserably day and night for her lost babies.

On the night the king's son was born, a fisherman was hauling up his net from the river. He saw that a wooden box had become caught in the net and suddenly he heard a faint wail. He snatched up the box and found a baby lying inside. He rushed home crying happily: "Look, wife, what I've brought you!'" When she saw the

baby now sleeping peacefully, she was filled with joy and gladness.

"We've no children ourselves. This must be a special gift to us," she laughed. When she picked up the baby she found rich clothes and gold pieces in the box. As she rocked the babe gently, she discovered the three tiny gold hairs behind his ear: so the happy couple called him Golden Hairs.

"We'll keep this money and the clothes in this box," they decided. "Little Golden Hairs may need them one day."

By a happy chance, the same man fished out a box from the river a year later. He found a darling baby girl lying inside, so he ran home to show her to his wife.

"Look, husband," cried his wife, "there are clothes and gold pieces the same as with Golden Hairs. I'm sure they are brother and sister! And see, there are three tiny stars behind her ear, so let us call her Golden Stars."

The two children lived happily with the fisherman and his wife until one day Golden Hairs and Golden Stars dashed inside after playing with their friends by the river.

"Mother, father, is it true?" they demanded, "that we are not really your children? Did father fish us out of the river?"

The couple sadly nodded their heads and brought out the

boxes of clothes and money which they had kept safely all these years.

"Thank you, dearest parents, for taking such great care of us," said the boy and girl, "but now we must go into the world and search for our real father and mother."

They packed their bags and set off. For weeks they wandered, seeking any news of their parents but nobody could tell them anything. When they reached the great city they decided to rest awhile. With their gold coins they bought a pretty house and garden and before long they had made everything so beautiful that all the townsfolk were chattering about clever Golden Hairs and Golden Stars. Their new house was near the king's castle so everyone at court heard about them too. As soon as she heard their names, the king's mother guessed who the children were. She knew she had to get rid of them.

She went to their house dressed as a poor old woman. She leaned over the garden gate and with sweet-sounding words, she praised everything. "What a wonderful house! Such a beautiful garden. What clever children you are! It would be perfect if only each tree had a tinkling bell, wouldn't it?"

"Where can I find these bells?" asked Golden Hairs eagerly.

"That's easy," said the cunning old woman. "You just climb yonder hill and you'll find a garden filled with trees. On one tree hangs a golden bell. Bring it back, hang it in your garden and see what happens!" Then she hobbled away but she did not tell the children that the garden was enchanted. Whoever stayed in it more than one hour would be turned into a tree.

"I'll fetch this golden bell at once," said Golden Hairs, but his sister was worried. "Something horrible may happen there. Promise me that you'll hurry back with the bell. Don't waste any time."

Golden Hairs promised and next day he climbed the hill and found the garden. He stretched on tiptoe and pulled off the bell then he raced back to his house. He hung the bell on a tree and next morning their garden was filled with silvery chimes from every tree.

Later the old woman returned. "What lovely tunes I can hear but your fountain needs golden fishes. You'll find some in a pool on the hill," she said before she slipped away.

Next day, Golden Hairs climbed the hill and found the pool. Quickly he scooped up a fish and ran home with it. Next morning a hundred fishes glittered and gleamed in the fountain.

The old woman was furious so she went to their house a third time. "It's wonderful," she sighed, "but you now need the Bird of Truth from the big house on the hill."

"Then I'll go tomorrow to this house," said Golden Hairs.

Golden Stars tried her best to stop him. She wept and cried: "Dearest brother, I've had such a fearful dream and I'm so frightened. Don't go. I'm sure you will get hurt."

But he set off. He found the house and this time he wandered through the gardens before he went inside. Each room was shining with gold, gleaming diamonds and sparkling silver. Slowly he looked around before he saw the Bird of Truth. As he stretched out his hand to catch it, the clock struck the hour and he fell to the ground – a tiny, sparkling piece of glass.

Golden Stars waited and waited for her brother. Then she too climbed the hill to the enchanted house. Face wet with tears, she wandered outside the garden calling her brother's name until she met a mysterious lady in black who said: "Go inside, child. Don't look at any treasures but fill your apron with pieces of glass from the floor. Take the Bird of Truth and fly away home. Hurry!"

Golden Stars did everything she had been told but the moment she stepped outside the magic garden the pieces of glass jumped from her apron! They were all children who had stayed too long in that house. She saw her dear brother and together they scampered home and put the Bird of Truth in a pretty cage.

Soon the news of the golden bells, the golden fishes and the Bird of Truth reached the ears of the king and queen. They visited the children's house and the queen asked the Bird of Truth about her children. Tears of joy streamed down her face as the bird chirped the story of Golden Hairs and Golden Stars. She hugged her long-lost children, but the king grew angry when the bird told about the old queen's wickedness.

"She shall float down the river in a wooden box," he ordered. "I will reward the fisherman and his wife for their kindness then we'll give a splendid feast for our new-found children."

But where the river carried the old queen, nobody knows.

THE HAPPY PRINCE

Oscar Wilde

High above the city, on a tall column, stood the statue of the Happy Prince. He was gilded all over with thin leaves of fine gold, for eyes he had two bright sapphires, and a large red ruby glowed on his sword-hilt.

He was very much admired indeed. "He is as beautiful as a weathercock," remarked one of the Town Councillors who wished to gain a reputation for having artistic tastes; "only not quite so useful," he added, fearing lest people should think him unpractical, which he really was not.

"Why can't you be like the Happy Prince?" asked a sensible mother of her little boy who was crying for the moon. "The Happy Prince never dreams of crying for anything."

"I am glad there is someone in the world who is quite happy," muttered a disappointed man as he gazed at the wonderful statue.

"He looks just like an angel," said the Charity Children as they came out of the cathedral in their bright scarlet cloaks and their clean white pinafores.

"How do you know?" said the Mathematical Master. "You have never seen one."

"Ah! but we have, in our dreams," answered the children; and the Mathematical Master frowned and looked very severe, for he did not approve of children dreaming.

One night there flew over the city a little Swallow. His friends had gone away to Egypt six weeks before, but he had stayed behind, for he was in love with the most beautiful Reed. He had met her early in the spring as he was flying down the river after a big yellow moth, and had been so attracted by her slender waist that he had stopped to talk to her. "Shall I love you?" said the Swallow, who liked to come to the point at once, and the Reed made him a low bow. So he flew round and round her, touching the water with his wings, and making silver ripples. This was his courtship, and it lasted all through the summer.

"It is a ridiculous attachment," twittered the other Swallows; "she has no money, and far too many relations;" and indeed the river was quite full of Reeds. Then, when autumn came they all flew away.

After they had gone he felt lonely, and began to tire of his lady-love. "She has no conversation," he said, "and I am afraid that she is a coquette, for she is always flirting with the wind." And certainly, whenever the wind blew, the Reed made the most graceful curtseys. "I admit that she is domestic," he continued, "but I love travelling, and my wife, consequently, should love travelling also."

"Will you come away with me?" he said finally to her, but the Reed shook her head, she was attached to her home.

"You have been trifling with me," he cried. "I am off to the Pyramids. Goodbye!" and he flew away.

All day long he flew, and at night-time he arrived at the city. "Where shall I put up?" he said.

Then he saw the statue on the tall column.

"I will put up there," he cried, "it is a fine position, with plenty of fresh air." So he alighted just between the feet of the Happy Prince.

"I have a golden bedroom," he said softly to himself as he looked round, and he prepared to go to sleep; but just as he was putting his head under his wing a large drop of water fell on him. "What a curious thing!" he cried, "there is not a single cloud in the sky, the stars are quite clear and bright, and yet it is raining. The climate in the north of Europe is really dreadful. The Reed used to like the rain, but that was merely her selfishness."

Then another drop fell.

"What is the use of a statue if it cannot keep the rain off?" he said, "I must look for a good chimney-pot," and he determined to fly away.

But before he had opened his wings, a third drop fell and he looked up, and saw – Ah! what did he see?

The eyes of the Happy Prince were filled with tears, and tears were running down his golden cheeks. His face was so beautiful in the moonlight that the little Swallow was filled with pity.

"Who are you?" he said.

"I am the Happy Prince."

"Why are you weeping then?" asked the Swallow; "you have quite drenched me."

"When I was alive and had a human heart," answered the statue, "I did not know what tears were, for I lived in the Palace of Sans-Souci, where sorrow is not allowed to enter. In the daytime I played with my companions in the garden, and in the evening I led the dance in the Great Hall. Round the garden ran a very lofty wall, but I never cared to ask what lay behind it, everything about me was so beautiful. My courtiers called me the Happy Prince, and happy indeed I was, if pleasure be happiness. So I lived, and so I died. And now that I am dead they have set me up here so high that I can see all the ugliness and all the misery of my city, and though my heart is made of lead yet I cannot choose but weep."

"What! Is he not solid gold?" said the Swallow to himself. He was too polite to make any personal remarks out loud.

"Far away," continued the statue in a low musical voice, "far away in a little street there is a poor house. One of the windows is open, and through it I can see a woman seated at a table. Her face is thin and worn, and she has coarse, red hands, all pricked by the needle, for she is a seamstress. She is embroidering passion flowers on a satin gown for the loveliest of the Queen's maids-of-honour to wear at the next Court Ball. In a bed in the corner of the room her little boy is lying ill. He has a fever, and is asking for oranges. His mother has nothing to give him but river water, so he is crying. Swallow, Swallow, little Swallow, will you not bring her the ruby out of my sword-hilt? My feet are fastened to this pedestal and I cannot move."

"I am waited for in Egypt," said the Swallow. "My friends are flying up and down the Nile, and talking to the large lotus flowers. Soon they will go to sleep in the tomb of the great King. The King is there himself in his painted coffin. He is wrapped in yellow linen, and embalmed with spices. Round his neck is a chain of pale green jade, and his hands are like withered leaves."

"Swallow, Swallow, little Swallow," said the Prince, "will you not stay with me for one night, and be my messenger? The boy is so thirsty, and the mother so sad."

"I don't think I like boys," answered the Swallow. "Last summer, when I was staying on the river, there were two rude boys, the miller's sons, who were always throwing stones at me. They never hit me, of course; we swallows fly far too well for that, and besides I come of a family famous for its agility; but still, it was a mark of disrespect."

But the Happy Prince looked so sad that the little Swallow was sorry. "It is very cold here," he said; "but I will stay with you for one night, and be your messenger."

"Thank you, little Swallow," said the Prince.

So the Swallow picked out the great ruby from the Prince's sword, and flew away with it in his beak over the roofs of the town.

He passed by the cathedral tower, where the white marble angels were sculptured. He passed by the Palace and heard the sound of dancing. A beautiful girl came out on the balcony with her lover. "How wonderful the stars are," he said to her, "and how wonderful is the power of love!"

"I hope my dress will be ready in time for the State Ball," she answered; "I have ordered passion flowers to be embroidered on it: but the seamstresses are so lazy."

He passed over the river, and saw the lanterns hanging to the masts of the ships. He passed over the Ghetto, and saw the old Jews bargaining with each other, and weighing out money in copper scales. At last he came to the poor house and looked in. The boy was tossing feverishly on his bed, and the mother had fallen asleep, she was so tired. In he hopped, and laid the great ruby on the table beside the woman's thimble. Then he flew gently round the bed, fanning the boy's forehead with his wings. "How cool I feel!" said the boy, "I must be getting better;" and he sank into delicious slumber.

Then the Swallow flew back to the Happy Prince, and told him what he had done. "It is curious," he remarked, "but I feel quite warm now, although it is so cold."

"That is because you have done a good action," said the

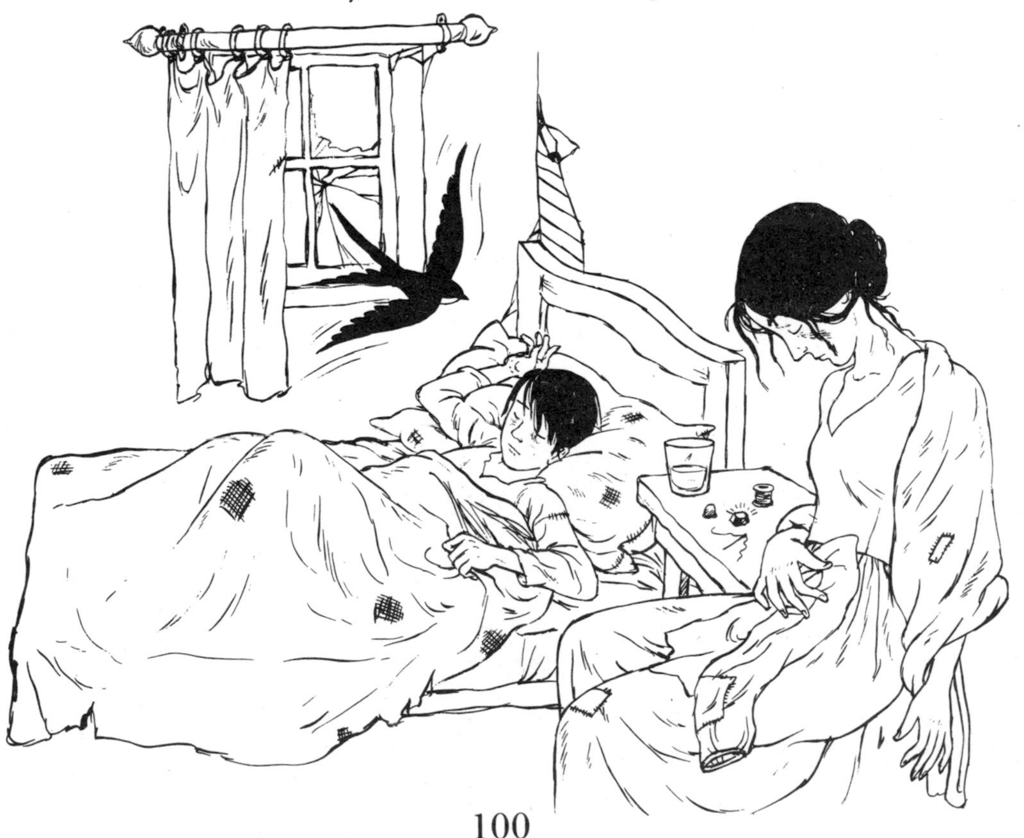

Prince. And the little Swallow began to think, and then he fell asleep. Thinking always made him sleepy.

When day broke he flew down to the river and had a bath. "What a remarkable phenomenon!" said the Professor of Ornithology as he was passing over the bridge. "A swallow in winter!" And he wrote a long letter about it to the local newspaper. Everyone quoted it, it was full of so many words that they could not understand.

"Tonight I go to Egypt," said the Swallow, and he was in high spirits at the prospect. He visited all the public monuments, and sat a long time on top of the church steeple. Wherever he went the Sparrows chirruped, and said to each other, "What a distinguished stranger!" so he enjoyed himself very much.

When the moon rose he flew back to the Happy Prince. "Have you any commissions for Egypt?" he cried; "I am just starting."

"Swallow, Swallow, little Swallow," said the Prince, "will you not stay with me one night longer?"

"I am waited for in Egypt," answered the Swallow. "Tomorrow my friends will fly up to the Second Cataract. The river-horse couches there among the bulrushes, and on a great granite house sits the God Memnon. All night long he watches the stars, and when the morning star shines he utters one cry of joy, and then he is silent. At noon the yellow lions come down to the water's edge to drink. They have eyes like green beryls, and their roar is louder than the roar of the cataract."

"Swallow, Swallow, little Swallow," said the Prince, "faraway across the city I see a young man in a garret. He is leaning over a desk covered with papers, and in a tumbler by his side there is a bunch of withered violets. His hair is brown and crisp, and his lips are red as a pomegranate, and he has large dreamy eyes. He is trying to finish a play for the Director of the Theatre, but he is too cold to write any more. There is no fire in the grate, and hunger has made him faint."

"I will wait with you one night longer," said the Swallow, who really had a good heart. "Shall I take him another ruby?"

"Alas! I have no ruby now," said the Prince; "my eyes are all that I have left. They are made of rare sapphires, which were brought out of India a thousand years ago. Pluck out one of them and take it to him. He will sell it to the jeweller, and buy firewood, and finish his play."

"Dear Prince," said the Swallow, "I cannot do that;" and he began to weep.

"Swallow, Swallow, little Swallow," said the Prince, "do as I command you."

So the Swallow plucked out the Prince's eye, and flew away to the student's garret. It was easy enough to get in, as there was a hole in the roof. Through this he darted, and came into the room. The young man had his head buried in his hands, so he did not hear the flutter of the bird's wings, and when he looked up he found the beautiful sapphire lying on the withered violets.

"I am beginning to be appreciated," he cried; "this is from some great admirer. Now I can finish my play," and he looked quite happy.

The next day the Swallow flew down to the harbour. He sat on the mast of a large vessel and watched the sailors hauling big chests out of the hold with ropes. "Heave a-hoy!" they shouted as each chest came up. "I am going to Egypt!" cried the Swallow, but nobody minded, and when the moon rose he flew back to the Happy Prince.

"I am come to bid you goodbye," he cried.

"Swallow, Swallow, little Swallow," said the Prince, "will you not stay with me one night longer?"

"It is winter," answered the Swallow, "and the chill snow will soon be here. In Egypt the sun is warm on the green palm trees, and the crocodiles lie in the mud and look lazily about them. My companions are building a nest in the Temple of Baalbec, and the pink and white doves are watching them, and cooing to each other. Dear Prince, I must leave you, but I will never forget you, and next spring I will bring you back two beautiful jewels in place of those you have given away. The ruby shall be redder than a red rose, and the sapphire shall be as blue as the great sea."

"In the square below," said the Happy Prince, "there stands a little match girl. She has let her matches fall in the gutter, and they are all spoiled. Her father will beat her if she does not bring home some money, and she is crying. She has no shoes or stockings, and her little head is bare. Pluck out my other eye, and give it to her, and her father will not beat her."

"I will stay with you one night longer," said the Swallow, "but I cannot pluck out your eye. You would be quite blind then."

"Swallow, Swallow, little Swallow," said the Prince, "do as I command you."

So he plucked out the Prince's other eye, and darted down with it. He swooped past the match girl, and slipped the jewel into the palm of her hand. "What a lovely bit of glass!" cried the little girl; and she ran home laughing.

Then the Swallow came back to the Prince, "You are blind now," he said, "so I will stay with you always."

"No, little Swallow," said the poor Prince, "you must go away to Egypt."

"I will stay with you always," said the Swallow, and he slept at the Prince's feet.

All the next day he sat on the Prince's shoulder, and told him stories of what he had seen in strange lands. He told him of the red ibises, who stand in long rows on the banks of the Nile, and catch goldfish in their beaks; of the Sphinx, who is as old as the world itself, and lives in the desert, and knows everything; of the merchants, who walk slowly by the side of their camels and carry amber beads in their hands; of the King of the Mountains of the Moon, who is as black as ebony, and worships a large crystal; of the great green snake that sleeps in a palm tree, and has twenty priests to feed it with honey cakes; and of the pygmies who sail over a big lake on large flat leaves, and are always at war with the butterflies.

"Dear little Swallow," said the Prince, "you tell me of marvellous things, but more marvellous than anything is the suffering of men and of women. There is no Mystery so great as Misery. Fly over my city, little Swallow, and tell me what you see there."

So the Swallow flew over the great city, and saw the rich making merry in their beautiful houses, while the beggars were sitting at the gates. He flew into dark lanes, and saw the white faces of starving children looking out listlessly at the black streets. Under the archway of a bridge two little boys were lying in one another's arms to try and keep themselves warm. "How hungry we are!" they said. "You must not lie here," shouted the watchman, and they wandered out into the rain.

Then he flew back and told the Prince what he had seen.

"I am covered with fine gold," said the Prince, "you must take it off, leaf by leaf, and give it to my poor; the living always think that gold can make them happy."

Leaf after leaf of the fine gold the Swallow picked off, till the Happy Prince looked quite dull and grey. Leaf after leaf of the fine gold he brought to the poor, and the children's faces grew rosier, and they laughed and played games in the street. "We have bread now!" they cried.

Then the snow came, and after the snow came the frost. The streets looked as if they were made of silver, they were so bright and glistening; long icicles like crystal daggers hung down from the eaves of the houses, everybody went about in furs, and the little boys wore scarlet caps and skated on the ice.

The poor little Swallow grew colder and colder, but he would not leave the Prince, he loved him too well. He picked up crumbs outside the baker's door when the baker was not looking, and tried to keep himself warm by flapping his wings.

But at last he knew that he was going to die. He had just enough strength to fly up to the Prince's shoulder once more.

"Goodbye, dear Prince!" he murmured, "will you let me kiss your hand?"

"I am glad that you are going to Egypt at last, little Swallow," said the Prince, "you have stayed too long here; but you must kiss me on the lips, for I love you."

"It is not to Egypt that I am going," said the Swallow. "I am going to the House of Death. Death is the Brother of Sleep, is he not?"

And he kissed the Happy Prince on the lips, and fell down dead at his feet.

At that moment a curious crack sounded inside the statue, as if something had broken. The fact is that the leaden heart had snapped right in two. It certainly was a dreadfully hard frost.

Early next morning the Mayor was walking in the square below in company with the Town Councillors. As they passed the column he looked up at the statue: "Dear me! How shabby the Happy Prince looks!" he said.

"How shabby, indeed!" cried the Town Councillors, who always agreed with the Mayor; and they went up to look at it.

"The ruby has fallen out of his sword, his eyes are gone, and he is golden no longer," said the Mayor; "in fact he is little better than a beggar!"

"Little better than a beggar," said the Town Councillors.

"And here is actually a dead bird at his feet!" continued the Mayor. "We must really issue a proclamation that birds are not to be allowed to die here." And the Town Clerk made a note of the suggestion.

So they pulled down the statue of the Happy Prince. "As he is no longer beautiful he is no longer useful," said the Art Professor at the University.

Then they melted the statue in a furnace, and the Mayor held a meeting of the Corporation to decide what was to be done with the metal. "We must have another statue, of course," he said, "and it shall be a statue of myself."

"Of myself," said each of the Town Councillors, and they quarrelled. When I last heard of them they were quarrelling still.

"What a strange thing!" said the overseer of the workmen at the foundry. "This broken lead heart will not melt in the furnace. We must throw it away." So they threw it on a dust heap where the dead Swallow was also lying.

"Bring me the two most precious things in the city," said God to one of His Angels; and the Angel brought Him the leaden heart and the dead bird.

"You have rightly chosen," said God, "for in my garden of Paradise this little bird shall sing for evermore, and in my city of gold the Happy Prince shall praise me."

THE BEAST WITH A THOUSAND TEETH

Terry Jones

A long time ago, in a land far away, the most terrible beast that ever lived roamed the countryside. It had four eyes, six legs and a thousand teeth. In the morning it would gobble up men as they went to work in the fields. In the afternoon it would break into lonely farms and eat up mothers and children as they sat down to lunch, and at night it would stalk the streets of the towns, looking for its supper.

In the biggest of all the towns, there lived a pastrycook and his wife, and they had a small son whose name was Sam. One morning, as Sam was helping his father to make pastries, he heard that the mayor had offered a reward of ten bags of gold to anyone who could rid the city of the beast.

"Oh," said Sam, "wouldn't I just like to win those ten bags of gold!"

"Nonsense!" said his father. "Put those pastries in the oven."

That afternoon, they heard that the king himself had offered a reward of a hundred bags of gold to anyone who could rid the kingdom of the beast.

"Oooh! Wouldn't I just like to win those hundred bags of gold," said Sam.

"You're too small," said his father. "Now run along and take those cakes to the palace before it gets dark."

So Sam set off for the palace with a tray of cakes balanced on his head. But he was so busy thinking of the hundred bags of gold that he lost his way, and soon it began to grow dark.

"Oh dear!" said Sam. "The beast will be coming soon to look for his supper. I'd better hurry home."

So he turned and started to hurry home as fast as he could. But he was utterly and completely lost, and he didn't know which way to turn. Soon it grew very dark. The streets were deserted, and everyone was safe inside, and had bolted and barred their doors for fear of the beast.

Poor Sam ran up this street and down the next, but he couldn't find the way home. Then suddenly – in the distance – he heard a sound like thunder, and he knew that the beast with a thousand teeth was approaching the city!

Sam ran up to the nearest house, and started to bang on the door.

"Let me in!" he cried. "I'm out in the streets, and the beast is approaching the city! Listen!" And he could hear the sound of the beast getting nearer and nearer. The ground shook and the windows rattled in their frames. But the people inside said no – if they opened the door, the beast might get in and eat them too.

So poor Sam ran up to the next house, and banged as hard as he could on their door, but the people told him to go away.

Then he heard a roar, and he heard the beast coming down the street, and he ran as hard as he could. But no matter how hard he ran, he could hear the beast getting nearer . . . and nearer . . . And he glanced over his shoulder – and there it was at the end of the street! Poor Sam in his fright dropped his tray, and hid under some steps. And the beast got nearer and nearer until it was right

on top of him, and it bent down and its terrible jaws went SNACK! and it gobbled up the tray of cakes, and then it turned on Sam.

Sam plucked up all his courage and shouted as loud as he could: "Don't eat me, Beast! Wouldn't you rather have some more cakes?"

The beast stopped and looked at Sam, and then it looked back at the empty tray, and it said: "Well . . . they *were* very nice cakes . . . I liked the pink ones particularly. But there are no more left, so I'll just have to eat you . . ." And it reached under the steps where poor Sam was hiding, and pulled him out in its great horny claws.

"Oh . . . p-p-please!" cried Sam. "If you don't eat me, I'll make you some more. I'll make you lots of good things, for I'm the son of the best pastrycook in the land."

"Will you make more of those pink ones?" asked the beast.

"Oh yes! I'll make you as many pink ones as you can eat!" cried Sam.

"Very well," said the beast, and put poor Sam in his pocket, and carried him home to his lair.

The beast lived in a dark and dismal cave. The floor was

littered with the bones of the people it had eaten, and the stone walls were marked with lines, where the beast used to sharpen its teeth. But Sam got to work right away, and started to bake as many cakes as he could for the beast. And when he ran out of flour or eggs or anything else, the beast would run back into town to get them, although it never paid for anything.

Sam cooked and baked, and he made scones and éclairs and meringues and sponge cakes and shortbread and doughnuts. But the beast looked at them and said, "You haven't made any pink ones!"

"Just a minute!" said Sam, and he took all the cakes and he covered every one of them in pink icing.

"There you are," said Sam, "they're *all* pink ones!"

"Great!" said the beast and ate the lot.

Well, the beast grew so fond of Sam's cakes that it shortly gave up eating people altogether, and it stayed at home in its cave eating and eating, and growing fatter and fatter. This went on for a whole year, until one morning Sam woke up to find the beast rolling around groaning and beating the floor of the cave. Of course you can guess what was the matter with it.

"Oh dear," said Sam, "I'm afraid it's all that pink icing that has given you toothache."

Well, the toothache got worse and worse and, because the beast had a thousand teeth, it was soon suffering from the worst toothache that anyone in the whole history of the world has ever suffered from. It lay on its side and held its head and roared in agony, until Sam began to feel quite sorry for it. The beast howled and howled with pain, until it could stand it no longer. "Please, Sam, help me!" it cried.

"Very well," said Sam. "Sit still and open your mouth."

So the beast sat very still and opened its mouth, while Sam got a pair of pliers and took out every single tooth in that beast's head.

Well, when the beast had lost all its thousand teeth, it couldn't eat people any more. So Sam took it home and went to the mayor and claimed ten bags of gold as his reward. Then he went to the king and claimed the hundred bags of gold as his reward. Then he went back and lived with his father and mother once more, and the beast helped in the pastryshop, and took cakes to the palace every day, and everyone forgot they had ever been afraid of the beast with a thousand teeth.

BRER RABBIT GETS HIMSELF A HOUSE

Joel Chandler Harris

Long ago an old man called Uncle Remus used to tell stories to a little boy. The two of them lived on a plantation in the southern states of America, and the stories were always about certain animals, Brer Rabbit and Brer Fox in particular, but several others too, Brer Bear and Brer Possum for instance.

One evening, Uncle Remus ate his supper as usual and then looked at the child over his spectacles and said,

"Now then, honey, I'll just rustle around with my memories and see if I can call to mind how old Brer Rabbit got himself a two-storey house without paying much for it."

He paused a moment, then told the following story:

It turned out one time that a whole lot of creatures decided to build a house together. Old Brer Bear he was among them, and Brer Fox and Brer Wolf and Brer Coon and Brer Possum, and possibly Brer Mink too. Anyway, there was a whole bunch of them, and they set to work and built a house in less than no time. Brer Rabbit, he pretended it made his head swim to climb the scaffolding, and that it made him feel dizzy to work in the sun, but he got a board, and he stuck a pencil behind his ear, and he went round measuring and marking, measuring and marking.

He looked so busy that all the other creatures were sure he was doing the most work, and folks going along the road said, "My, my, that Brer Rabbit is doing more work than the whole lot of them put together." Yet all the time Brer Rabbit was doing nothing, and he had plenty of time to lie in the shade scratching fleas off himself.

Meanwhile, the other creatures, they built the house, and it sure was a fine one. It had an upstairs and a downstairs, and chimneys all round, and it had rooms for all the creatures who had helped to make it.

Brer Rabbit, he picked out one of the upstairs rooms, and he got a gun and a brass cannon, and when no one was looking he put

them up in the room. Then he got a big bowl of dirty water and carried it up there when no one was looking.

When the house was finished and all the animals were sitting in the parlour after supper, Brer Rabbit, he got up and stretched himself, and made excuses, saying he believed he'd go to his room. When he got there, and while all the others were laughing and chatting and being sociable downstairs, Brer Rabbit stuck his head out of the room and hollered:

"When a big man wants to sit down, whereabouts is he going to sit?" says he.

The other creatures laughed and called back, "If a big man like you can't sit in a chair, he'd better sit on the floor."

"Watch out, down there," says old Brer Rabbit, "because I'm going to sit down," says he.

With that, *bang!* went Brer Rabbit's gun. The other creatures looked round at one another in astonishment as much as to say, "What in the name of gracious is that?"

They listened and they listened, but they didn't hear any more fuss and it wasn't long before they were all chatting again.

Then Brer Rabbit stuck his head out of his room again, and hollered, "When a big man like me wants to sneeze, whereabouts is he going to sneeze?"

The other creatures called back, "A big man like you can sneeze anywhere he wants."

"Watch out down there, then," says Brer Rabbit, "because I'm going to sneeze right here," says he.

With that Brer Rabbit let off his cannon – *bulder-um-m-m!* The window panes rattled. The whole house shook as though it would come down, and old Brer Bear fell out of his rocking chair – *kerblump!*

When they all settled down again Brer Possum and Brer Mink suggested that as Brer Rabbit had such a bad cold they would step outside and get some fresh air. The other creatures said that they would stick it out, and before long they all got their hair smoothed down and began to talk again.

After a while, when they were beginning to enjoy themselves once more, Brer Rabbit hollered out:

"When a big man like me chews tobacco, where is he going to spit?"

The other creatures called back as though they were getting pretty angry:

"Big man or little man, spit where you please!"

Then Brer Rabbit called out, "This is the way a big man spits," and with that he tipped over the bowl of dirty water, and when the other creatures heard it coming sloshing down the stairs, my, how they rushed out of the house! Some went out the back door, some went out the front door, some fell out of the windows, some went one way and some another way; but they all got out as quickly as they could.

Then Brer Rabbit, he shut up the house, and fastened the windows and went to bed. He pulled the covers up round his ears, and he slept like a man who doesn't owe anybody anything.

"And neither did he owe them," said Uncle Remus to the little boy, "for if the other creatures got scared and ran off from their own house, what business is that of Brer Rabbit? That's what I'd like to know."

JOSEPH AND HIS COAT OF MANY COLOURS

Old Testament

Over two thousand years ago there lived a good man called Israel. He had twelve sons but he loved Joseph the best of all, and one day he gave him a gorgeous coat of many colours. Joseph's brothers, except baby Benjamin, were jealous for their father never gave them any presents.

Once Joseph had a dream and foolishly he told his brothers about it. "I dreamed that we were stacking sheaves of corn in the fields when suddenly your sheaves bowed down to my sheaf!"

"What! We'll never bow down to you," they shouted and they hated him even more and planned to get rid of him.

One day the brothers were guarding their father's sheep in some faraway fields when Israel sent Joseph to see that all was well with his brothers. When they saw him coming they whispered, "This is our chance. Let us kill Joseph and throw him into a deep

hole. Then we'll tell father that a wild animal ate him."

But Reuben, the eldest son, did not agree. "Put him down this empty well and leave him," he suggested because secretly he planned to come back later and rescue Joseph. The rest agreed so when Joseph arrived, they beat him and tore off his lovely coat before throwing him into a well. Then they calmly ate their dinner in the fields.

Before long, some merchants on their way to Egypt passed by. The brothers decided to sell Joseph to them for twenty pieces of silver. He was hauled out of the well and the merchants took him with them to Egypt where they sold him as a slave.

Later, the brothers killed a goat and dipped Joseph's coat in its blood. They showed this to their father who cried piteously: "It is Joseph's coat. My son has been killed. Woe is me!" From that day on, he would not let little Benjamin out of his sight.

In Egypt Joseph was sold to Potiphar, the captain of the Pharaoh's guard, and he worked well because he thought it was his duty to God.

Before long Potiphar trusted him to look after everything in his house. But Potiphar's wife fell in love with the young and clever Joseph. She was furious when he did not return her love. In revenge, she told Potiphar many lies and wicked stories about him. Potiphar believed his wife and he threw Joseph into prison. Here he was kept with the Pharaoh's prisoners, but he refused to be downhearted for he knew he had done nothing wrong.

It chanced that the Pharaoh's chief baker and chief winekeeper were also in prison and one night both of them had puzzling dreams. The winekeeper dreamed about a vine with three branches from which he picked many grapes. Then he squeezed their juice into the Pharaoh's cup. Joseph, who knew all about dreams, said this meant Pharaoh would send for his winekeeper in three days and forgive him.

The baker dreamed he was carrying three baskets of delicious cakes on his head but birds flew down and ate them all. Joseph felt sad because he knew this meant that in three days the baker would be put to death on the Pharaoh's orders.

All this came to pass – the winekeeper was let out of prison and Joseph begged him to tell Pharaoh about the lies of Potiphar's wife. But for two years the man forgot about Joseph until one night Pharaoh had two strange dreams. He dreamed he was standing by the River Nile where seven fat cows were eating grass. Seven thin scrawny ones appeared and swallowed them up. Then he noticed seven ripe ears of wheat but they were eaten up by seven shrivelled ears of wheat. Nobody could tell Pharaoh what these dreams meant, until the winekeeper remembered Joseph. Pharaoh sent for him and Joseph told him that the seven fat cows and the seven ripe ears of wheat meant the same thing. There would be plenty of good food in Egypt for seven years. Then there would be seven years of famine when nothing would grow. Joseph said Pharaoh must build barns and store plenty of food in the good years, to use during the bad years.

Pharaoh thanked Joseph and made him Chief Ruler of Egypt. He gave him fine clothes, a gold ring and chain, a lovely Egyptian wife, a wonderful chariot and many slaves.

For seven years the harvests were good just as Joseph foretold. They stored so much grain in the cities each year that nobody could count it. Then the years of plenty ended and people began to starve. Joseph was able to hand out wheat from the barns and before long, people from countries far and wide came to Egypt to buy corn. Joseph believed God had been helping him and he remembered to pray each day for his father and family.

In Canaan where Israel and his sons lived there was also famine, so Israel sent them to Egypt to buy wheat before they starved to death. He did not let Benjamin go.

The others journeyed to Egypt where they found Joseph the Ruler. He knew them at once but they did not realize that this important person was Joseph and they bowed down before him. Joseph's first dream had come true. He spoke roughly to them and pretended he could not understand them. "You are spies," he said, but they answered, "No, no, my lord. We are honest men who have come to buy food for our starving families."

Next, Joseph asked them many questions. They told him that Israel still felt sad about his lost son and that he loved little Benjamin very dearly. Then Joseph said sternly: "Take the food you need and go. Leave Simeon behind and bring Benjamin to see me. Then I'll know you are not spies and you can all go home."

Joseph heard the brothers say sadly that this was a punishment from God for their cruelty to Joseph long ago. They filled their sacks with wheat but when they arrived home they found money inside the sacks. They were worried and did not dare return to Egypt lest they be accused of stealing.

But soon the famine in Canaan grew worse. The brothers were forced to return to Egypt and this time they took Benjamin.

Joseph was overjoyed when they arrived with his youngest brother. Simeon joined them and all the brothers sat down to a feast. Joseph spoke kindly to everyone but when Benjamin told him his father was alive and well tears came to his eyes.

Israel's sacks were filled with wheat and in Benjamin's little sack Joseph hid his own silver cup. Next day they set off but they had not travelled far when Joseph's men galloped up.

"Our master says you are thieves. We must search your belongings."

Of course they found the silver cup in Benjamin's sack and they accused him of stealing it. Everyone went back to the city where Joseph said, "The one in whose sack the cup was found must stay as my slave. The rest of you can go free."

The brothers knew Benjamin had not taken the cup. They begged Joseph to change his mind and Judah fell on his knees.

"Our father will die of sorrow," he pleaded, "if we go back without Benjamin. Let me take his place and be your slave."

When he heard this, Joseph could not pretend any longer. He burst into tears and in their own language he cried:

"I am Joseph, your brother, whom you sold as a slave. With God's help I have become rich and powerful. I have forgiven you, my brothers, for I know you are sorry now. But you must go quickly to Canaan. Tell my father the good news and bring him, his goods and your families to Egypt, for this famine will last for five more years. You will be safe here. Hurry, hurry!"

When the brothers reached Israel's house they called joyfully: "Joseph lives! He is a great and good man in Egypt."

Israel could scarcely believe his ears but when he heard the whole story he thanked God for all these blessings. Then Israel, his sons and their wives packed all their belongings and went to Egypt where they lived in peace and plenty for many many years.

THE COMING OF KING ARTHUR

Arthurian Legend

In Britain's West Countrie long ago there lived a king called Uther Pendragon who had many enemies. The king's closest friend, the wizard Merlin, advised the king to take his son Arthur away to a safer place. So it was that Arthur was taken to the castle of Sir Hector, a noble knight.

Arthur grew up with Kay, Sir Hector's son and together the two boys learned to use their swords like true knights. Arthur had no idea he was a king's son until one day Merlin visited the castle and watched Arthur and Kay jousting together. He summoned Sir Hector: "Uther Pendragon is dead," he said. "His subjects need a strong leader to fight their enemies, so it is time for Arthur, heir to Uther's throne, to show himself. This is my plan."

He told Sir Hector about a tournament at Camelot and said Arthur and Kay should learn to do battle against the men there who did not want Arthur to become king after his father.

The boys were very excited at the prospect of being true knights. "I trust you have forgotten nothing," said Sir Hector as they rode into Camelot. Kay seemed uncomfortable but Arthur only had eyes for the flags and shields of the knights. He put his hand on his sword. Just then Kay grabbed his arm. "I've forgotten my sword," he whispered. "I can't take part in the tournament! What shall I do?" At once Arthur handed his sword to Kay. "Take mine. I'll find another somewhere," and he slipped away.

He wandered along until he came to a huge stone with a sword buried right up to its hilt. "What luck!" he exclaimed. "Someone has left his sword here. I'll take it for the tournament and return it afterwards." A crowd soon gathered round to watch. He put one foot firmly on the stone then he tugged at the hilt, using both hands. The sword came out so easily that he almost fell backwards! The crowd gasped in astonishment and murmured uneasily while Arthur rushed happily back to the tournament. Kay had already suffered defeat, so Arthur attacked the nearest swordsman. Knight after knight he conquered and before long a cry arose: "The Sword in the Stone! This boy pulled out the Sword!"

Soon Mordred, young Arthur's chief enemy, heard these shouts. He was troubled because he knew the words carved at the bottom of the stone:

'Only the true king can draw this sword from the stone.'

He himself had tried to drag out the sword to prove that he was the rightful king but he had failed. He saw Arthur approaching, so he clasped his sword. "Mordred," shouted Arthur, "you wanted to steal my father's kingdom when he died. Now I, Arthur Pendragon, have come to claim his crown."

"I'm not afraid of a boy like you," jeered Mordred, "you will have to kill me first!" and he lunged forward with his sword.

Back and forth they fought, swords clashing and whirling. Then Arthur struck one mighty blow and Mordred fell. The crowds cheered their young rightful king and were glad he had overcome the wicked cruel Mordred.

So Arthur became king, but alas, there were some rulers in the West Countrie who treated their people very badly. King Arthur decided to do something to help them. With banners flying and trumpets sounding, Arthur set out with his warriors, riding on a powerful white horse. Along the road he saw burned-out farms, cottages and starving villagers and at every turn he heard: "King Pellenore killed our men. King Pellenore took our food. King Pellenore is wicked."

But Pellenore had heard about Arthur so he sent this message to the young king: "Let us settle our quarrel in a single fight outside my castle: man to man, without any of our warriors."

Arthur agreed to this challenge and he rode alone to meet Pellenore. They fought grimly, then slowly but surely Arthur drove Pellenore back. Suddenly Pellenore gave a secret signal. His knights poured out from the castle and attacked Arthur. His horse was cut down and as Arthur fell, his sword from the stone shattered and his armour was torn away. He was close to death when Sir Lancelot, his most trusted knight, galloped up and pierced Pellenore's wicked heart with his lance. His followers ran away and Lancelot carried Arthur into the castle to recover from his terrible wounds.

Arthur grieved over his lost sword when suddenly Merlin appeared. "Send your men back to Camelot," he whispered, "then follow me and I will lead you to a mightier sword."

Arthur gave his orders and Merlin led him along winding paths to a lonely, silent place. A wonderful lake appeared and Arthur gasped fearfully, for in the lake's centre a long and slender arm, covered with white silk, held up a sword.

"Take that boat and fetch the sword," ordered Merlin. "The Lady of the Lake is lending you Excalibur. Use it to help others for as long as you live. Guard it well: it has magic powers."

Arthur rowed out and withdrew the sword carefully and as he did so the arm sank beneath the waters. He noticed some letters on the blade: 'Keep me' and 'Cast me away'. He rowed back to Merlin and the wizard spoke seriously: "When your death is near, promise that you will come back to this place and return Excalibur to the Lady of the Lake."

"Faithfully, I promise." Young King Arthur thanked Merlin then off he galloped to Camelot, eager for adventures with his new sword Excalibur.

THE BOY WHO CRIED WOLF

Aesop's Fables

There was once a shepherd boy who loved to play jokes on his friends in the village where he lived.

One day when he was tending the sheep on the hillside, he saw that his mother and the other women were collecting water in big stone jars at the stream down below. "Help, mother, help!" he shouted. "Wolves are attacking me – come quickly. Help!"

The women stopped what they were doing and ran over the rough ground to help him. All the water in their jars was spilt but that naughty boy only laughed. "Fooled you, didn't I?" he shouted.

Another day he waited until all the men were sitting down to eat their supper after a hard day's work. "Wolves, wolves," he shouted. The villagers rushed to his side but he had fooled them again and their supper was cold when they got back home.

This unkind shepherd boy played this trick many times until one day he was alone outside the village with his flock. A wolf silently crept up and attacked his sheep. He screamed and he shouted but the villagers smiled and nodded to each other. "He's up to his old tricks," they all agreed.

The boy bellowed "Wolf!" until he was hoarse but no help came. All the sheep were killed. That foolish boy had cried 'wolf' so often that when he did tell the truth nobody believed him.

CLUMSY HANS

Hans Andersen

In a big house in the country there lived a rich man who had three sons. The two eldest boys thought they were twice as clever as anyone else, especially their younger brother, whom they nicknamed 'Clumsy Hans'.

The two older brothers wanted to marry the king's daughter and she had declared that she would only marry a suitor who spoke clearly and cleverly and was not afraid of anything.

So, one brother learned the whole of the English dictionary by heart as well as every word in the newspapers for the past five years, while the other brother decided to learn the rules of every trade as well as all the laws in the kingdom.

"The princess will marry *me!*" they both declared. Their father was very proud of them and he gave a wonderful horse to each son. The one who knew so many words received a black horse and the other who knew all about the law was given a white one. Before they set out for the palace they rubbed their lips with cod liver oil to make their lips move quickly when they spoke to the princess.

Everybody had gathered by the stables to give the brothers a good send-off, when the youngest son turned up. "You're wearing your best clothes," he said, "where are you going?"

"Oh, Clumsy Hans," they said, "haven't you heard that whoever can speak the most clearly will win the king's daughter for his wife?"

"What a splendid idea! I'll come with you," exclaimed Clumsy Hans. But they simply burst out laughing and rode off.

"Father, I must have a horse," Hans said. "I think I'd like to get married. If the princess chooses me, that will be good, but if she doesn't want me, I'll marry her all the same!"

"What nonsense," scoffed his father. "I certainly won't give you a horse for you can't think properly and you know nothing You're not like your two clever brothers."

"Very well, if I can't have a horse, I'll take my billy goat. He'll carry me." Away he raced after his brothers, singing loudly as he clung to the goat's curved horns.

The two older brothers were riding slowly for they were practising all the clever words they thought would be useful.

"Hey," called Clumsy Hans, "here I am. Look what I've found on the road. Isn't it beautiful?" And he held up a dead crow.

"Ugh, how horrible," said one brother. "What are you going to do with that, may I ask?"

"With this crow? Give it to the princess, of course," he replied.

"She'll love that!" both brothers laughed unkindly as they rode on. Clumsy Hans rode after them on his billy goat.

"Hey! It's me again," he shouted. "Look what I've found this time. You can't find things like this every day, you know."

The brothers turned round. "That's just an old battered clog. Surely you're not planning to give it to the princess, you silly boy?"

"Of course I am," laughed Clumsy Hans as his brothers spurred on their horses. This time they rode very quickly away from him. But before long he caught up with them as they took a rest.

"Hey, here I am again," chuckled Clumsy Hans, "with something wonderful."

"What is it this time?" sighed the brothers.

"It's marvellous," came the boast, "the princess will love it."

"Why, it's plain smelly mud from the ditch!" they both said.

"That's right," was the reply. "Best ditch mud. See, it will run through my fingers. I'll fill up my pockets with it."

This time the brothers galloped away and reached the city gates more than an hour before their brother on his goat. So many young men wanted to win the princess that they had to wait packed together in tight lines until their name was called. Inside the palace many townsfolk stood around to listen to all these clever suitors, but strange to say, as soon as they were called inside, these selfsame suitors seemed to lose their tongues.

"He's no good," the princess kept shouting. "Throw him out!"

At last it was the turn of the brother who knew every word in the dictionary. Once inside, he thought he was standing upside-down for the ceiling was covered with mirrors. There were many clerks by each window, busily scribbling down every single word each young man uttered. There was one chief printer in charge who made sure that all that he heard was printed in the newspapers the next day. The floorboards creaked. The stoves were red-hot so the hall was extremely warm. The young man quivered and shook and then muttered: "It's terribly hot in here."

"True," agreed the princess, "my father is frying chickens today."

He stood there like a dummy. He forgot all the long words he had learned. He forgot the clever things he had practised. He stood there and could not think of a single sensible word!

"He's no good," said the princess. "Throw him out," and the first clever brother had to leave the hall.

Now the second brother tried his luck.

"Phew, how hot it is in here," he gasped.

"True. The king is frying chickens," said the princess.

"Eh, umm, er," he stammered, "er, umm, eh," and the clerks carefully wrote down "er, umm, eh," in their notebooks.

"No good. Throw him out," and that was the end of the second brother.

Now it was Clumsy Hans' turn. He rode into the hall on his billy goat.

"It's far too hot in here," he complained.

"True. The king is frying chickens," said the princess.

"Splendid," Clumsy Hans told her, "in that case I will fry my black crow with his chickens."

"That's fine," said the princess, "but I'm afraid that I haven't a pot or a frying pan. Have you got anything you can fry a crow in?"

"Oh, that's simple enough. I've got the very thing. Here is a good cooking pot for you," and he pulled out the old clog and pushed the dead and rather smelly crow inside.

"We'll have a fine feast," the princess smiled, "but I'd like to start with soup, if you please. Where can we get some?"

"I happen to have some in my pocket," said Clumsy Hans. "In fact, I have so much that I can throw some away." He put one hand into his pocket and scattered a little mud behind him.

"I like this suitor," exclaimed the princess. "You seem to be the only one who talks sensibly and gives good answers to all my questions. But do you know that every word we say together in this hall is being written down by those reporters over there? It will be printed in the newspapers tomorrow and the townsfolk will be able to read our secrets. Of course they don't understand a word they are writing and that old man who is in charge is the worst. He can't understand anything at all!"

The princess laughed behind her hand for she wanted to test Clumsy Hans a little more. The clerks whispered together and each one deliberately dropped an ink blob on the floor.

"Reporters, did you say?" exclaimed Clumsy Hans. "Do you mean that everybody believes what these stupid people write or say? Then the chief printer shall receive my last gift and best gift." With that, he threw all the mud he had left into the head printer's face!

"Bravo! Well done," the princess clapped her hands. "I have never been brave enough to do that to newspaper reporters. You are clever with words and you are not afraid of anything or anyone so let us ask my father if we can be married today."

So Clumsy Hans won the princess for his wife, much to his brothers' surprise, and in the end he was crowned king. He was a Clever Hans now!

THE BLACK BULL OF NORROWAY

Scottish & Scandinavian Traditional

Long ago, in a country far away in the north there lived a widow and her three daughters. She had once been a queen, but her husband, the king, had been killed in a battle and she was now very, very poor.

One day her eldest daughter said to her, "Mother, bake me a cake to take to the fortune-teller so that she will tell me my fortune."

The fortune-teller accepted the fine cake the girl had brought, and then she said to her, "Stand by the back door, my dear, and tell me if anything comes down the road." By and by the girl cried out that a carriage drawn by six grey horses was coming towards them.

"Go with it," said the fortune-teller, "for there your fortune lies." The coachman stopped for the girl to climb in, and away they went.

Before long the second daughter asked her mother to bake a cake for the fortune-teller, for she too wanted to know what life had to offer her. "Stand by the back door, my dear," said the fortune-teller, "and tell me if anything comes down the road." Then, when a carriage drawn by six gleaming chestnut horses came by, she told the girl to get into it, for there lay her fortune.

In time the youngest daughter asked her mother to bake a cake for her to take to the fortune-teller. Just as before, the fortune-teller said, "Stand by the back door, my dear, and tell me if anything comes down the road." Soon the girl said:

"I can see a great black bull coming down the road."

"Go with the bull, girl," said the fortune-teller, "for your fortune lies with the bull."

The young girl was very disappointed, for she wanted to drive away in a fine carriage like her sisters, but she did as the fortune-teller told her.

She rode on the back of the great black bull for many miles, until she was faint with hunger and thirst. "Eat out of my left ear," said the bull, "and drink out of my right." The girl did as he suggested and to her amazement found in each ear all the food and drink she wanted.

In the evening they came to a fine castle. "We will spend the night here," said the bull. "It is my brother's castle." The girl was lifted off his back and taken into the castle while the bull was led into a field. To her surprise she found her eldest sister living there as the lady of the house. They greeted each other joyfully, then her sister said, "The black bull you were riding on is really the Lord of Norroway. A spell was cast many years ago which turned him into a bull." That night the girl slept in great luxury and the next day her sister gave her a beautiful apple. "Keep it," she said, "and do not break it, until you are in great trouble."

All that day the girl travelled on the black bull's back, until evening when they came to an even grander castle. "We will stay the night here, in this castle where my second brother lives," said the bull. This time she was not as surprised as before to find her

other sister living there as a grand lady. She spent the night in a fine room filled with beautiful furniture and hung with blue and gold tapestries. In the morning her sister gave her a pear. "Keep it safe," she was told, "until the day when you are in great need. Only then should you break it open."

That day, the girl and the black bull travelled on again. Further and further they journeyed – further than the girl thought possible. She was exhausted when they arrived in the evening at a castle that was grander than any she had seen before.

"This is my home," said the bull, "and we will stay here for tonight." The girl was well looked after as before and the next morning she was given a beautiful plum.

"Keep this carefully," she was told, "until the day when you are in great need. Only then should you break it open."

On the fourth day the great black bull took her to a deep dark valley, where he asked her to get off his back. "You must stay here," he said, "while I go and fight the devil. You will know if I win, for everything around will turn blue, but if I lose, everything

you see will turn red. Sit on this boulder and remember you must not move, not even a hand or a foot until I return. For if you move, I shall never find you again."

The girl promised to do as she was told, for by now she loved and trusted the bull. For hours and hours she sat on the boulder without moving, then, just when she felt she could wait no longer, everything around her suddenly went blue. She was so delighted that she moved one foot. She moved it only a little, just enough to cross it over the other, forgetting her promise for a moment.

The bull returned after his victory but, just as he had said, he could not find her anywhere. The girl stayed in the valley for hours, weeping for what she had done, and at last she set off alone, although she did not know where to go.

After she had wandered from valley to valley for several days, the young girl came to a glass mountain. She tried to climb it, but each time her feet slipped backwards, and eventually she gave up. Soon after this she met a blacksmith who told her that if she worked for him for seven years he would make her special shoes of iron that would take her over the glass mountain.

For seven long years she worked hard for the blacksmith, and at the end of that time he kept his promise and made her the shoes to take her on her way. On the other side of the mountain she stopped at a little house where a washerwoman and her daughter were scrubbing some bloodstained clothes in a tub.

"The finest lord I have ever seen left these clothes here seven years ago," said the washerwoman. "He told us that whoever washed out the bloodstains would be his wife. But for seven long years we have washed and rinsed, and the stains remain."

"Let me try," said the girl, and the first time she washed the clothes the bloodstains disappeared. Absolutely delighted, the washerwoman rushed off and told the lord of the castle nearby that the clothes were clean. Now this lord was the Lord of Norroway, and the old woman lied to him, saying that it was her own daughter who had done the task. She thought it would be a fine thing for her daughter to marry a lord. The wedding was arranged for the next day, and there seemed nothing the young girl could do to stop it.

Then she remembered the apple she had been given so long

ago. Surely the time had come to open it. Inside were jewels, which sparkled and shone. She showed these to the washerwoman, and asked if she could see the lord alone that evening. "The jewels will all be yours if you arrange this for me," she said. The washerwoman took the jewels greedily, but before she allowed the girl to go to the lord's room, she put a sleeping potion in his drink, so that he slept deeply the whole night through. The girl sat by his bedside, and she cried,

> *"Seven long years I served for thee,*
> *The glassy hill I climbed for thee,*
> *The blood-stained clothes I washed for thee,*
> *Wilt thou not wake, and turn to me?"*

but the Lord of Norroway slept on.

The next day the girl was overcome with grief, for she could not think how to stop the wedding, so she broke open the pear, and found it contained even more lovely jewels than the apple. She took these once again to the washerwoman. "Marry your daughter

tomorrow," she begged, "not today, and let me see the lord alone once more. In return the jewels will be yours." The washerwoman agreed, but again slipped a sleeping potion in the lord's drink.

For the second time the girl tried to waken the Lord of Norroway.

> *"Seven long years I served for thee,*
> *The glassy hill I climbed for thee,*
> *The blood-stained clothes I washed for thee,*
> *Wilt thou not wake and turn to me?"*

she cried over and over again, but he slept on, the whole night through.

The next morning the girl broke open the beautiful plum she had been given, and found an even greater collection of splendid jewels. She offered them to the greedy washerwoman who agreed to put off the wedding for one more day. That night, while allowing the girl to visit the bridegroom, she once more put the sleeping potion into his drink. But this time the lord poured away the drink when the washerwoman was not looking for he suspected trickery of some kind. When the girl came to his room for the third time and cried,

> *"Seven long years I served for thee,*
> *The glassy hill I climbed for thee,*
> *The blood-stained clothes I washed for thee,*
> *Wilt thou not wake and turn to me?"*

he turned and saw her.

As they talked he told her his story: how a spell had been cast on him turning him into a bull, how he had fought and beaten the devil and the spell had been broken. "Ever since then," he said, "I have been searching for you."

The Lord of Norroway and the youngest daughter were married next day, and lived happily in the castle. "I little thought," she said, "the day I saw the black bull coming down the road, that I had truly found my fortune."

ARION AND THE DOLPHIN

Greek Legend

There was once a musician called Arion, who wandered about the country singing songs, and wherever he sang people stopped to listen.

When the King of Corinth heard his music he invited Arion to live with him in the royal palace.

One day Arion received an invitation to compete at the music festival in Sicily.

"You must go," said the king, "for I am sure you will win the competition, and the prize is a bag of gold."

"The gold does not interest me," said Arion, "but I would like to compete and of course I would like to win!"

"You may go in one of my ships," said the king, "but promise you'll return, for I shall miss your music."

Arion promised to return, and away he sailed in the king's ship over the sea to the island of Sicily.

All the best musicians in the world were there to compete. One by one they played their instruments and sang their songs, and then it was Arion's turn. He sang so beautifully that the King of Sicily awarded him the first prize, a bag of gold, and all his admirers gave him wonderful gifts of jewels and other treasure. They tried to persuade him to stay on in Sicily, but Arion refused.

"I have promised the King of Corinth I shall return," said he, "and his ship waits there in the harbour to carry me home."

So the King of Sicily and all Arion's friends and admirers saw him off and waved him farewell.

Arion stood on the prow waving to them until they were out of sight, but when he turned to go to the cabin, he found himself surrounded by the captain and an angry crew. They had seen the gold and treasure Arion had carried on board, and had plotted among themselves how they would take it from him.

"You must die," said the captain. "It is the wish of the entire crew."

"Why, what have I done to hurt you?"

"You are too rich," said the captain.

"Spare my life, and I will give you the bag of gold and all the other treasures that were given to me," pleaded Arion.

"No, we cannot do that, for when you reach Corinth you may change your mind, regret your gift, and make us return it," said the captain. "No, it is too dangerous. You must die!"

"Very well," said Arion, "I see that your minds are made up. But please, grant me my last wish. Allow me to sing one more song before I die."

"You may do that," said the captain, "if, when the last note has been sung, you leap overboard into the sea."

Arion promised to do that and, dressed in his finest clothes, he stood on the prow of the ship and sang more sweetly than he had ever sung before. Then he took a great leap into the sea; and the ship sailed on.

Now, a school of dolphins had gathered round to listen to Arion's songs, for dolphins are very fond of music. When he leapt from the ship, one of them swam under him, caught him on its back and saved him from drowning. Then the dolphin swam with

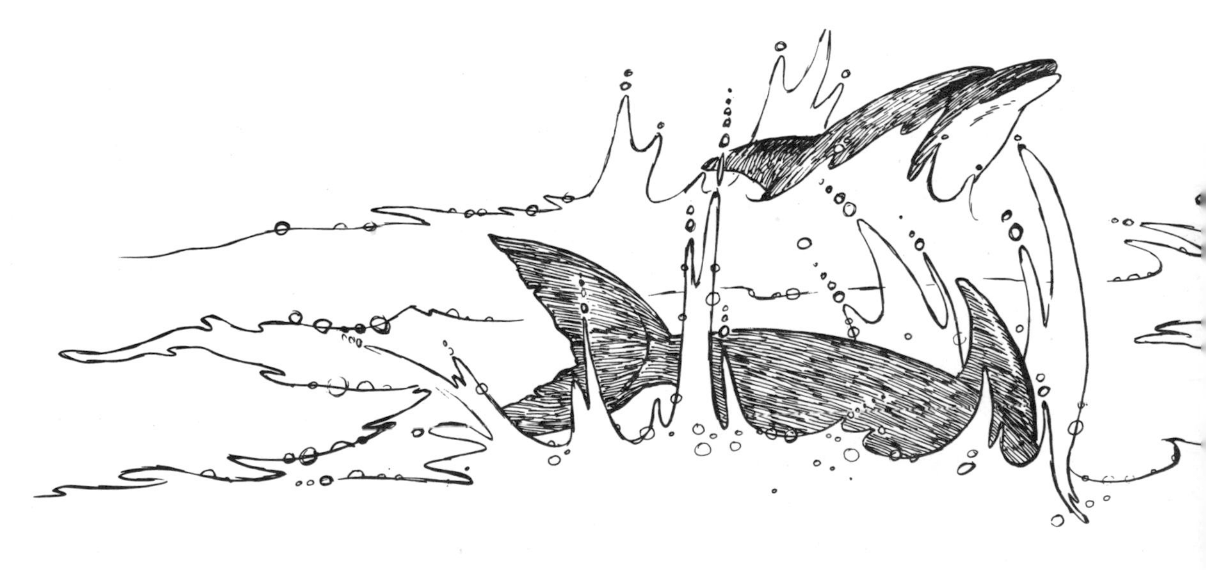

Arion on its back and reached Corinth long before the ship.

The king was delighted to see Arion, but when he heard how the ship's crew had treated him he was very angry indeed.

"I am astonished my sailors could behave so badly," he said.

When at last the ship arrived in port, the king sent for the crew.

"Where is Arion?" he asked, pretending he did not know.

"He stayed in Sicily," said those rascals. "He was enjoying himself so much he refused to return with us, although we waited several days for him."

"Is that so?" said the king, frowning with anger.

Then Arion himself came into the room. He was wearing the same clothes in which he had leapt from the ship and, when they saw him, the captain and the crew were terrified.

"A ghost! A ghost!" they cried out. "Arion was drowned and this must be his ghost!" And in their fright they confessed to the king all that they had done to Arion. The king punished them and ordered them to leave Greece for ever.

As for Arion, he stayed at Corinth and became one of the greatest musicians in all Greece.

How the Rhinoceros Got His Skin

Rudyard Kipling

Once upon a time, on an uninhabited island on the shores of the Red Sea, there lived a Parsee from whose hat the rays of the sun were reflected in more-than-oriental splendour. And the Parsee lived by the Red Sea with nothing but his hat and his knife and a cooking-stove of the kind that you must particularly never touch. And one day he took flour and water and currants and plums and sugar and things, and made himself one cake which was two feet across and three feet thick. It was indeed a Superior Comestible (*that's* Magic), and he put it on the stove because *he* was allowed to cook on that stove, and he baked it and he baked it till it was all done brown and smelt most sentimental.

But just as he was going to eat it there came down to the beach from the Altogether Uninhabited Interior one Rhinoceros with a horn on his nose, two piggy eyes, and few manners. In those days the Rhinoceros's skin fitted him quite tight. There were no wrinkles in it anywhere. He looked exactly like a Noah's Ark Rhinoceros, but of course much bigger. All the same, he had no manners then, and he has no manners now, and he never will have any manners. He said, "How!" and the Parsee left that cake and climbed to the top of a palm-tree with nothing on but his hat, from which the rays of the sun were always reflected, in more-than-oriental splendour. And the Rhinoceros upset the oil-stove with his nose, and the cake rolled on the sand, and he spiked that cake on the horn of his nose, and he ate it, and he went away, waving his tail, to the desolate and Exclusively Uninhabited Interior which abuts on the islands of Mazanderan, Socotra, and the Promontories of the Larger Equinox. Then the Parsee came down from his palm-tree and put the stove on its legs and recited the following *Sloka*, which, as you have not heard, I will now proceed to relate:

"Them that takes cakes
Which the Parsee-man bakes
Makes dreadful mistakes."

And there was a great deal more in that than you would think.

Because, five weeks later, there was a heat-wave in the Red Sea, and everybody took off all the clothes they had. The Parsee took off his hat; but the Rhinoceros took off his skin and carried it over his shoulder as he came down to the beach to bathe. In those days it buttoned underneath with three buttons and looked like a waterproof. He said nothing whatever about the Parsee's cake, because he had eaten it all; and he never had any manners, then, since, or henceforward. He waddled straight into the water and blew bubbles through his nose, leaving his skin on the beach.

Presently the Parsee came by and found the skin, and he smiled one smile that ran all round his face two times. Then he danced three times round the skin and rubbed his hands. Then he went to his camp and filled his hat with cake-crumbs, for the Parsee never ate anything but cake, and never swept out his camp. He took that skin, and he shook that skin, and he scrubbed that skin, and he rubbed that skin just as full of old, dry, stale, tickly cake-crumbs and some burned currants as ever it could *possibly* hold. Then he climbed to the top of his palm-tree and waited for the Rhinoceros to come out of the water and put it on.

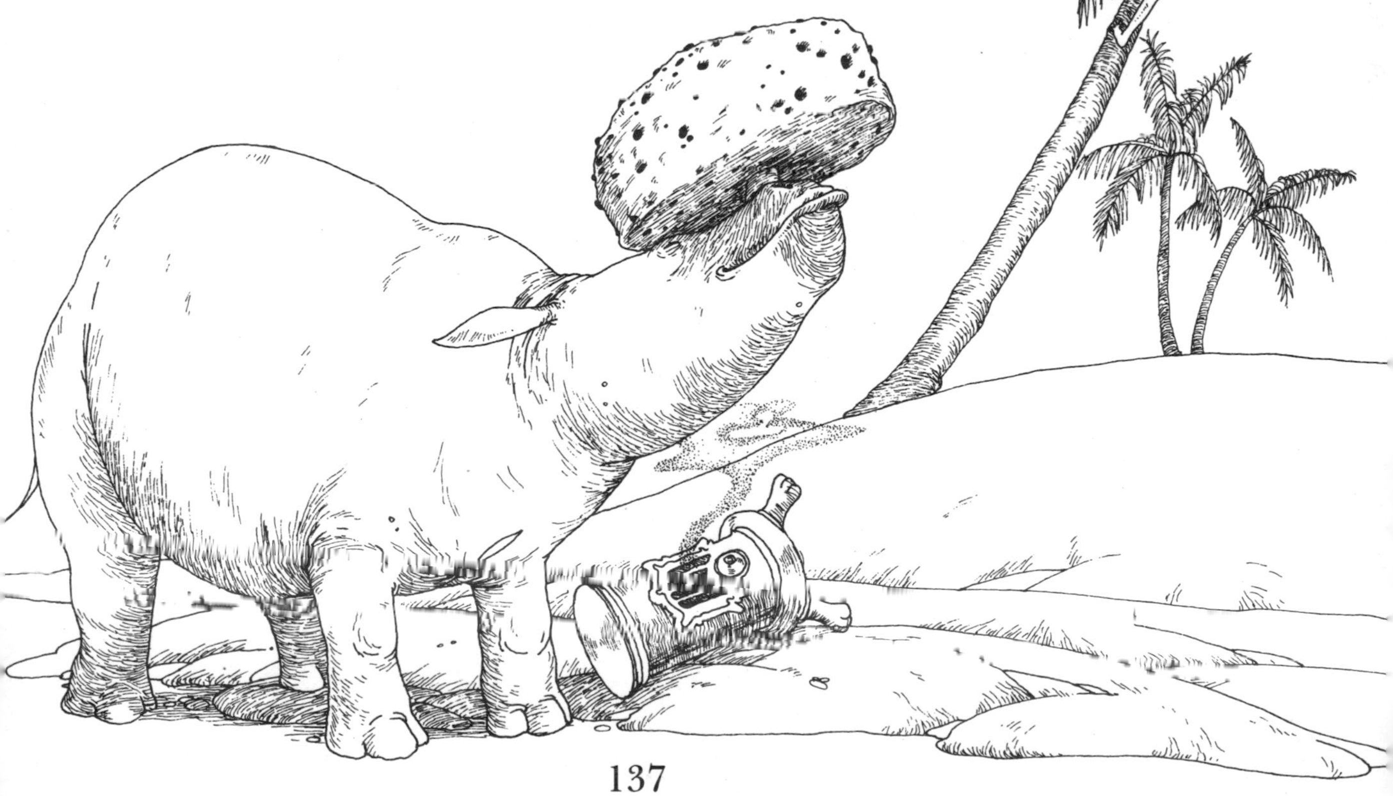

And the Rhinoceros did. He buttoned it up with the three buttons, and it tickled like cake-crumbs in bed. Then he wanted to scratch, but that made it worse; and then he lay down on the sands and rolled and rolled and rolled, and every time he rolled the cake-crumbs tickled him worse and worse and worse. Then he ran to the palm-tree and rubbed and rubbed and rubbed himself against it. He rubbed so much and so hard that he rubbed his skin into a great fold over his shoulders, and another fold underneath, where the buttons used to be (but he rubbed the buttons off), and he rubbed some more folds over his legs. And it spoiled his temper, but it didn't make the least difference to the cake-crumbs. They were inside his skin and they tickled. So he went home, very angry indeed and horribly scratchy; and from that day to this every rhinoceros has great folds in his skin and a very bad temper, all on account of the cake-crumbs inside.

But the Parsee came down from his palm-tree, wearing his hat, from which the rays of the sun were reflected in more-than-oriental splendour, packed up his cooking-stove, and went away in the direction of Orotavo, Amygdala, the Upland Meadows of Antananarivo, and the Marshes of Sonaput.

THE NECKLACE OF PRINCESS FIORIMONDE

Mary de Morgan

Long ago, a king had a most beautiful daughter called Fiorimonde. Princesses are supposed to be charming, happy and good as well as beautiful but this one was wicked and black-hearted. She learned to use black magic from a hideous old witch who lived on a lonely mountain faraway. Nobody knew about her except the princess who often went to her hut when everyone was asleep. This witch had used her magic to make Fiorimonde beautiful and the princess helped her with all her witchcraft in return.

The king decided it was time that his daughter should get married. He sent messengers to nearby kings and princes and invited them to his court to meet the princess. When she heard about this, she trembled with rage for she knew that a husband would soon discover she visited a witch and her beauty would vanish if she could not continue to do so.

That night when everyone was sleeping, the princess called to a small bird sitting on the window-sill. She scattered some special seeds and as the bird pecked them, it grew and grew until it was as large as an ostrich. She climbed out of the window and perched on the bird's back. Instantly it flew away over the countryside till it reached the witch's dark dreary hut on the mountain.

"Who is bothering me? Go away!" a voice croaked when the princess whispered something through the keyhole.

"Let me in," she said, "I must have your help."

The door opened and when the princess went inside she sat near the witch and told her the whole story.

"Mm," croaked the witch, "we'll stop this nonsense! What shall we do with these princes when they come? Turn them into animals or shall we change them into beads to wear like a necklace?"

"Oh, a necklace," the princess laughed horribly, "Just imagine pushing princes on a string! They'll be my best jewels."

"Be careful," the witch warned, "lest you yourself become a

bead," and she pulled a long gold thread out of a dirty black bag. She put it over Fiorimonde's head and round her neck and said: "This thread will never break! You must make those who wish to marry you close their fingers around this cord. They'll be strung along it like beads! They cannot escape unless the thread is cut."

"Wonderful," cried the princess, "you can be sure I'll never close my fingers round it. Oh, how I long to try this out."

The bird carried the princess back in a flash. She gave it some magic drops and it changed back into a tiny bird. It hopped outside and the princess fell fast asleep after her busy night.

Later on, the princess told her father she would be happy to meet any prince or king who came to the court. The king was pleased and told her that King Pierrot was arriving that very day.

When Pierrot saw her he was overcome by her beauty and it was agreed that he would be a suitable husband for the princess. A marriage was arranged and on the night before the wedding a great feast was held. The princess was wearing a gown of softest pink but she wore no jewels except for her shimmering gold chain.

After the feast, she glided into the garden and King Pierrot followed her. He took her delicate hand and said: "Tomorrow, sweetest princess, you will be my queen. What gift can I give you as fine as your beauty?"

"I'd like a necklace of gold and diamonds exactly the same length as this gold cord," she told him.

"It's very plain," he said. "Why do you wear it?"

"It's very special," she laughed, "it's as light as a feather but stronger than iron. Here, hold it in both hands and try to break it. You won't be able to, I'm sure."

Pierrot took the cord and pulled hard but as soon as his fingers closed round it, he vanished into thin air. Yet on the cord there was now a shining crystal bead.

With a wicked laugh Princess Fiorimonde looked down and touched the bead carefully. "My valuable necklace! The best in the world," she gloated before she went inside and spoke to her father.

"Please send someone to find King Pierrot. He suddenly left me while we were talking. I hope I haven't upset him."

Servants were sent to make a search but Pierrot could not be found anywhere. "I'm sure he will be here for the wedding tomorrow," the king said, "but I don't like his manners at all!"

That night, the princess's maid Yolanda was brushing her mistress's hair. She saw the gold string with its one lovely bead and she noticed that the princess kept touching it, over and over again.

"That's a lovely bead, madam," she said. "Is it a wedding present from King Pierrot?"

"It certainly is," replied her mistress slowly, "the best gift he could give me, and soon I'll get more and more lovely beads." Her voice was so strange that Yolanda shivered inside with fear.

Next day everything was ready for the wedding. The princess wore a white satin gown with a long train embroidered with pearls, and her ladies-in-waiting said she was the loveliest bride they'd ever seen. She was just leaving her room when her father came along and sent her ladies downstairs to join the wedding guests.

"Daughter," he whispered, "my soldiers have looked everywhere for King Pierrot but he cannot be found. I fear something dreadful has happened to him, but we cannot have a wedding without a bridegroom!"

"We must put it off, dear father," the princess said, "and who

knows, we may have a wedding or a funeral tomorrow." She pretended to cry but she was laughing into her handkerchief.

Nothing was heard about the missing king and everybody felt sure he was dead and felt sad. The princess wore black clothes and she asked to be left alone for four weeks because she was so upset. But in her bedroom she laughed until she cried. Yolanda grew more fearful and she noticed that her mistress wore the gold cord under her black gown, night and day.

The four weeks ended and the king showed his daughter the picture of Prince Hildebrand. He looked fair and strong so she happily and obediently agreed to marry him. She put away her black gowns and another grand wedding was arranged.

When Prince Hildebrand arrived, he could not take his eyes away from Fiorimonde and he gazed at her beauty all night. This time she stayed at her father's side but at sunrise next morning she arose early. She put on a simple white dress and crept downstairs into the gardens. Quietly she walked until she was standing beneath Hildebrand's window where she sang a sweet magical song.

Hildebrand sprang out of bed and looked outside to see who was singing. When he saw the princess, who looked so lovely in the early sunshine, he dressed hurriedly and went outside to greet her.

"Lovely lady," he exclaimed, "why are you singing here all alone?"

"I love to see the colours in the sky," she replied, "I've never seen anything finer except in this bead on my golden cord."

"Where did the bead come from?" he asked.

"From far away," came the reply. "Here, look closely at it."

He put out his hands and grasped the cord. At that instant, he vanished. Another bead appeared on the cord around Fiorimonde's neck while she laughed cruelly. "Oh lovely necklace. How I love you!"

She crept back to bed and slept soundly until Yolanda came to help her with the wedding gown and veil. At once she saw that there were now two glittering beads on the gold string.

The princess was all ready when the king rushed into her room.

"Prince Hildebrand has disappeared," he bellowed. "Put

away your wedding clothes." She pretended to cry and once again she stayed in her room for four weeks wearing black clothes. Then she said: "I don't want people to think that nobody wants to marry me so please ask more princes and lords to visit the court."

So the king sent messengers all over the world and one by one kings and princes arrived at the palace. They all wanted to marry the princess but as soon as the wedding was arranged, the bridegroom would vanish. Only Yolanda saw how many more beads were fastened on the gold chain around her mistress's neck. Meanwhile, she grew ever more beautiful and no one guessed how wicked she really was.

Now it happened that a prince called Florestan saw Fiorimonde's portrait and he told his good friend Gervase that he wanted to visit her father as he wished to marry her. Gervase was worried. "Something evil happens at that court," he said. "Prince after prince has disappeared. I beg you not to go."

"That doesn't worry me," replied Florestan, "she must be my bride!" And off he rode, closely followed by his faithful friend, Gervase.

The king welcomed them heartily when they reached his palace.

"This is a fine prince," he said to himself, "I'd like him to marry my daughter so I pray nothing will go wrong this time."

The princess was sitting in the garden when she heard that Prince Florestan had arrived. "Send him out here," she said. "I'll agree to marry him tomorrow if he can get himself to the church!" She laughed so horribly that her ladies-in-waiting were shocked.

As soon as Florestan saw her beauty he was dazzled and he did not notice the wicked look in her beautiful eyes.

"Come and sit down," she said sweetly, "let us talk about happy things. Send away your friend so we may be alone together."

Florestan agreed to this and Gervase wandered sadly along a path until he met Yolanda. She stopped him and whispered: "Are you the prince's friend? Do you love him truly?"

"Of course, more than anyone else," said Gervase. "Why do you ask?"

"If he is with the princess, you'll never see him again."

"Why ever not? Who are you to say such things?"

"I am Yolanda, Princess Fiorimonde's maid. Ten princes have come to marry her. All have disappeared. I alone know where they are."

"Where have they gone? Why don't you tell somebody?" cried Gervase.

"I'm scared, that's why," Yolanda looked round fearfully. "The princess is a witch. She wears each prince as a bead on her necklace which she never takes off. Ten good men have gone. The eleventh will be your friend, Prince Florestan, I fear."

"How wicked," Gervase was shocked. "I'll kill this princess!" Yolanda shook her head, "Take care. Killing her might not break the spell or bring back the princes. How can I show you the necklace?"

"When she is asleep, you can lead me to her room," he told her.

So later on, Gervase and Yolanda met near the princess's room. "Don't make a sound," she said, "remember she is a witch."

"I myself may be turned into a bead," whispered Gervase, "but if I get rid of this wicked woman, what will be my reward?"

"Whatever I can offer you," said Yolanda shyly.

"Then I'd like you to marry me and come to my country with me." Gervase kissed her hand as he spoke. "I promise," she smiled. "First though, the prisoners must be set free."

They crept into the bedroom. Fiorimonde looked so sweet that Gervase wondered if Yolanda was telling the truth about her. She pulled his arm and pointed to the necklace. It had eleven beads now, alas!

"I'll show you the gold cord which must be cut," she said. But even as she gently clasped the cord, she vanished. Gervase was in despair. "Ten, eleven, twelve beads," he counted. "Oh, Yolanda, oh, princes! Now I understand this horrible secret." He crept away and all night he wondered how he could rescue Yolanda and his friend, Florestan.

Fiorimonde was puzzled next morning when she got up and counted her beads. "Twelve lovely beads!" she exclaimed. "Someone has touched my necklace when I was asleep. But they've been punished so I've nothing to worry about."

All that day a fierce storm raged. Fiorimonde laughed as the thunder roared and she clapped her hands at each lightning flash. When the wind was howling its loudest, the servants told her that someone had come to visit her but he would not give his name.

"Show him in," she cried. "Prince or peasant. It matters not."

As the stranger entered the hall he threw off his wet cloak. The princess noticed his wonderful rich robes but she did not notice that it was Florestan's friend, Gervase, who stood before her.

"Welcome," she said, "you've come through thunder and lightning to visit me, pray tell me what you've heard about me."

"I've heard you're the most beautiful woman in the world," he said.

"And is that not true?" she demanded proudly.

Gervase looked and in his heart he said: "It is true, wicked one. You are indeed fair but hateful too." Aloud he said: "Alas, Princess, you are lovely but there lives a woman who is fairer still than you."

"Fairer than I? Impossible!" Fiorimonde raged. "How dare you tell me this. Who are you? Where do you come from?"

"I've come to marry you," replied Gervase, "but I must tell the truth. I have seen a fairer woman than you."

"Who is she?" the princess almost screeched. "Bring her to me so I may see for myself. You must be telling a lie."

"What will you give me," he said, "if I bring her to you? I'd like that necklace you're wearing." Fiorimonde shook her head.

"That's the one thing you cannot have," and she ordered her servants to bring diamonds, rubies, gold and pearls to give to him.

"I want none of these," he said calmly, "you can see her in exchange for your necklace. Nothing else will do."

"Take it off then," shouted the princess furiously.

"Certainly not, I don't know how to undo it," he answered. She raged at him but he would not touch the cord. He would not be tricked by her this time.

Next morning Gervase went into the woods where he picked acorns and berries to make a necklace which he hid under his coat. The princess wore her prettiest dress and went down into the garden where she met Gervase coming back from the woods.

"Good prince," she said, "yesterday was dark and stormy. You could not see me properly. In the sunlight am I not beautiful?" She smiled sweetly but Gervase remembered Yolanda! "You are lovely," he said, "so why do you worry because someone is lovelier still?"

She clenched her fists. "You say you've seen a lovelier woman but you've surely never seen such shining beads as these?"

"I've never seen beads like yours, princess. But I like my necklace better." He smiled as he pulled out his simple woodland string. "There is no necklace like mine anywhere in the world."

"Is it magic? What can it do?" cried she, wondering if it had been worn by the beautiful woman he had spoken of.

"Let us exchange necklaces," Gervase offered, "give me yours and when mine is around your throat I'll say truthfully how fair you are."

"Take it," she shouted gleefully. She forgot the witch's warning and lifted the cord. It fell to the ground and Fiorimonde vanished. Gervase smiled. He counted thirteen beads on the necklace now. "Oh wicked woman, you were too vain and not so clever after all." He picked up the necklace with his sword and carried it to the king and his courtiers.

"Where is your daughter?" Gervase asked. "She seems to have disappeared."

Of course she could not be found and Gervase slipped the necklace onto the floor. He pulled out a sharp dagger and cut the cord in two. A mighty explosion was heard as he pulled the first bead away from the cord. King Pierrot appeared! Then, prince after prince appeared, ending with Florestan. "Here is the one you must thank, noble princes," he said as he pulled off the twelfth bead. Yolanda stood there, crying with happiness as Gervase told the king all that had happened.

"I am ashamed," he groaned, "my daughter must be punished."

"Let her be given the punishment she chose herself," said Gervase. "Hang this, the thirteenth bead, outside the town hall and when it swings and glitters, everybody will know it is the wicked Fiorimonde!"

The king agreed to this and there the bead still hangs, shimmering in the moonlight and reminding everyone of the beautiful, but evil, Princess Fiorimonde.

THE WATER OF LIFE

Grimm Brothers

In a faraway land long ago, there lived a king who became very ill. His three sons were walking sadly around the palace gardens wondering how they could help their father when an odd little gnome stopped them. "I know the king is dying," he said, "but if you could give him a dose of the Water of Life, he'd get well again. However, this Water of Life is hard to find."

"I'll find it," said the eldest son boldly, and he set off.

"My father will give me his kingdom if I bring this water to him," he thought as he rode along. He entered a deep valley where he noticed an ugly little manikin who called cheerily: "Prince, prince, where are you going?"

"What's that to you, ugly creature?" the prince answered rudely. He rode on but not for long. Huge trees sprang up around him. He was a prisoner. He heard a mocking laugh and he knew that the manikin was paying him back for his rudeness.

Soon the second son said he would search for the Water of Life. "My brother must be dead," he thought, "now I will get my father's kingdom if I find this magic water for him." Off he rode and in time he rode into the deep valley and met the ugly manikin. "Prince, prince, where are you going?" he was asked.

"Mind your own business," answered the second prince rudely. Oh dear, the manikin put a spell on him, and he joined his elder brother in the magic forest.

When the second prince did not return, the youngest son decided to search for the Water of Life. The manikin met him in the same place and called: "Prince, prince, where are you going?"

"My father is ill," the prince replied politely, "I'm looking for the Water of Life which will cure him. Please can you help me?"

"Aren't you afraid to talk to an ugly creature like me?"

The prince was astonished. "I didn't notice your looks," he said. "Your voice is kind so I beg you to help me if you can." The manikin smiled. "Gentle prince, I will tell you what to do. The Water is in the well of an enchanted castle. You need two things to reach this well safely. First, take this iron stick. Strike the gate of the castle three times and it will open. Two hungry lions will be waiting inside. Throw them these two loaves of bread and they will let you pass. Run to the well and take some of the Water of Life before the clock strikes twelve. If you stay any later the gates will shut you inside the castle for ever."

The prince thanked his new friend and journeyed on through many lands until he spied the enchanted castle. The gates flew open when he used the stick and the lions quietly ate the bread he threw them. He entered a magnificent hall where a lovely princess greeted him joyfully. "If you will come back here in a year and marry me, the spell that keeps me here will be broken. This castle and all my kingdom will belong to you," she told him.

Gladly he promised to return. Then she pointed out the way to the well. He went on and he came across a sword and a loaf of bread. He picked them up and carried them into the gardens. It was so peaceful that the prince decided to have a short rest.

The clock was striking a quarter to twelve when he awoke. In horror, he ran to the well and filled a bottle with the precious

water. He raced through the gates just as the clock struck twelve. The iron doors clanged behind him. He was safe!

Overjoyed, he set off for home and on the way he met the little manikin again. "Your sword will kill whole armies," he told the prince, "and your loaf will never be finished."

"I'm grateful for your help," said the prince. "Please can you tell me anything about my brothers? They were searching for the Water of Life before me, but they never came back."

"They were rude and ill-mannered!" the manikin replied. "They are my prisoners."

"Please set them free," begged the prince. Reluctantly, the manikin let the brothers go. "Take care," he warned the youngest prince, "for I fear your brothers have evil hearts!"

The brothers asked many questions and their kind brother told them everything. All three rode away until they came to a land where enemies from other countries had burned the crops and people had nothing to eat. The prince handed the king of this land his bread and at once his subjects had as much to eat as they wanted. Then he lent the king his sword. With it he killed his enemies in one day. The same thing happened in two more countries the brothers passed through.

One night, while the young prince slept, the elder brothers chatted together. "Our brother has found the Water of Life and our father will reward him with his kingdom. We must ruin him somehow and spoil his chances." They looked around. Quietly they poured the Water of Life into their own bottle and put bitter-tasting water back in its place.

When at last the three reached home, the youngest son took his bottle to the sick king and poured him a drink. The bitter water made him worse than before and he groaned miserably. The other brothers rushed in. "He is poisoning you, father. Quickly, drink this Water of Life which we have found for you."

As soon as the water touched the king's lips his illness left him and he felt strong again. The princes went outside. "Thank you, little brother, for finding the water for us," they sneered. "Our father hates you now and you'll be punished. Next year one of us will return for the princess and marry her!"

The king was indeed very angry. He felt sure that his youngest son had tried to poison him. He decided that he must die.

Shortly afterwards, the good prince and the king's chief huntsman went hunting in the woods. After a while the huntsman said: "The king has ordered me to shoot you."

The prince was shocked. "Let me live," he said. "Here, take my royal coat and show it to the king. Meanwhile, I'll hide far away."

"Gladly," said the huntsman, "I don't want to kill you."

Some days later, three grand lords arrived at the king's palace with gold and jewels for his youngest son. "These are gifts from three kings," they explained, "whose people were saved from starvation by your son who lent them his sword and his bread."

"My poor son!" the king cried. "Why did I have him killed?" The huntsman stepped forward. "I did not kill him, Sire," he said. "He is still alive." The king was delighted. "If he will only return to my court I will forgive him anything," he cried.

Meanwhile the princess was waiting eagerly for one year to pass. She ordered her servants to build a road of solid gold up to the palace gate. Then she spoke to her guards:

"Whoever rides straight up to the gate is my true love. Whoever rides to the right or left must be turned away."

At the end of the year, the eldest brother thought he would go to the princess and tell her that he was the one who had broken the spell. He travelled to her palace but when he saw the gleaming gold he thought: "I don't want to damage this gold," so he rode on the right-hand side up to the gate. "Be off with you," the guards shouted, "you're not the true prince."

Then the second prince set out. He came to the golden road and stopped. "It would be a pity to spoil this gold," he said, so he rode up on the left-hand side. "You're not the true prince," shouted the guards. "Away with you!"

The third prince came out of his hiding place to claim his bride. He was thinking about her all the time so he did not even notice the golden road. He went straight to the gate which flew open. The princess welcomed him joyfully. At once they went to the king and he was furious when they told him how his other sons had cheated him, but before he could punish them they ran away. The prince and the princess had a wonderful wedding and they gave the seat of honour to the ugly little manikin!

THE DRAGON AND THE MONKEY

Chinese Traditional

Far away in the China Seas lived a dragon and his wife. She was fretful and rather difficult, but he was a kind and loving dragon. As they swam in the warm seas together she was forever complaining and asking her husband to fetch her different foods. He always thought, "This time I will really make her happy, and then how easy and lovely life will be." Yet somehow, whatever delicacy he fetched her, she was never satisfied and always wanted something else.

One day she twitched her tail more than usual, and told her husband that she was not feeling well and that she had heard a monkey's heart was the only thing to cure her.

"You are certainly looking pale, my love," said the dragon, "and you know I would do anything for you, but how can I possibly find you a monkey's heart? Monkeys live up trees, and I could never catch one."

"Now I know you don't love me," cried his wife. "If you did you would find a way to catch one. Now I shall surely die!"

The dragon sighed and swam off across the seas to an island where he knew some monkeys lived. "Somehow," he thought desperately, "I must trick a monkey into coming with me, for I cannot let my wife die."

When he reached the island, he saw a little monkey sitting in a tree. The dragon called out,

"Hello, monkey! It's good to see you! Come down and talk to me. That tree looks so unsafe, you might fall out!"

At that the monkey roared with laughter. "Ha! Ha! Ha! You are funny, dragon. Whoever heard of a monkey falling out of a tree?"

The dragon thought of his wife and tried again.

"I'll show you a tree covered with delicious juicy fruit, monkey. It grows on the other side of the sea."

Again the monkey laughed and laughed. "Ha! Ha! Ha!

Whoever heard of a monkey swimming across the sea, dragon?"

"I could take you on my back, little monkey," said the dragon.

The monkey liked this idea and swung out of the tree on to the dragon's back. As he swam across the sea, the dragon thought there was no way the monkey could escape, so he said,

"I am sorry, little monkey, I've tricked you. There are no trees with delicious fruit where we are going. I am taking you to my wife who wishes to eat your heart. She says it is the only thing that will cure her of her illness."

The monkey looked at the water all around him and saw no way to escape, but he thought quickly, and said,

"Your poor wife! I am sorry to hear she's not well. There is nothing I'd like more than to give her my heart. But what a pity you did not tell me before we left. You obviously did not know, dragon, that we monkeys never carry our hearts with us. I left it behind in the tree where you found me. If you would be kind enough to swim back there with me, I shall willingly fetch it."

So the dragon turned round and swam back to the place where he had found the monkey. With one leap the monkey was in the branches of the tree, safe out of the dragon's reach.

"I'm sorry to disappoint you, dragon," he called out, "but I had my heart with me all the time. You won't trick me out of this tree again. Ha! Ha! Ha!"

There was no way the dragon could reach him and whether or not he ever caught another monkey I do not know. Perhaps he is still looking while his wife swims alone in the China Seas.

THE RIDDLEMASTER

Catherine Storr

Sitting on one of the public benches in the High Street one warm Saturday morning, Polly licked all round the top of an ice-cream cornct.

A large person sat down suddenly beside her. The bench swayed and creaked, and Polly looked round.

"Good morning, Wolf!"

"Good morning, Polly."

"Nice day, Wolf."

"Going to be hot, Polly."

"Mmm," Polly said. She was engaged in trying to save a useful bit of ice-cream with her tongue before it dripped on to the pavement and was wasted.

"In fact it is hot now, Polly."

"I'm not too hot," Polly said.

"Perhaps that delicious looking ice is cooling you down," the wolf said enviously.

"Perhaps it is," Polly agreed.

"I'm absolutely boiling," the wolf said.

Polly fished in the pocket of her cotton dress and pulled out a threepenny bit. It was more than half what she had left, but she was a kind girl, and in a way she was fond of the wolf, tiresome as he sometimes was.

"Here you are Wolf," she said, holding it out to him. "Go into Woolworths and get one for yourself."

There was a scurry of feet, a flash of black fur, and a little cloud of white summer dust rose off the pavement near Polly's feet. The wolf had gone.

Two minutes later he came back, a good deal more slowly. He was licking his ice-cream cornet with a very long red tongue and it was disappearing extremely quickly. He sat down again beside Polly with a satisfied grunt.

"Mm! Just what I needed. Thank you very much, Polly."

"Not at all, Wolf," said Polly, who had thought that he might have said this before.

She went on licking her ice in a happy dream-like state, while the wolf did the same, but twice as fast.

Presently, in a slightly aggrieved voice, the wolf said, "Haven't you nearly finished?"

"Well no, not nearly," Polly said. She always enjoyed spinning out ices as long as possible. "Have you?"

"Ages ago."

"I wish you wouldn't look at me so hard, Wolf," Polly said, wriggling. "It makes me feel uncomfortable when I'm eating."

"I was only thinking," the wolf said.

"You look sad, then, when you think," Polly remarked.

"I generally am. It's a very sad world, Polly."

"Is it?" said Polly, in surprise.

"Yes. A lot of sad things happen."

"What things?" asked Polly.

"Well, I finish up all my ice-cream."

"That's fairly sad. But at any rate you did have it," Polly said.

"I haven't got it Now," the wolf said. "And it's Now that I want it. Now is the only time to eat ice-cream."

"When you are eating it, it is Now," Polly remarked.

"But when I'm not, it isn't. I wish it was always Now," the wolf sighed.

"It sounds like a riddle," Polly said.

"What does?"

"What you were saying. When is Now not Now or something like that. You know the sort I mean, when is a door not a door?"

"I love riddles," said the wolf in a much more cheerful voice. "I know lots. Let's ask each other riddles."

"Yes, let's," said Polly.

"And I tell you what would make it really amusing. Let's say that whoever wins can eat the other person up."

"Wins how?" Polly asked, cautiously.

"By asking three riddles the other person can't answer."

"Three in a row," Polly insisted.

"Very well. Three in a row."

"And I can stop whenever I want to."

"All right," the wolf agreed, unwillingly. "And I'll start," he added quickly. "What made the penny stamp?"

Polly knew it was because the threepenny bit, and said so. Then she asked the wolf what made the apple turnover, and he knew the answer to that. Polly knew what was the longest word in the dictionary, and the wolf knew what has an eye but cannot see. This reminded him of the question of what has hands but no fingers and a face but no nose, to which Polly was able to reply that it was a clock.

"My turn," she said with relief. "Wolf, what gets bigger, the more you take away from it?"

The wolf looked puzzled.

"Are you sure you've got it right, Polly?" he asked at length. "You don't mean it gets smaller the more you take away from it?"

"No, I don't."

"It gets bigger?"

"Yes."

"No cake I ever saw did that," the wolf said, thinking aloud. "Some special kind of pudding, perhaps?"

"It's not a pudding," Polly said.

"I know!" the wolf said triumphantly. "It's the sort of pain you get when you're hungry. And the more you don't eat the worse the pain gets. That's getting bigger the less you do about it."

"No, you're wrong," Polly said. "It isn't a pain or anything to eat, either. It's a hole. The more you take away, the bigger it gets, don't you see, Wolf?"

"Being hungry is a sort of hole in your inside," the wolf said. "But anyhow it's my turn now. I'm going to ask you a new riddle, so you won't know the answer already, and I don't suppose you'll be able to guess it, either. What gets filled up three or four times a day, and yet can always hold more?"

"Do you mean it can hold more after it's been filled?" Polly asked.

The wolf thought, and then said, "Yes."

"But it couldn't, Wolf! If it was properly filled up it couldn't hold any more."

"It does though," the wolf said triumphantly. "It seems to be quite bursting full and then you try very hard and it still holds a little more."

Polly had her suspicions of what this might be, but she didn't want to say in case she was wrong.

"I can't guess."

"It's me!" the wolf cried, in delight. "Got you, that time, Polly! However full up I am, I can always manage a little bit more. Your turn next, Polly."

"What," Polly asked, "is the difference between an elephant and a pillar-box?" The wolf thought for some time.

"The elephant is bigger," he said, at last.

"Yes. But that isn't the right answer."

"The pillar-box is red. Bright red. And the elephant isn't."

"Ye-es. But that isn't the right answer either."

The wolf looked puzzled. He stared hard at the old-fashioned Victorian pillar-box in the High Street. It had a crimped lid with a knob on top like a silver teapot. But it didn't help him. After some time he said crossly, "I don't know."

"You mean you can't tell the difference between an elephant and a pillar-box?"

"No."

"Then I shan't send you to post my letters," Polly said, triumphantly. She thought it was a very funny riddle.

The wolf, however, didn't.

"You don't see the joke, Wolf?" Polly asked, a little disappointed that he was so unmoved.

"I see it, yes. But I don't think it is funny. It's not a proper riddle at all. It's just silly."

"Now you ask me something," Polly suggested. After a minute or two's thought, the wolf said, "What is the difference between pea soup and a clean pocket handkerchief?"

"Pea soup is hot and a pocket handkerchief is cold," said Polly.

"No. Anyhow you could have cold pea soup."

"Pea soup is green," said Polly.

"I expect a clean pocket handkerchief could be green too, if it tried," said the wolf. "Do you give it up?"

"Well," said Polly, "of course I do know the difference, but I don't know what you want me to say."

"I want you to say you don't know the difference between them," said the wolf, crossly.

"But I do," said Polly.

"But then I can't say what I was going to say!" the wolf cried.

He looked so disappointed that Polly relented.

"All right, then, you say it."

"You don't know the difference between pea soup and a clean pocket handkerchief?"

"I'll pretend I don't. No, then," said Polly.

"You ought to be more careful what you keep in your pockets," the wolf said. He laughed so much at this that he choked, and Polly had to beat him hard on the back before he recovered and could sit back comfortably on the seat again.

"Your turn," he said, as soon as he could speak.

Polly thought carefully. She thought of a riddle about a man going to St Ives; of one about the man who showed a portrait to another man; of one about a candle; but she was not satisfied with any of them. With so many riddles it isn't really so much a question of guessing the answers, as of knowing them or not knowing them already, and if the wolf were to invent a completely new riddle out

of his head, he would be able to eat her, Polly, in no time at all.

"Hurry up," said the wolf.

Perhaps it was seeing his long red tongue at such very close quarters, or it may have been the feeling that she had no time to lose, that made Polly say, before she had considered what she was going to say, "What is it that has teeth, but no mouth?"

"Grrrr," said the wolf, showing all his teeth for a moment. "Are you quite sure he hasn't a mouth, Polly?"

"Quite sure. And I'm supposed to be asking the questions, not you, Wolf."

The wolf did not appear to hear this. He had now turned his back on Polly and was going through some sort of rapid repetition in a subdued gabble, through which Polly could hear only occasional words.

"... Grandma, so I said the better to see you with, gabble, gabble, gabble, Ears you've got, gabble, gabble better to hear gabble gabble gabble gabble gabble TEETH gabble eat you all up."

He turned round with a satisfied air.

"I've guessed it, Polly. It's a GRANDMOTHER."

"No," said Polly, astonished.

"Well then, Red Riding Hood's grandmother if you are so particular. The story mentions her eyes and her ears and her teeth, so I expect she hadn't got anything else. No mouth anyhow."

"It's not anyone's grandmother."

"Not a grandmother," said the wolf slowly. He shook his head. "It's difficult. Tell me some more about it. Are they sharp teeth, Polly?"

"They can be," Polly said.

"As sharp as mine?" asked the wolf, showing his for comparison.

"No," said Polly, drawing back a little. "But more tidily arranged," she added.

The wolf shut his jaws with a snap.

"I give up," he said, in a disagreeable tone. "There isn't anything I know of that has teeth and no mouth. What use would the teeth be to anyone without a mouth? I mean what is the point of taking a nice juicy bite out of something if you've got to find someone else's mouth to swallow it for you? It doesn't make sense."

"It's a comb," said Polly, when she got a chance to speak.

"A what?" cried the wolf in disgust.

"A COMB. What you do your hair with. It's got teeth, hasn't it? But no mouth. A comb, Wolf."

The wolf looked sulky. Then he said in a bright voice, "My turn now, and I'll begin straight away. What is the difference between a nice fat young pink pig and a plate of sausages and bacon? You don't know, of course, so I'll tell you. It's – "

"Wolf!" Polly interrupted.

"It's a very good riddle, this one, and I can't blame you for not having guessed it. The answer is – "

"WOLF!" Polly said, "I want to tell you something."

"Not the answer?"

"No, not the answer. Something else."

"Well, go on."

"Look, Wolf, we made a bargain, didn't we, that whoever lost three lives running by not being able to answer riddles, might be eaten up by the other person?"

"Yes," the wolf agreed. "And you've lost two already, and now you're not going to be able to answer the third and then I shall eat you up. Now I'll tell you what the difference is between a nice fat little pink – "

"No!" Polly shouted. "Listen, Wolf! I may have lost two lives already, but you have lost three!"

"I haven't!"

"Yes, you have! You couldn't answer the riddle about the hole, you didn't know the difference between an elephant and a pillar-box – "

"I do!" said the wolf indignantly.

"Well, you may now, but you didn't when I asked you the riddle; and you didn't know about the comb having teeth and no mouth. That was three you couldn't answer in a row, so it isn't you that is going to eat me up."

"What is it then?" the wolf asked, shaken.

"It's me that is going to eat you up!" said Polly.

The wolf moved rather further away.

"Are you really going to eat me up, Polly?"

"In a moment, Wolf. I'm just considering how I'll have you cooked," said Polly.

"I'm very tough, Polly."

"That's all right, Wolf. I can simmer you gently over a low flame until you are tender."

"I don't suppose I'd fit very nicely into any of your saucepans, Polly."

"I can use the big one Mother has for making jam. That's an enormous saucepan," said Polly, thoughtfully, measuring the wolf with her eyes.

The wolf began visibly to shake where he sat.

"Oh please, Polly, don't eat me. Don't eat me up this time," he urged. "Let me off this once, I promise I'll never do it again."

"Never do what again?" Polly asked.

"I don't know. What was I doing?" the wolf asked himself, in despair.

"Trying to get me to eat," Polly suggested.

"Well, of course, I'm always doing that," the wolf agreed.

"And you would have eaten me?" Polly asked.

"Not if you'd asked very nicely, I wouldn't," the wolf said. "Like I'm asking now."

"And if I didn't eat you, you'd stop trying to get me?"

The wolf considered.

"Look," he said, "I can't say I'll stop for ever, because after all a wolf is a wolf, and if I promised for ever I wouldn't be a wolf any more. But I promise to stop for a long time. I won't try any more today."

"And what about after today?" Polly insisted.

"The first time I catch you," the wolf said dreamily, "if you ask me *very* nicely I'll let you go because you've let me off today. But after that, no mercy! It'll be just Snap! Crunch! Swallow!"

"All right," Polly said, recollecting that so far the wolf had not ever got as far as catching her successfully even once. "You can go."

The wolf ducked his head gratefully and trotted off. Polly saw him threading his way between busy shoppers in the High Street.

But she sat contentedly in the hot sun and wondered what was the difference between a fat pink pig and a plate of sausages and bacon. Not much, if she knew her wolf!

GOAT'S EARS

Serbian Traditional

Once upon a time a king called Trojan had floppy hairy ears just like a goat and he was furious if anyone mentioned this to him. Every morning a barber came to the royal palace to shave him. "Have you noticed anything peculiar about me?" the king always demanded.

"Your Majesty has goat's ears," each barber replied. At once the poor barber's head would be chopped off by the king himself.

Well, before long there were no barbers left in the kingdom except for the Worshipful Master of Barbers himself. Strange to say, he fell ill the morning he should have visited the palace so he sent his young apprentice to shave the king instead.

"What are you doing here?" Trojan roared.

"My master is sick so I was given the honour of shaving Your Majesty," the young man replied as he calmly started to lather the royal chin. He noticed the royal goat's ears but he said not a word!

"Have you noticed anything different about me?" the king asked as he usually did.

"No, not a thing, Your Majesty," came the quiet reply.

"I appoint you the Royal Barber from now on," the delighted king declared. "Here, take these gold coins as your reward."

The young apprentice then went back to his master, who was quite surprised to see him.

"What happened?" he asked anxiously. "How did you get on with the king?"

"Very well," the young man said cheerfully. "He says I'm to shave him every day and he gave me these twelve gold coins too." He did not mention the king's goat's ears!

The young barber went each morning to the palace as the king had commanded and each morning he received twelve gold coins. He kept his secret to himself but after some months he felt as though the secret was burning something inside him and he longed to share it with someone. The Worshipful Master of

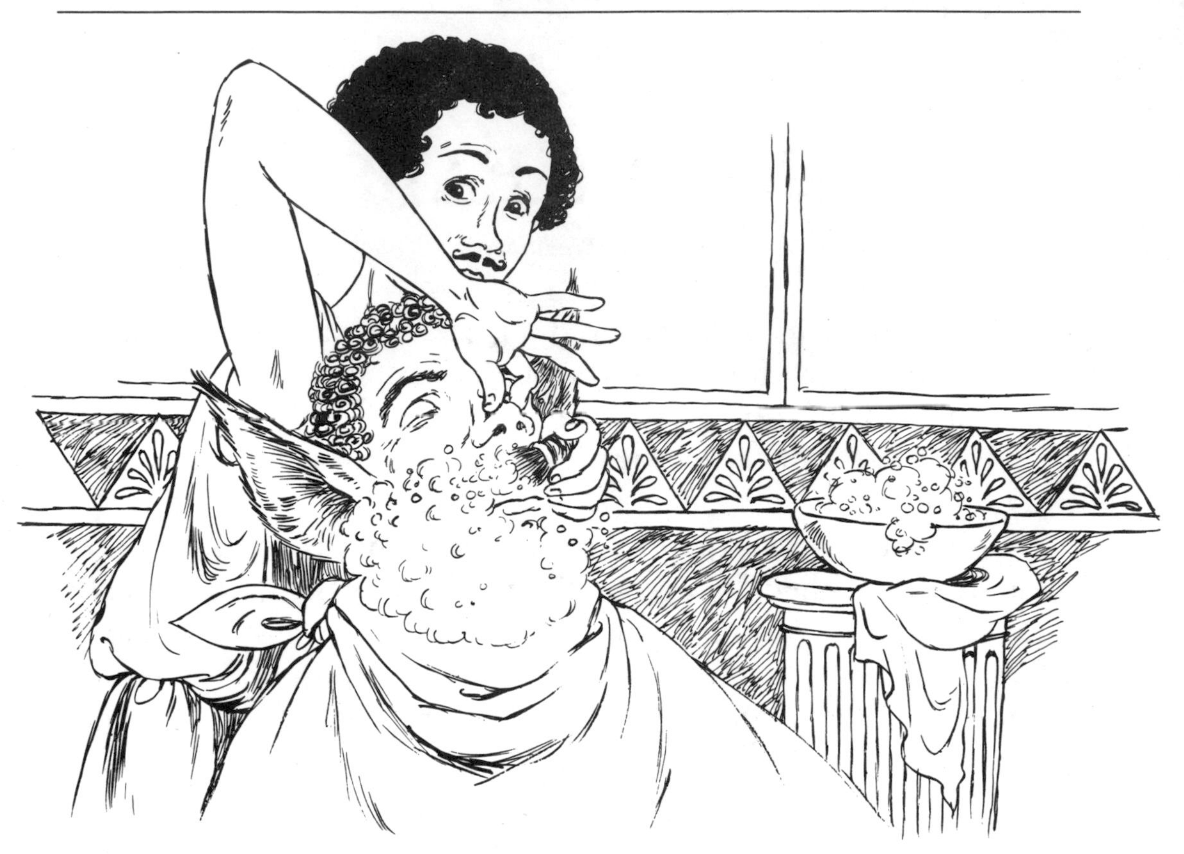

Barbers noticed that the young man was worried and uneasy.

"What ails you?" he asked gently one day.

"I know something very secret," came the reply. "I know I mustn't give anything away, yet I long to tell someone about it."

"You can trust me," the master said, "I can keep things to myself, you know that. However, if you don't want to tell me, why not tell the priest? Or better still, you can go into the countryside, find a field and dig a hole there. Then when you've dug deep down, you must kneel down and whisper your secret three times into the hole. Lastly, you must put back the earth, smooth it over and come back here."

"That plan seems to be the best one," the young barber said. "Thank you for your advice."

He went at once to a field outside the city walls where he dug a deep hole. He made sure nobody was listening then he knelt down and whispered three times: "King Trojan has goat's ears." He felt better at once so he shovelled the earth back and rushed back home.

Months later, an elder tree with three straight stems sprang out of that same hole. Some shepherds noticed the tree and one of them cut off a stem and made a fine flute for himself. As soon as he started to play the flute sang sweetly: "King Trojan has goat's ears," over and over again.

Before long, all the townspeople heard of this wonderful flute and its wonderful song. The news reached King Trojan in his palace. He sent for his barber and demanded angrily: "What have you been telling my subjects about me?"

"N-n-nothing, Your Majesty," the poor man stuttered. "I've never told anyone about your ears!"

This made the king even angrier. He drew out his sword and the terrified barber called out: "I only whispered the secret to the earth. Now a tree has grown there and people have made flutes from its branches which keep repeating my secret, Your Majesty."

"Bring me my coach," the king shouted. "We'll soon see if you are telling the truth," and his guards bundled the trembling barber into the coach behind the king. They drove to the field where they found that the elder tree had only one stem left.

"Cut it down and make another flute," the king ordered his attendants. When it was ready, he examined it carefully then he handed it to the chief court musician.

"Play a tune on this flute," he commanded.

Nothing came out except the words:

"King Trojan has goat's ears."

Everybody held their breath. The barber bowed his head, certain that he would lose his head. Then a really funny thing happened. King Trojan gave a mighty laugh and he put away his sword.

"I see that even our wonderful Mother Earth has to give up her secrets sometimes," he declared, "so I cannot keep my ears secret any longer either. You were telling the truth, so you can keep your head for you kept the secret well."

"Your Majesty is very kind," the barber replied. "As a matter of fact, nobody in the kingdom has such fine ears as yours."

All the people cheered. The king looked pleased and tossed his ears. Perhaps he'd call himself King Goat's Ears from now on – perhaps!

The Little Jackal and the Crocodile

African Traditional

There was once a little jackal who lived in the jungle. He was a greedy little jackal, and one of his favourite meals was fresh crabs from thc river. One day he went down to the big river near his home and put his paw in the water to pull out a crab.

Snap! A large, lazy crocodile who had been lying in the water snapped his jaws and caught the jackal's paw. The little jackal did not cry out, although he was very frightened. Instead he laughed.

"Ha! Ha! That crocodile in the river thinks he has caught my paw, but the stupid animal does not realize he has snapped up a piece of wood and is holding it in his jaws."

The crocodile immediately opened his mouth for he did not want to be seen with a log of wood in his jaws. Quickly the little jackal danced away and called cheekily from a safe distance, "I'll catch some crabs another day, Mr Crocodile." The crocodile lashed his tail with rage and resolved to catch the little jackal and eat him the next time he came to the river.

A week later, when his paw was healed, the jackal came back to the river. He wanted to catch some crabs, but did not want to be eaten by the crocodile. This time he called out from a safe distance, "I can't see any crabs lying on the bank, so I'll have to dip my paw into the water near the edge," and he watched the river for a few minutes. The crocodile thought, "Now is my chance to catch the jackal," and he swam close to the river bank.

When the little jackal saw the water move, he called out, "Thank you, Mr Crocodile. Now I know you are there, I'll come back another day."

The crocodile lashed his tail with rage until he stirred up the mud from the bottom of the river. He swore he would not let the little jackal trick him again.

The jackal could not stop thinking about the crabs, so a few days later he went down to the river again. He could not see the crocodile so he called out, "I know crabs make bubbles in the water, so as soon as I see some bubbles I'll dip my paw in and then I'll catch them easily."

When he heard this, the crocodile, who was lying just beneath the water, started to blow bubbles as fast as he could. He was sure that the jackal would put his paw in where the bubbles were rising and *Snap!* This time he would have the little jackal.

But when the jackal saw the bubbles, he called out:

"Thank you, Mr Crocodile, for showing me where you are. I'll come another day for the crabs."

The crocodile was so angry at being tricked again that he waited till the jackal's back was turned, then he jumped out of the river and followed the jackal, determined to catch him and eat him this time.

Now the jackal, who was very hungry, made his way to the fig grove to eat some figs. By the time the crocodile arrived, he was having a lovely feast munching the ripe blue fruit, and licking his lips with pleasure.

The crocodile was exhausted by walking on land which he found was much more difficult than swimming in the river. "I am too tired to catch the jackal now," he said to himself. "But I'll set a trap and catch him next time he comes for the figs."

The next day, the greedy jackal returned to the fig grove. He did love eating figs! To his surprise he saw a large and rather untidy pile of figs that had not been there before. "I wonder if my friend the crocodile has anything to do with this?" he said to himself, and he called out:

"What a lovely pile of figs! All I need to do is to see which figs

wave in the breeze, for it is always the ripest and most delicious figs that wave in the breeze. I shall then know which ones to eat."

Of course the crocodile was buried under the pile of figs and when he heard this he smiled a big toothy crocodile smile. "All I have to do is to wriggle a bit," he thought. "When the jackal sees the figs move he will come and eat them and this time I will certainly catch him."

The little jackal watched as the crocodile wriggled under the pile of figs, and he laughed and laughed.

"Thank you, Mr Crocodile," he said, "I'll come back another day when you are not here."

Now the crocodile was really in a rage so he followed the little jackal to his house to catch him there. There was no one at home when the crocodile got there, but the crocodile thought, "I will wait here, and catch him when he comes home tonight."

He was too big to go through the gate, so he broke it and then he was too big to go through the door, so he smashed that. "Never mind," he said to himself. "I will eat the little jackal tonight whatever happens," and he lay in wait for the jackal in the jackal's little house.

When the jackal came home he saw the broken gate, and smashed door, and he said to himself, "I wonder if my friend the crocodile has anything to do with this?" Then he called out:

"Little house, why haven't you said 'hello' to me as you do each night when I come home?"

The crocodile heard this, and thought he ought to make everything seem as normal as possible, so he shouted out, "Hello, little jackal!"

Then a wicked smile appeared on the jackal's face. He fetched some twigs and branches, piled them up outside his house, and set fire to it. As the house burned he called out:

"A roast crocodile is safer than a live crocodile! I shall go and build myself a new house by the river where I can catch all the crabs I want."

With that he skipped off to the river bank and for all I know he is still there today, eating crabs all day long, and laughing at the way he tricked the crocodile.

THE FOX AND THE CROW

Aesop's Fables

A crow was sitting on the branch of a tree one day, with a large piece of cheese in his mouth. A fox caught the scent of the cheese and, following his nose, found himself at the foot of the tree where the crow sat. The cheese looked and smelt so delicious that it made the fox's mouth water and he longed to eat it. The cheese, however, was well out of his reach, and the fox knew only too well that the crow would not drop it without some good reason. The fox thought a little, and decided to talk to the crow: "Good day, Mr Crow! How fine you look sitting there. How glossy and black your feathers are. But tell me, is your voice as fine as your plumage? If it is, you would be proclaimed by all to be the most splendid creature in the whole wood!"

The crow was greatly impressed by the fox's words. He was proud that the fox admired his sleek black feathers and gleaming beak and eyes, so he decided to show off his fine voice too. The fox would then see that indeed he was the most splendid creature in the whole wood.

He opened his beak wide to sing and, as he did so, the cheese fell to the ground. In a flash the fox snatched it up and from a safe distance he said:

"My dear Sir, you should know that flattery gets nowhere unless those who hear it believe it. This lesson, as you can see, has cost you a fine piece of cheese."

The crow realized he had been foolish, and vowed, a little too late, that he would never be tricked the same way again.

THE WRESTLING PRINCESS

Judy Corbalis

Once upon a time there was a princess who was six feet tall, who liked her own way and who loved to wrestle. Every day, she would challenge the guards at her father's palace to wrestling matches and every day, she won. Then she would pick up the loser and fling him on the ground, but gently, because she had a very kind nature.

The princess had one other unusual hobby. She liked to drive forklift trucks. Because she was a princess, and her father was very rich, she had three forklift trucks of her own – a blue one, a yellow one, and a green and purple striped one with a coronet on each side. Whenever there was a royal parade, the king would ride in front in his golden carriage, behind him would ride a company of soldiers and behind them came the princess driving her striped

royal forklift truck. The king got very cross about it but the princess simply said, "If I can't drive my forklift truck, I won't go," and because she was such a good wrestler, the king was too scared to disagree with her.

One day, when the princess had wrestled with sixteen soldiers at once and had beaten them all, the king sent a page to tell her to come to see him in the royal tea-room.

The princess was annoyed.

"Is it urgent?" she asked the page. "I was just greasing the axle of my blue forklift truck."

"I think you should come, Your Highness," said the page, respectfully, "His Majesty was in a terrible temper. He's burnt four pieces of toast already and dripped butter all over his second-best ermine robe."

"Oh gosh," said the princess, "I'd better come right away."

So she got up, picked up her oilcan and went into the royal bathroom to wash her hands for tea. She left oil marks all over the gold taps and the page sent a message to the palace housekeeper to clean them quickly before the king saw them.

The princess went down to the tea-room and knocked loudly on the door. A herald opened it. "The Princess Ermyntrude!" he announced.

"About time, too," said the king. "And where have you been?"

"Greasing the axle of the blue forklift truck," answered the princess politely.

The king put his head in his hands and groaned.

"This can't go on," he sighed tragically. "When *will* you stop messing about with these dirty machines, Ermyntrude? You're nearly sixteen and you need a husband. I must have a successor."

"I'll succeed you, Father," cried the princess cheerfully. "I'd love to be a king."

"You can't be a king," said the king sadly. "It's not allowed."

"Why not?" asked the princess.

"I don't know," said the king. "I don't make the laws. Ask the judges – it's their affair. Anyway, you can't and that's that. You have to have a husband."

He picked up his tapestry and moodily started sewing.

"Ermyntrude," he said after a long silence, "you won't get a husband if you don't change your ways."

"Why ever not?" asked the princess, in surprise.

"To get a husband you must be enchantingly beautiful, dainty and weak," said the king.

"Well, I'm not," said Ermyntrude cheerfully. "I'm nothing to look at, I'm six feet tall and I'm certainly not weak. Why, Father, did you hear, this morning I wrestled with sixteen guards at once and I defeated them all?"

"Ermyntrude!" said the king sternly, as he rethreaded his needle with No. 9 blue tapestry cotton. "Ermyntrude, we are not having any more wrestling and no more forklift trucks either. If you want a husband, you will have to become delicate and frail."

"I *don't* want a husband," said the princess and she stamped her foot hard. The toast rack wobbled. "*You* want me to have a husband. I just want to go on wrestling and looking after my trucks and driving in parades."

"Well, you can't," said the king. "And that's that. I shall lock up the forklift trucks and instruct the guards that there is to be no more wrestling and we shall have a contest to find you a husband."

The princess was furiously angry.

"Just you wait," she shouted rudely, "I'll ruin your stupid old contest. How dare you lock up my forklift trucks. You're a rotten mean old pig!"

"Ermyntrude," said the king sternly, putting down his tapestry, "you will do as you are told." And he got up and left the royal tea-room.

Princess Ermyntrude was very very angry. She bent the toasting fork in half and stamped on the bread.

"Stupid, stupid, stupid," she said crossly. And she went away to think out a plan.

The first contest to find a prince to marry the Princess Ermyntrude took place next day. The king had beamed a message by satellite to all the neighbouring countries, and helicopters with eligible princes in them were arriving in dozens at the palace heliport.

The princess watched them from the window of her room where she was sulking.

"Stupid, stupid," she said. "Why, not one of them even pilots his own helicopter."

And she went on sulking.

After lunch, the king sent a messenger to announce that the princess was to dress in her best robes and come to the great hall of the palace.

She put on her golden dress and her fur cape and her small golden crown and her large golden shoes (for she had big feet) and down she went.

At the front of the throne room she stopped to give the herald time to announce her name, then she went in.

Seated inside were seventy-two princes, all seeking her hand in marriage.

The princess looked at them all. They all looked back.

"Sit here, my dear," said the king loudly, and under his breath, he added, "and behave yourself!"

The princess said nothing.

"Good afternoon and welcome to you all," began the king. "We are here today to find a suitable husband for the lovely Princess Ermyntrude, my daughter. The first competition in this contest will be that of height. As you know the princess is a very tall girl. She cannot have a husband shorter than herself so you will all line up while the Lord Chamberlain measures you."

The seventy-two princes lined up in six rows and the Lord Chamberlain took out the royal tape measure and began to measure them.

"Why can't I have a shorter husband?" whispered the princess.

"Be quiet. You just can't," said the king.

"Forty-eight princes left in the contest, Your Majesty," cried the Lord Chamberlain.

"Thank you," said the king. "I'm sorry you gentlemen had a wasted journey but you are welcome at the banquet this evening."

And he bowed very low.

"The second competition," said the king, "will be that of disposition. The Princess Ermyntrude has a beautiful disposition, none better, but she does have a slightly hasty temper. She cannot have a husband who cannot match her temper. So we shall have a face-pulling, insult-throwing contest. The Lord Chamberlain will call your names one by one and you will come forward and confront the princess, pull the worst face you can manage, put on a temper display and insult her."

"Your Majesty, is this wise? Twenty-four of the princes have retired in confusion already," hissed the Lord Chamberlain.

"Weaklings," murmured the princess sweetly.

The first prince stepped forward. The Princess Ermyntrude pulled a repulsive face and he burst into tears.

"Eliminated," said the Lord Chamberlain running forward with a box of tissues. "Next!"

The next and the next after him and the prince following *them* were all eliminated and it was not until the fifth competitor crossed his eyes, stuck out his tongue and shouted, "Silly cry baby," at the princess, making her so angry that she forgot to shout back, that anyone succeeded at all.

The fifth prince inspired the next four after him but the princes after that were no match for Princess Ermyntrude until the eighteenth and nineteenth princes called her, "Crow face" and "Squiggle bum" and made her giggle.

By the end of the contest, there were seven princes left, all taller and more insulting than the princess.

"And now," said the king, "for the third and final contest. The third competition," he continued, "will be that of strength. As you may know, the Princess Ermyntrude is very strong. She cannot have a weaker husband so you will all line up and wrestle with her."

"Why can't I have a weaker husband?" whispered the princess.

"Be quiet. You just can't," said the king.

So the Lord Chamberlain lined up the seven princes and just as they were being given their instructions, the princess, who was flexing her arm muscles, glanced over at the watching crowd of commoners and noticed a short man covered in helicopter engine oil standing at the back. Because she was so tall, Princess Ermyntrude could see him clearly and, as she looked, he looked back at her and winked quite distinctly. The princess looked again. The short man winked again.

"*Helicopter* engine oil!" thought the princess. "That's the sort of man I like."

Just then the short man looked at her and, forming his mouth carefully, whispered silently, "Choose the seventh. Don't beat him."

The princess felt strangely excited. She looked again. The little man pointed discreetly to the tall, rather nervous looking prince at the end of the line-up. "That one," he mouthed.

Princess Ermyntrude didn't much like the look of the seventh prince but she did want to please the helicopter mechanic so she nodded discreetly, rolled up her golden sleeves and stepped forward to take on the first prince.

CRASH! He hit the mat with staggering force.

CRASH, CRASH, CRASH, CRASH, CRASH.

The next five princes followed. The poor seventh prince was looking paler and paler and his knees were beginning to buckle under him. The princess looked quickly at the mechanic who nodded briefly, then she moved towards the seventh prince. He seized her feebly by the arm.

"Good heavens, I could floor him with one blow," thought the princess, but she didn't. Instead, she let herself go limp and floppy and two seconds later, for the first time in her life, she lay flat on her back on the floor.

The crowd let out a stupendous cheer. The king and the Lord Chamberlain rushed forward and seized the hands of the young prince.

The poor prince looked very pale.

"This is terrible, terrible," he muttered desperately.

"Nonsensc," cried the king. "I award you the hand of the princess and half my kingdom."

"But Sire . . ." stammered the prince. "I can't."

"Can't!" shouted the king. "What do you mean can't. You can and you will or I'll have you beheaded!"

There was a scuffle in the crowd and the helicopter mechanic darted forward and bent low at the king's feet.

"Majesty," he murmured reverently, "Majesty, I am the prince's helicopter pilot, mechanic and aide. Prince Florizel is overcome with shock and gratitude. Is that not so, Sire?" he asked turning to the prince.

"Um, yes, yes, that's right," said the prince nervously.

The mechanic smiled.

"Prince Florizel, of course, must have the blessing of *his* father, the King of Buzzaramia, whose kingdom adjoins your own, before the ceremony can take place. Is that not so, Sire?"

"Definitely," said the prince.

"Quite, quite," said the king, "I favour these old customs myself. The princess will fly there tomorrow to meet him, in her own royal helicopter."

"And I shall pilot myself," said the princess.

"We shan't go into *that* now," said the king. "Here, you may kiss the princess."

With a small sigh, the prince fainted dead away.

"Shock," said the pilot hastily. "Clearly shock, Your Majesty. It's not every day he wins the hand of such a beautiful, charming and talented young lady."

And he looked deep into the princess's eyes.

The prince was carried out to his helicopter and flown off by his pilot, with instructions that the Princess Ermyntrude would fly in the following day.

The rest of the contestants and the princess had a large and elegant banquet with a six-metre chocolate cake in the shape of a heart and litres of ice-cream.

"Who made that heart?" asked Ermyntrude.

"I ordered it from Cook," said the king.

"Well, *I* think it's soppy. A heart!" said the princess in disgust.

Next morning she was up early and, dressed in her frog-green flying suit and bright red aviator goggles, she slipped out to her helicopter before the king was up, climbed in and was just warming up the engine when the Lord Chamberlain came rushing out into the garden.

"Stop, stop," he cried waving his arms wildly. "Stop. His Majesty, your father, is coming too."

The Princess Ermyntrude turned off the master switch and leaned out of the window.

"Well, he'd better hurry and I'm piloting," she said carelessly. "I'll wait three minutes and I'm going if he hasn't come by then."

The Lord Chamberlain rushed into the palace and returned

with the king hastily pulling his ermine robe over his nightshirt and replacing his nightcap with a crown.

"You're a dreadful girl, Ermyntrude," he said sadly. "Here I am with a hangover from the chocolate cake and you insist on being selfish."

"I'm *not* selfish," said Ermyntrude. "I'm by far the best pilot in the palace and it's your own fault you've got a hangover if you will encourage Cook to put rum in the chocolate cake. Anyway, all this was your idea. I'm not marrying that silly prince and I'm flying over to tell him so."

"Ermyntrude," cried the king, scandalized. "How can you do such a thing? I'll be ruined. He won the contest. And besides, you've got to marry someone."

"I haven't and I won't," said the princess firmly and she set the rotor blades in action.

Within an hour, they were flying into the next kingdom and soon they could see the palace shining golden on the highest hilltop.

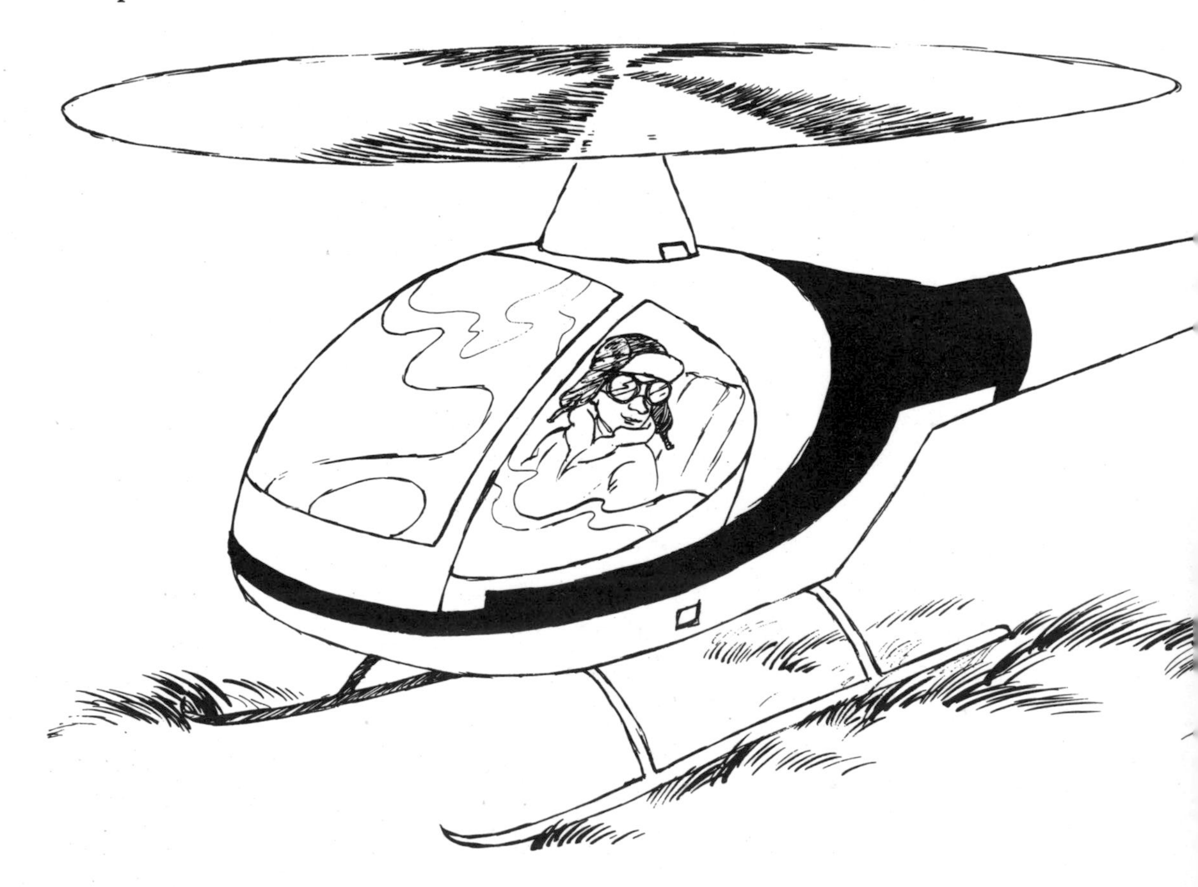

"Over there," said the king mournfully. "Please change your mind, Ermyntrude."

"Never," said the princess positively. "Never, never, never, never, never."

Below them they could see the landing pad with ostrich feathers and fairy-lights along the strip.

Princess Ermyntrude settled the helicopter gently on the ground, waited for the blades to stop turning and got out.

The prince's mechanic was standing on the tarmac.

"A perfect landing," he cried admiringly.

The Princess Ermyntrude smiled. Just then, an older man in ermine trimmed pyjamas came running across the grass.

"Florizel, Florizel, what is all this?" he cried.

The mechanic picked up an oilcan from beside his feet.

"Put that down, you ninny," cried the man in ermine pyjamas. "Don't you know this is a royal princess?"

"You're being ridiculous, Father," said the mechanic. "Of course I know she's a princess. I'm going to marry her."

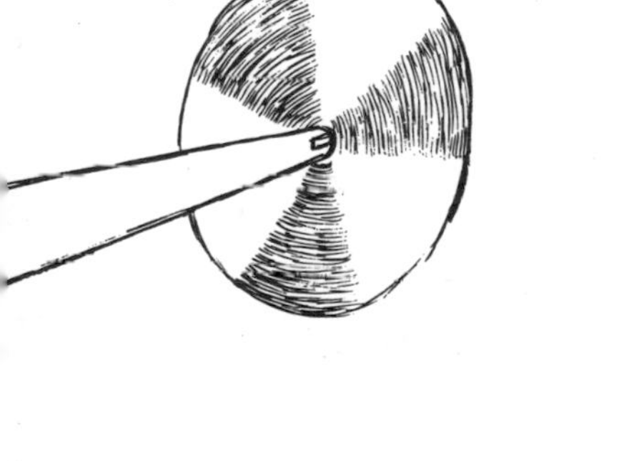

"*You* are?" cried Princess Ermyntrude's father. "My daughter's not marrying you. She's marrying your prince."

"I am marrying him," said the Princess Ermyntrude.

"She certainly is," said the mechanic. "And in case you're wondering, I *am* Prince Florizel. The other one was an imposter."

"But how?" asked the princess.

"Well," said Prince Florizel, "it was all my father's idea that I should go so I persuaded my mechanic to change places with me. I thought my father would never find out. Then, when I saw the Princess Ermyntrude, I fell instantly in love with her. She had axle grease on her neck and she was so big and strong. Then I realized it was lucky I'd changed places or you'd have eliminated me on height."

"That's right. You're too short," said the king.

"He's not," said the princess.

"No, I'm not, I'm exactly right and so is she," said Prince Florizel. "Then when I saw her pulling faces and shouting insults and throwing princes to the ground, I knew she was the one person I could fall in love with."

"Really?" asked the princess.

"Truly," said Prince Florizel. "Now, come and see my mechanical digger."

And holding the oilcan in one hand and the princess's hand in the other, he led the way to the machine shed.

The king looked at Prince Florizel's father.

"There's nothing I can do with her once she's made up her mind," he said wearily.

"I have the same trouble with Florizel," said the second king. "I say, would you like an Alka Seltzer and some breakfast?"

"Would I?" said the princess's father, "I certainly would."

So arm-in-arm they went off together to the palace.

And so Princess Ermyntrude and Prince Florizel were married in tremendous splendour.

The Princess Ermyntrude had a special diamond and gold thread boiler suit made for the wedding and she drove herself to the church in a beautiful bright red forklift truck with E in flashing lights on one side and F picked out in stars on the other and with garlands of flowers on the forks.

Prince Florizel, who had parachuted in for the wedding, wore an emerald and silver thread shirt with silver lamé trousers and had flowers in his beard. On the steps of the church he reached up on tiptoe to kiss the princess as the television cameras whirred and the people cheered, then they ran down the steps and jumped into the royal forklift and steered away through the excited crowds.

"I'm terribly happy," murmured the prince.

"So am I," said the princess. "I say did you bring the hamburgers and the ketchup?"

"All there in the back," said the prince.

"And I remembered the wedding cake. Look at it," said the princess proudly.

"Good heavens," cried Prince Florizel. "It's magnificent."

For the wedding cake was shaped like a giant oilcan.

"Perfect, don't you think?" murmured the princess.

"Absolutely," said the prince.

And they both lived happily ever after.

WHOSE SHADOW?

Aaron Judah

In the afternoon Bruno's friends, Elephancy, Camello, Horso, Oxy, Donkin, Kangar, and Teddy, waved goodbye to Bruno, and set off on the long road back to town. It was afternoon, and the sun was still hot. It seemed to have got hotter. They walked one behind the other, not talking very much. There were seven of them, making seven shadows across the road. Elephancy was leading, with Camello behind, followed by Horso, then Oxy, Donkin, Kangar, and last and littlest of all, Teddy.

Now as they plodded silently along, Camello noticed that Elephancy's shadow in front was larger than his own. He also realized it would be cooler in the shadow, so he called to Elephancy from behind:

"I say, d'you mind if I walk in your shadow?"

"Not in the least," Elephancy generously replied. "You're welcome."

So Camello quickly loped up to his side, and, by keeping his head low, carried on walking with every bit of him in the cool of his big friend's shadow.

It certainly was a relief. The sun was so hot Camello was afraid he'd get sunstroke. Indeed, Horso behind him was thinking much the same, and no sooner had Camello slipped into Elephancy's shadow, when Horso called out:

"I say, Elephancy, d'you mind if I get into your shadow?"

"Not a bit," was the prompt reply. "Join us."

So Horso trotted up and began to walk in the shadow next to Camello. However, when he did this, Camello looked at him from the corner of his eye, and said, "As a matter of fact, Horso, do you realize you're walking in *my* shadow? It's *my* permission you should have asked."

"Rot!" retorted Horso with a toss of his head. "I'm walking in Elephancy's shadow. Any fool can see that."

"Any fool can see it's *my* shadow you're in!" contradicted Camello in a blustering voice. "The proof – "

"Oh, do shut up, Camello!" snarled Elephancy, who was a bit short-tempered on account of the heat. "It's perfectly obvious he's in my shadow! You're *both* in my shadow! Now keep quiet, I don't wish to hear another word about it."

Camello fumed, but didn't utter a word. He was scared if he protested too much Elephancy would turn him out of his shadow. So he looked daggers at Horso and muttered under his breath.

Meanwhile Oxy had come trotting up. "Elephancy," he requested, "may I walk in your shadow too?"

And he was granted kind permission also. Thus Camello, Horso, and Oxy walked on in the cool of Elephancy's shadow. Then Donkin, closely followed by Kangar, ran up, and they too begged permission of Elephancy to walk in his shadow. Pretty soon Camello, Horso, Oxy, Donkin, and Kangar were all walking in the cool of Elephancy's shadow. Only the littlest, Teddy, still walked alone behind. Hot and sweating, his face was screwed up not only to keep out the sun, but in an expression of deep perplexity. He mopped his brow with a sodden handkerchief. The sun blazed relentlessly down. And still Teddy trudged behind.

"Come on, Teddy," urged Kangar, looking round, "come into our shadow."

"Who said that?" roared Elephancy, raising clouds of dust with his great feet. "Who's offering my shadow so freely around? If Teddy wants to come into my shadow he should ask *me*! And that means *me*, and no one else!"

"That's just the trouble," piped up Teddy from behind. "I don't know *whom* to ask. Suppose I get into the shadow beside Kangar, and by and by you go away, I'd still be in the shade, shouldn't I? Whose shadow would that be?"

"Mine!" shouted Camello. "Mine!"

"So I should beg Camello's permission," said Teddy. "But," he continued, "if *you* then went away, Camello, I should still be in the shade. Whose shadow would that be?"

"Mine!" claimed Horso. "Mine!"

"So I should beg your permission, Horso. But if *you* went away, and *Oxy* went away, and *Donkin* went away, I should still be in the shade. Whose shadow would *that* be?"

"Mine, of course!" cried Kangar, raising his head proudly.

"Undoubtedly," agreed Teddy, "because if *you* went away and left me, I'd have no shade at all."

"In that case," decided Kangar, "it's *my* permission you should beg."

"And in that case," interrupted Donkin, "it's my permission *Kangar* should beg."

"Well, then," claimed Oxy, "Donkin should beg *my* permission."

"And Oxy should beg *mine*," claimed Horso.

"And Horso should beg *mine*," stated Camello in tones of finality. "That's what I said from the very beginning! It's all settled now, let's talk no more about it."

"*Nothing's* settled!" roared Elephancy, who'd been boiling up all this time. "You should *all* beg *my* permission! Because if I *did* go away – yes, I'll go away now, and you'll *see* what'll happen!" So saying he rushed over to the other side of the road, taking his great shadow with him, and causing it to fall into the ditch. And he continued marching proudly on that side of the road by himself.

Meanwhile, the heat of the sun had got too much for little Teddy, and without another word he slipped into the shadow beside Kangar. Poor Camello was now, of course, caught in the full glare of the burning sun, while the others continued as they were in the shade. This didn't last long, however. Camello looked down at the others marching comfortably in the shadow, and cried, "I certainly don't see why I should struggle along in the heat while you enjoy the benefits of my shadow!"

So saying, he rushed to the other side of the road, and fell in behind Elephancy. And Horso, who didn't want to suffer in the sun while the others got the benefits of *his* shadow, also rushed to the other side of the road and fell in behind Camello. Then Oxy crossed over and fell in behind Horso, to put Donkin in the sun. Then Donkin fell in behind Oxy to put Kangar in the sun, and finally Kangar fell behind Donkin, leaving Teddy alone, marching in the middle of the road, also in the sweltering heat of the sun. And they tramped proudly on with everyone taking jolly good care that not an inch of his shadow covered another. While all this time, of course, the sun beat unceasingly and mercilessly upon them.

"I warned you this would happen," gloated Elephancy in

front again. "*You're* the ones that are suffering, not I. *I* never had *any* shade in the *first* place! I feel sorry for you, but you must learn, my shadow is *my* shadow, and I'm the one who says who may walk in it, see?"

"*My* shadow is *my* shadow too!" chorused Camello, Horso, Oxy, Donkin, and Kangar just as proudly. At that moment little Teddy, still marching in the middle of the road, suddenly noticed a squirrel trotting next to him.

"Gosh," he said, looking gratefully up at Teddy, "it certainly makes a difference walking in the shade."

"Get away!" cried Teddy, brandishing his fist at the tiny fellow. "You impertinent scoundrel, you're trespassing on my shadow!"

"I'm not doing any harm, please let me stay," pleaded the little fellow.

In reply Teddy gave him a resounding cuff across the ear. The poor squirrel went scuttling up a tree to the cheers and jeers of the others.

"That's the way to deal with people who treat your shadow as if they own it!" they cried. And they marched on well pleased with themselves in spite of the sun. "From now on," declared Teddy, puffing out his chest, "anyone who wants to walk in my shadow will have to pay me a penny."

"I'll charge tuppence," said Kangar, "because my shadow's bigger."

"And I'll charge sixpence," said Donkin.

"And I'll charge one shilling and sixpence!" cried Oxy.

"I'll charge a pound!" shouted Horso.

"I'll charge a hundred pounds!" screamed Camello.

"And I'll charge thousands! Thousands!" trumpeted Elephancy in such a great voice, it echoed from the sky.

However, they had not gone another five yards, when all of a sudden their precious shadows – all seven of them – vanished into thin air. This was because a vast dark cloud that had all this time been creeping up, now covered the face of the sun. So it got cooler at once, but they had little time to enjoy the comfort of it, because the great dark cloud was followed in rapid succession by many other clouds, till soon the whole sky was black. A sharp wind began to blow. It became cooler and cooler. Then with a sudden pitter-patter, large icy drops of rain began to fall.

With a cry, Elephancy, followed by Camello, Horso, Oxy, Donkin, Kangar and Teddy began to run. But long before they reached the outskirts of the town, the storm had caught them. They'd never known anything like it. The rain came down in buckets! It drenched their clothes, ran down their necks, and filled their boots. They sloshed through puddles, shivering and falling over one another. They could hardly see for raindrops! When they were absolutely soaked and bedraggled, the rain stopped. The black clouds began to move away, but before they had gone there appeared in the dark sky something that surprised and dazzled their eyes. It was the biggest, brightest rainbow they had ever seen. They all stopped together and stared up at it in silence.

Donkin said, "I wonder whose rainbow that is."

"Don't be silly!" snorted Elephancy. "Rainbows belong to nobody."

"You're wrong," said Teddy. "Rainbows belong to everybody. And so do shadows."

THE TORTOISES' PICNIC

English Traditional

There were once three tortoises – a father, a mother, and a baby. And one fine spring day they decided that they would like to go for a picnic. They picked the place they would go to, a nice wood at some distance off, and they began to get their stuff together. They got tins of salmon and tins of tongue, and sandwiches, and orange squash, and everything they could think of. In about three months they were ready, and they set out, carrying their baskets.

They walked and walked and walked, and time went on, and after about eighteen months they sat down and had a rest. But they knew just where they wanted to go and they were about halfway to it, so they set out again. And in three years they reached the picnic place. They unpacked their baskets and spread out the cloth, and arranged the food on it and it looked lovely.

Then Mother Tortoise began to look into the picnic baskets. She turned them all upside down, and shook them, but they were all empty, and at last she said, "We've forgotten the tin-opener!" They looked at each other, and at last Father and Mother said, "Baby, you'll have to go back for it."

"What!" said the baby, "me! Go back all that long way!"

"Nothing for it," said Father Tortoise, "we can't start without a tin-opener. We'll wait for you."

"Well, do you swear, do you promise faithfully," said the baby, "that you won't touch a thing till I come back?"

"Yes, we promise faithfully," they said, and Baby plodded away, and after a while he was lost to sight among the bushes.

And Father and Mother waited. They waited and waited and waited, and a whole year went by, and they began to get rather hungry. But they'd promised, so they waited. And another year went by, and another, and they got really hungry. "Don't you think we could have just one sandwich each?" said Mother Tortoise. "He'd never know the difference."

"No," said Father Tortoise, "we promised. We must wait till he comes back."

So they waited, and another year passed, and another, and they got ravenous.

"It's six years now," said Mother Tortoise. "He ought to be back by now."

"Yes, I suppose he ought," said Father Tortoise. "Let's just have one sandwich while we're waiting."

They picked up the sandwiches, but just as they were going to eat them, a little voice said, "Aha! I knew you'd cheat." And Baby Tortoise popped his head out of a bush. "It's a good thing I didn't start for that tin-opener," he said.

WALI DAD THE SIMPLE-HEARTED

Indian Traditional

Years ago a poor old man called Wali Dad lived in a mud hut somewhere in India. He was all alone in the world. Every day he cut grass in the jungle which he sold as fodder for horses. He only earned five annas a day but after he had bought his daily rice he still managed to save half an anna which he would toss into an earthenware chatti that he kept hidden in a hole in the floor.

One night he suddenly decided to count his savings. He tugged the jar from its hole and he gasped in astonishment as a great pile of coins tumbled out.

"Whatever can I do with them?" he wondered. "I don't need anything. I'm happy as I am." So he packed the money into an old sock, rolled himself in a ragged blanket and went to sleep.

Early next morning he staggered away with the sack to a jeweller's shop in a nearby town where he exchanged his savings for a beautiful gold bracelet which he hid under his robe. Next he visited a good friend who travelled over many lands buying and selling goods and camels. They greeted each other politely then Wali Dad said: "Who is the most beautiful and virtuous woman you've ever met?"

"The Princess of Khaistan," the merchant replied instantly. "She is beautiful, good, kind, generous. Everybody agrees on this."

"Well," said Wali Dad, "next time you visit Khaistan give her this gold bracelet. Tell her it is from an old man who believes goodness and kindness are more important than money." With these words he pulled out the bracelet and gave it to his astonished friend. "I'll do what you ask, old friend," he promised.

After some time the merchant journeyed to Khaistan. He found the palace where the princess lived and he delivered the bracelet to her. He also passed on Wali Dad's simple message to the princess.

"Who could have sent this gift?" she wondered. "He must be rewarded."

The princess gave the merchant a camel-load of rich silks for Wali Dad and some money for himself. He set out for home and on reaching Wali Dad's hut he handed the princess's gift to him. The dear old man marvelled at the silks but he was worried. "How can I possibly use them?" he wondered. After thinking hard, he asked his friend if he knew any young and noble princes who could make use of this valuable present.

"I know all the princes from Delhi to Baghdad," the man smiled, "but the most gallant and noble is the Prince of Nekabad."

"Excellent! Take these silks to him with my blessing," Wali Dad exclaimed, very happy to have got rid of them so easily.

The merchant set off and in time, he reached Nekabad. When he was admitted to see the prince he spread out the silks and begged him to accept them as a gift from someone who greatly admired the prince's goodness and nobility.

"How generous," the prince declared, "here is gold for you, honest merchant, and for the giver, you must take twelve of my finest horses."

The merchant travelled back to Wali Dad who, when he

saw the horses coming, rushed into the jungle. "Wonderful," he thought. "They'll need plenty of grass." When he returned with a huge bundle of grass he had a marvellous idea. "Take the horses to the Princess of Khaistan," he told his friend, "and keep two for yourself."

Off went the merchant and this time the princess asked him many questions which he could not answer easily. He simply could not tell her that Wali Dad was a ragged, wrinkled old man! So he said his friend had heard so much about her goodness that he wanted to lay the most precious things he owned at her feet.

The princess asked her father what she should do in return. "You cannot refuse these gifts," he advised, "so we must send him such a valuable present that he cannot send anything better. Then he'll feel ashamed and will stop sending anything more." He ordered that twice as many mules loaded with silver should be sent to Wali Dad as a present from the princess.

The poor merchant hurried back. He arrived at last at Wali Dad's hut. "Excellent," cried he again. "Now I can repay the prince for his gift of those magnificent horses. First, dear friend, you must take six mules then please take the rest to Nekabad."

Off went the merchant and this time the prince also asked many questions. The merchant praised Wali Dad so much that the old man would not have known himself if he had been there! The prince decided that he would send a magnificent royal present back so he ordered his servants to bring twenty horses with gold and silver saddles, twenty camels which could travel many days without a rest and twenty elephants covered with pearls and silver beads. The merchant needed guards to protect this caravan as it streamed back home across the country. Wali Dad saw the dust clouds which the caravan raised and he rushed to cut plenty of grass to sell. When he got back the merchant called out: "Congratulations! All these riches are for you."

"Riches," cried Wali Dad, "what does an old man like me, almost ready to die, want with riches? Take it to the lovely princess but keep two horses, two camels and two elephants for yourself."

The merchant was getting rich but he was getting worried. He decided to make one more journey and this would be the last one.

When the King of Khaistan saw the glittering caravan he felt sure 'Prince' Wali Dad wished to marry his daughter so he decided they should pay him a visit. His best camels, elephants, jewellery and silks were made ready and the merchant was ordered to lead the procession. Poor man, he was now deeply worried.

At last they were only one day's march from the hut and the merchant was ordered to ride ahead to ask Wali Dad to receive the King and Princess of Khaistan.

Wali Dad was eating dry bread and onions when his friend arrived. He tore his beard when he heard the news. He begged the merchant to hold back the royal procession for one day.

After the merchant left, Wali Dad was so upset by the results of his foolish kindness that he decided to end his miserable life. At midnight he went to a high cliff where a deep river flowed far below. He took a little run and – stopped at the very edge. He could not kill himself. He wept with shame. Suddenly soft light shone around him and two lovely spirits appeared.

"Why are you crying?" they whispered. "What are you doing here?"

"I came here to die. Let me tell you my story . . ." The two spirits smiled when they heard the tale and touched him. Instantly his rags changed into rich robes. A jewelled turban covered his head. His grass cutter became a glittering sword. He turned round and saw a magnificent shining palace. He was speechless and frightened too. "Fear not," said the spirits. "Allah rewards the simple and pure-hearted."

They vanished and when the merchant arrived he was just as surprised as Wali Dad, who described what had happened. Hurriedly the king and princess were escorted to the palace where a wonderful feast was ready. Later that day, the king asked Wali Dad if he wished to marry his daughter but he said he was far too old and ugly for the lovely princess. "Wait until you meet my young friend," he said. Hastily he sent the merchant to the Prince of Nekabad, begging him for a visit. The prince could not refuse and as soon as he arrived he fell head over heels in love with the princess. They were married in Wali Dad's magnificent palace and after the wedding everybody went home. Wali Dad lived many more years but though he was now so rich he remained as simple-hearted as when he was Wali Dad the Grass Cutter.

THE ELEPHANT'S CHILD

Rudyard Kipling

In the High and Far-Off Times the Elephant, O Best Beloved, had no trunk. He had only a blackish, bulgy nose, as big as a boot, that he could wriggle about from side to side; but he couldn't pick up things with it. But there was one Elephant – a new Elephant – an Elephant's Child – who was full of 'satiable curtiosity, and that means he asked ever so many questions. *And* he lived in Africa, and he filled all Africa with his 'satiable curtiosities. He asked his tall aunt, the Ostrich, why her tail-feathers grew just so, and his tall aunt the Ostrich spanked him with her hard, hard claw. He asked his tall uncle, the Giraffe, what made his skin spotty, and his tall uncle, the Giraffe, spanked him with his hard, hard hoof. And still he was full of 'satiable curtiosity! He asked his broad aunt, the Hippopotamus, why her eyes were red, and his broad aunt, the Hippopotamus, spanked him with her broad, broad hoof; and he asked his hairy uncle, the Baboon, why melons tasted just so, and his hairy uncle, the Baboon, spanked him with his hairy, hairy paw. And *still* he was full of 'satiable curtiosity! He asked questions about everything he saw, or heard, or felt, or smelt, or touched, and all his uncles and his aunts spanked him. And still he was full of 'satiable curtiosity!

One fine morning in the middle of the Precession of the Equinoxes this 'satiable Elephant's Child asked a new fine question that he had never asked before. He asked, "What does the Crocodile have for dinner?" Then everybody said, "Hush!" in a loud and dretful tone, and they spanked him immediately and directly, without stopping, for a long time.

By and by, when that was finished, he came upon Kolokolo Bird sitting in the middle of a wait-a-bit thorn-bush, and he said, "My father has spanked me, and my mother has spanked me; all my aunts and uncles have spanked me for my 'satiable curtiosity; and *still* I want to know what the Crocodile has for dinner!"

The Kolokolo Bird said, with a mournful cry, "Go to the banks of the great grey-green greasy Limpopo River, all set about with fever-trees, and find out."

That very next morning, when there was nothing left of the Equinoxes, because the Precession had preceded according to precedent, this 'satiable Elephant's Child took a hundred pounds of bananas (the little short red kind), and a hundred pounds of sugar-cane (the long purple kind), and seventeen melons (the greeny-crackly kind), and said to all his dear families, "Goodbye. I am going to the great grey-green, greasy Limpopo River, all set about with fever-trees, to find out what the Crocodile has for dinner." And they all spanked him once more for luck, though he asked them most politely to stop.

Then he went away, a little warm, but not at all astonished, eating melons, and throwing the rind about, because he could not pick it up.

He went from Graham's Town to Kimberley, and from Kimberley to Khama's Country, and from Khama's Country he went east by north, eating melons all the time, till at last he came to the banks of the great grey-green, greasy Limpopo River, all set about with fever-trees, precisely as Kolokolo Bird had said.

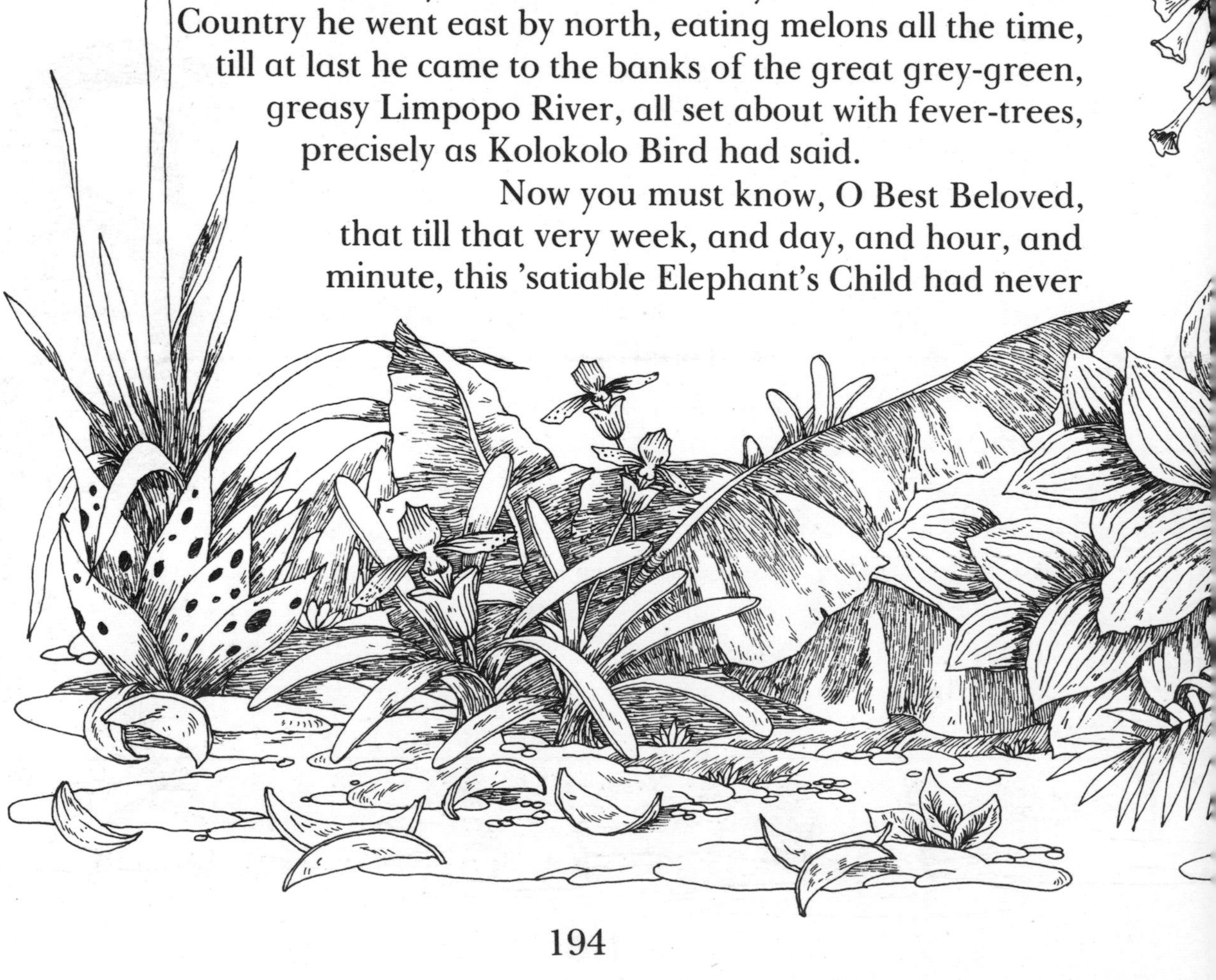

Now you must know, O Best Beloved, that till that very week, and day, and hour, and minute, this 'satiable Elephant's Child had never seen a Crocodile, and did not know what one was like. It was all his 'satiable curtiosity.

The first thing that he found was a Bi-Coloured-Python-Rock-Snake curled round a rock.

"'Scuse me," said the Elephant's Child politely, "but have you seen such a thing as a Crocodile in these promiscuous parts?"

"*Have* I seen a Crocodile?" said the Bi-Coloured-Python-Rock-Snake, in a voice of dretful scorn. "What will you ask me next?"

"'Scuse me," said the Elephant's Child, "but could you kindly tell me what he has for dinner?"

Then the Bi-Coloured-Python-Rock-Snake uncoiled himself very quickly from the rock, and spanked the Elephant's Child with his scalesome, flailsome tail.

"That is odd," said the Elephant's Child, "because my father and my mother, and my uncle and my aunt, not to mention my other aunt, the Hippopotamus, and my other uncle, the Baboon, have all spanked me for my 'satiable curtiosity – and I suppose this is the same thing."

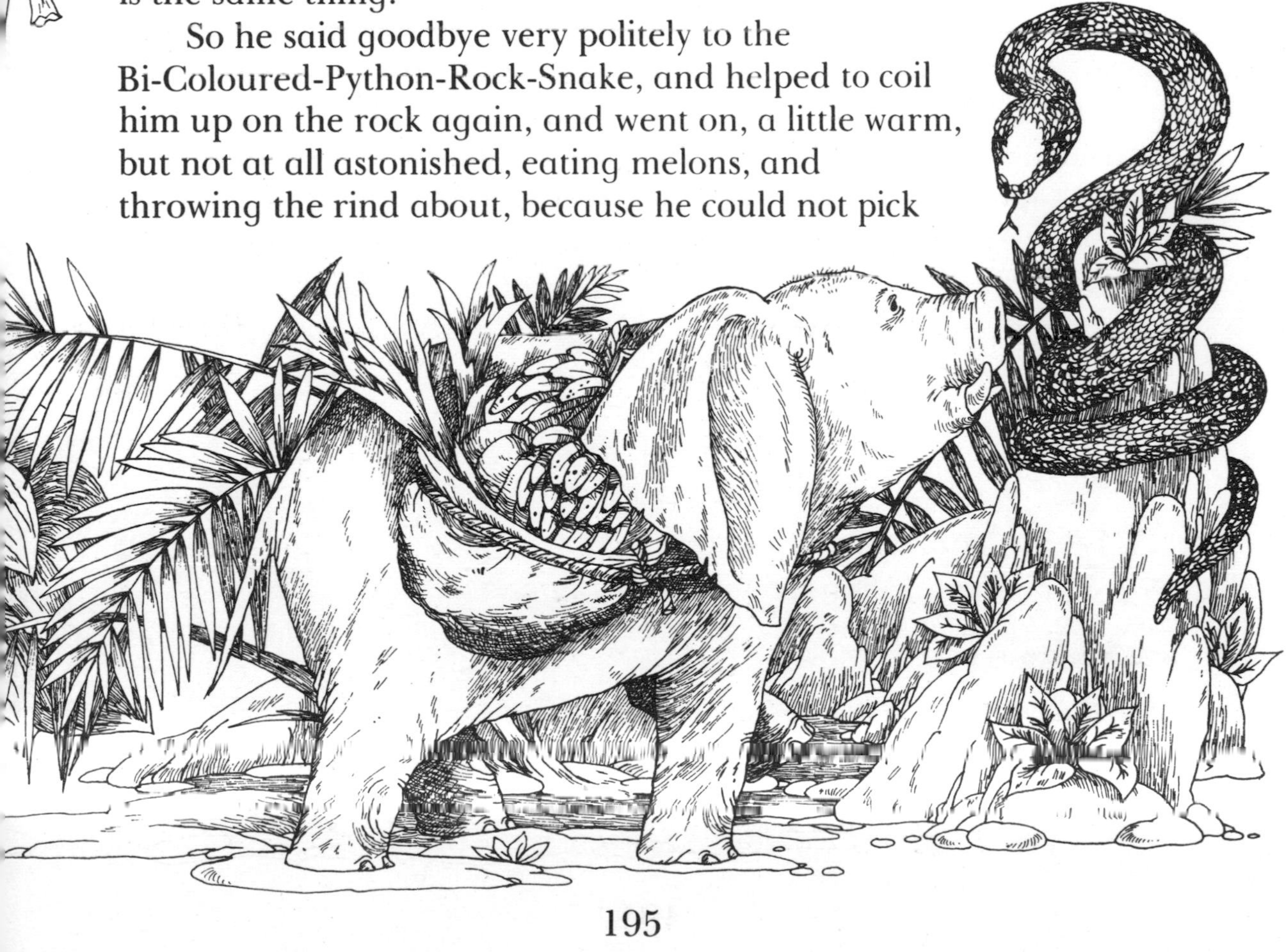

So he said goodbye very politely to the Bi-Coloured-Python-Rock-Snake, and helped to coil him up on the rock again, and went on, a little warm, but not at all astonished, eating melons, and throwing the rind about, because he could not pick it up, till he trod on what he thought was a log of wood at the very edge of the great grey-green, greasy Limpopo River, all set about with fever-trees.

But it was really the Crocodile, O Best Beloved, and the Crocodile winked one eye – like this!

"'Scuse me," said the Elephant's Child politely, "but do you happen to have seen a Crocodile in these promiscuous parts?"

Then the Crocodile winked the other eye, and lifted half of his tail out of the mud; and the Elephant's Child stepped back most politely, because he did not wish to be spanked again.

"Come hither, Little One," said the Crocodile. "Why do you ask such things?"

"'Scuse me," said the Elephant's Child most politely, "but my father has spanked me, my mother has spanked me, not to mention my tall aunt, the Ostrich, and my tall uncle, the Giraffe, who can kick ever so hard, as well as my broad aunt, the Hippopotamus, and my hairy uncle, the Baboon, *and* including the Bi-Coloured-Python-Rock-Snake, with the scalesome tail, just up the bank, who spanks harder than any of them; and *so*, if it's all the same to you, I don't want to be spanked any more."

"Come hither, Little One," said the Crocodile, "for I am the Crocodile," and he wept crocodile-tears to show it was quite true.

Then the Elephant's Child grew all breathless, and panted, and kneeled down on the bank and said, "You are the very person I have been looking for all these long days. Will you tell me what you have for dinner?"

"Come hither, Little One," said the Crocodile, "and I'll whisper."

Then the Elephant's Child put his head down close to the Crocodile's musky, tusky mouth, and the Crocodile caught him by his little nose, which up to that very day, hour, and minute, had been no bigger than a boot, though much more useful.

"I think," said the Crocodile – and he said it between his teeth, like this, "I think today I will begin with the Elephant's Child!"

At this, O Best Beloved, the Elephant's Child was much annoyed, and he said, speaking through his nose, like this, "Led go! You are hurtig be!"

Then the Bi-Coloured-Python-Rock-Snake scuffled down

from the bank and said, "My young friend, if you do not now, immediately and instantly, pull as hard as ever you can, it is my opinion that your acquaintance in the large-pattern leather ulster" (and by this he meant the Crocodile) "will jerk you into yonder limpid stream before you can say Jack Robinson."

This is the way Bi-Coloured-Python-Rock-Snakes always talk.

Then the Elephant's Child sat back on his little haunches, and pulled, and pulled, and pulled, and his nose began to stretch. And the Crocodile floundered into the water, making it all creamy with great sweeps of his tail, and *he* pulled, and pulled, and pulled.

And the Elephant's Child's nose kept on stretching; and the Elephant's Child spread all his little four legs and pulled, and pulled, and pulled, and his nose kept on stretching; and the Crocodile threshed his tail like an oar, and *he* pulled, and pulled, and pulled, and at each pull the Elephant's Child's nose grew longer and longer – and it hurt him hijjus!

Then the Elephant's Child felt his legs slipping, and he said through his nose, which was now nearly five feet long, "This is too butch for be!"

Then the Bi-Coloured-Python-Rock-Snake came down from the bank, and knotted himself in a double-clove-hitch round the Elephant's Child's hind legs, and said, "Rash and inexperienced traveller, we will now seriously devote ourselves to a little high tension, because if we do not, it is my impression that yonder self-propelling man-of-war with the armour-plated upper deck" (and by this, O Best Beloved, he meant the Crocodile) "will permanently vitiate your future career."

That is the way Bi-Coloured-Python-Rock-Snakes always talk.

So he pulled, and the Elephant's Child pulled, and the Crocodile pulled; but the Elephant's Child and the Bi-Coloured-Python-Rock-Snake pulled hardest; and at last the Crocodile let go of the Elephant's Child's nose with a plop that you could hear all up and down the Limpopo.

Then the Elephant's Child sat down most hard and sudden; but first he was careful to say "Thank you" to the Bi-Coloured-Python-Rock-Snake; and next he was kind to his poor pulled nose, and wrapped it all up in cool banana leaves, and hung it in the great grey-green, greasy Limpopo to cool.

"What are you doing that for?" said the Bi-Coloured-Python-Rock-Snake.

"'Scuse me," said the Elephant's Child, "but my nose is badly out of shape, and I am waiting for it to shrink."

"Then you will wait a long time," said the Bi-Coloured-Python-Rock-Snake. "Some people do not know what is good for them."

The Elephant's Child sat there for three days waiting for his nose to shrink. But it never grew any shorter, and, besides, it made him squint. For, O Best Beloved, you will see and understand that the Crocodile had pulled it out into a really truly trunk the same as all Elephants have today.

At the end of the third day a fly came and stung him on the shoulder, and before he knew what he was doing he lifted up his trunk and hit that fly dead with the end of it.

"'Vantage number one!" said the Bi-Coloured-Python-Rock-Snake. "You couldn't have done that with a mere-smear nose. Try and eat a little now."

Before he thought what he was doing the Elephant's Child put out his trunk and plucked a large bundle of grass, dusted it clean against his fore-legs, and stuffed it into his own mouth.

"'Vantage number two!" said the Bi-Coloured-Python-Rock-Snake. "You couldn't have done that with a mere-smear nose. Don't you think the sun is very hot here?"

"It is," said the Elephant's Child, and before he thought what he was doing he schlooped up a schloop of mud from the banks of the great grey-green, greasy Limpopo, and slapped it on his head, where it made a cool schloopy-sloshy mud-cap all trickly behind his ears.

"'Vantage number three!" said the Bi-Coloured-Python-Rock-Snake. "You couldn't have done that with a mere-smear nose. Now how do you feel about being spanked again?"

"'Scuse me," said the Elephant's Child, "but I should not like it at all."

"How would you like to spank somebody?" said the Bi-Coloured-Python-Rock-Snake.

"I should like it very much indeed," said the Elephant's Child.

"Well," said the Bi-Coloured-Python-Rock-Snake, "you will find that new nose of yours very useful to spank people with."

"Thank you," said the Elephant's Child, "I'll remember that; and now I think I'll go home to all my dear families and try."

So the Elephant's Child went home across Africa frisking and whisking his trunk. When he wanted fruit to eat he pulled fruit down from a tree, instead of waiting for it to fall as he used to. When he wanted grass he plucked grass up from the ground, instead of going on his knees as he used to do. When the flies bit him he broke off the branch of a tree and used it as a fly whisk; and he made himself a new, cool, slushy-squshy mud-cap whenever the sun was hot. When he felt lonely walking through Africa he sang to himself down his trunk, and the noise was louder than several

brass bands. He went specially out of his way to find a broad Hippopotamus (she was no relation of his), and he spanked her very hard, to make sure that the Bi-Coloured-Python-Rock-Snake had spoken the truth about his new trunk. The rest of the time he picked up the melon-rinds that he had dropped on his way to the Limpopo – for he was a Tidy Pachyderm.

One dark evening he came back to all his dear families, and he coiled up his trunk and said, "How do you do?" They were very glad to see him, and immediately said, "Come here and be spanked for your 'satiable curtiosity."

"Pooh," said the Elephant's Child. "I don't think you peoples know anything about spanking; but *I* do, and I'll show you."

Then he uncurled his trunk and knocked two of his dear brothers head over heels.

"O Bananas!" said they, "where did you learn that trick, and what have you done to your nose?"

"I got a new one from the Crocodile on the banks of the great, grey-green, greasy Limpopo River," said the Elephant's Child. "I asked him what he had for dinner, and he gave me this to keep."

"It looks very ugly," said his hairy uncle, the Baboon.

"It does," said the Elephant's Child. "But it's very useful," and he picked up his hairy uncle, the Baboon, by one hairy leg, and hove him into a hornets' nest.

Then that bad Elephant's Child spanked all his dear families for a long time, till they were very warm and greatly astonished. He pulled out his tall Ostrich aunt's tail-feathers; and he caught his tall uncle, the Giraffe, by the hind-leg, and dragged him through a thorn bush; and he shouted at his broad aunt, the Hippopotamus, and blew bubbles into her ear when she was sleeping in the water after meals; but he never let anyone touch Kolokolo Bird.

At last things grew so exciting that his dear families went off one by one in a hurry to the banks of the great grey-green, greasy Limpopo River, all set about with fever-trees, to borrow new noses from the Crocodile. When they came back nobody spanked anybody any more; and ever since that day, O Best Beloved, all the Elephants you will ever see, besides all those that you won't, have trunks precisely like the trunk of the 'satiable Elephant's Child.

THE PEAR TREE

Joan Aiken

Long ago, near the beginning of things, when the earth was almost all covered in forest, God sent down the angel Gabriel to see how people were getting along, and if they had enough to eat. There were three poor brothers living at that time who owned nothing in the world but one pear tree. This tree, though, was as beautiful as a miracle, for it was very tall, and bore leaves, flowers, and fruit, all at the same time; the leaves were green as emerald, the flowers white as snow, and the pears fine, large, and glossy, big as your two fists put together. And the tall tree arched over at the top in a graceful curve like a shepherd's crook, as if it were looking down to admire itself.

Well, the angel Gabriel disguised himself as a poor beggar and walked through the forest until he came to this pear tree. The eldest brother was lying under the tree, keeping guard over it to make sure nobody stole the fruit, while the other two took some pears to market.

"Oh, kind Sir," Gabriel besought him, "I am so tired and hungry from travelling through the forest. Could you spare me just one of your beautiful pears?"

"Certainly, poor old man," said the eldest brother. And he picked a basketful of the pears and gave them to Gabriel. "These are from my share of the fruit," he said, "for I can't give you the pears that belong to my brothers."

Next day Gabriel returned to the tree. This time the middle brother was keeping guard over it while the other two carried some of the fruit to market.

"Oh, kind Sir," begged Gabriel, "could you give me a pear or two, just to keep a poor old traveller from dying of hunger?"

"Willingly, you poor old fellow," said the middle brother, and he gave Gabriel some choice pears. "These are mine," he said, "for naturally I can't give you pears from my brothers' share."

On the third day Gabriel came again to the tree and found the youngest brother keeping watch. And he, too, when asked, gave the angel some fruit from his share, explaining that he could not give away his brothers' pears.

Next day Gabriel took the form of a monk and returned to the tree; this time he found all three brothers lying under it in the shade and talking together, while the white blossom fell on them like snow. For it was Sunday and there was no market.

"Come with me, poor brothers," Gabriel said to them, "and I will give you a better life." So, very much astonished, they followed him through the forest.

Presently they came to a great waterfall.

Here Gabriel said to the eldest brother, "Because of your kindness to the poor traveller, you can make any wish and it will be granted."

"In that case," said the eldest brother, "I wish that this waterfall should all be turned to wine, and that the wine should all belong to me."

"Your wish is granted," said Gabriel, making the sign of the

cross with his staff. And on that very instant the waterfall was turned to red wine, and there were men with staves, making casks, men stoking furnaces to make bottles, men collecting the wine. "All this is yours," Gabriel told the eldest brother. "See you put it to good use." And he went on his way with the other two.

Next they came to a clearing in the forest where they saw a great flock of doves.

"Now it is your turn for a wish," Gabriel said to the second brother. "Ask for anything you like, because you gave some of your fruit to the poor beggar."

"In that case," said the second brother, "I wish all these doves could be turned into a herd of cattle, and I wish they belonged to me."

Directly he spoke, Gabriel made the sign of the cross, and all the doves were turned into cattle. Moreover there were herdsmen looking after them, and girls milking them, and women churning butter and making cheese.

"All this is for you," Gabriel said to the second brother. "You will be able to earn yourself a proper living."

And he went on his way with the youngest brother until they came to a long glade in the forest.

"Now," said Gabriel to the youngest brother, "it is your turn for a wish. What would you like?"

The youngest brother said, "I should like a good Christian girl for a wife."

Gabriel scratched his head at that.

"You ask a most awkward thing," he said. "There are only three such girls in the world. One is married already, one has declared that she will never take a husband, and the third has two suitors after her as it is. However, we shall see what we can do."

So he took the youngest brother to the village where the good Christian girl lived. Her name was Militsa. When they entered her house they saw that the table was already covered with gold and silver gifts from the other two suitors, with woven cloth, silks and velvets, and embroidered slippers and carved ornaments. All the youngest brother could put down for his gift was a basket of pears.

"What kind of a present is that?" exclaimed the girl's father scornfully.

But Militsa had seen the youngest brother and liked his looks. "Let it be decided this way," she said to her father. "Let each of them plant a vine, and I will marry the man whose vine first bears fruit."

So this was done, and on the very next day fine grapes were found hanging on the youngest brother's vine. The girl's father could make no further objection, so the two of them were married directly, and went to live in the forest.

Gabriel went back and told God what he had done for the three brothers.

"Are you sure you did right?" said God.

"Of course I did!" said the angel Gabriel.

"Well," said God, "we shall see. Leave them for a year, and then go back to find out how they are getting on."

At the end of a year Gabriel went to visit the eldest brother. As before, he disguised himself in beggar's clothes, and hobbled into the village which had sprung up around the river of wine. There were inns and stalls, shops, swings, and merry-go-rounds; all the

money from these things went to the eldest brother. So Gabriel knocked at the door of his fine large house and asked for a cup of wine.

"The idea! If I gave a cup of wine to every vagabond who came whining to my door, how do you imagine I would make a living?" exclaimed the eldest brother. "Be off, before I call the constables!"

"Humph," said the angel Gabriel at this, and he made the sign of the cross. Directly he did so, the whole village, shops, inns, stalls, and people, and the river of wine, all vanished away; nothing remained but the waterfall dashing over its crag. "That good luck was not for you," Gabriel told the eldest brother. "You were better as you were before. Go back to your pear tree!"

Then Gabriel went to visit the second brother, who was now running a great farm, with dairies, and butcheries where they sold meat, and tanneries where they sold boots and saddles and all kinds of things made out of leather. Gabriel knocked at the second brother's door and asked for a drink of milk.

"A likely thing it would be if I were to give a drink of milk to every beggar who passed through!" exclaimed the second brother. "Be off, before I set the dogs on you!"

"Humph," muttered Gabriel at this, and he made the sign of the cross. At once the farm, the cattle, the shops and stalls, houses and barns, men and women, vanished clean away. Nothing was left but a clearing in the forest and a flock of doves who rose up into the air, wheeled round, and flew off.

"That good luck was not for you. I can see you were better as you were before," Gabriel told the second brother. "Go back to your pear tree."

And he went on his way, scratching his head.

Now he came to the youngest brother, who was living in a tiny hut in the forest with his young wife Militsa. They were so poor that they had to grind up the bark of trees to make flour for their bread.

Gabriel knocked at the door and asked if they could give him a bed for the night and a bite to eat.

"Willingly," said Militsa, and she put a loaf of bark bread in the ashes to bake. And she gave Gabriel a mossy stone to sit on, and a pillow of leaves. But, much to her surprise, when the bread was baked and she took it out, she found that it had turned to a beautiful large loaf of the finest wheat flour.

"God be thanked," she said to her husband, "now we have something better to offer our guest." And she put it before Gabriel on a wooden plate and gave him a wooden cup full of water. But when they came to drink they found the water had changed to wine. And in the morning, when they went outside their hut to speed the traveller on his way, they found that the poor little cabin had turned into a handsome mansion, with everything around it that they could possibly need. So they lived happily for many years.

Gabriel went back to heaven.

"What about the other two brothers?" asked God.

"Some people are best left alone," said Gabriel, and he looked down to where the eldest and the middle brother were lying peacefully under their beautiful tree, with its green leaves, and its glossy fruit, and the white blossom falling like snow.

THE GIANT'S CLEVER WIFE

Irish Traditional

Finn McCoul was a giant who lived in the north of Ireland long ago. He was building a bridge across the sea to Scotland which, to this day, is called The Giant's Causeway. Now Finn wanted a sight of his wife Oonagh whom he loved dearly, so he pulled up a whole fir tree, lopped off its roots and branches to make a walking stick and he set off. Clean over the mountain tops he stepped and was soon at home at the top of Knockmany Hill.

His wife greeted him with a great kiss. "It's pleased I am to see you. Sit down and have the fine dinner I've ready for you." Finn ate twenty eggs, a whole oxen, fifty cabbages and a great pile of delicious loaves, hot from the oven.

They were happy together, chatting over this and that, but Oonagh saw that Finn was troubled. "Why are you putting that great thumb in your mouth?" says she. She knew that Finn was touching a special tooth which could warn him of danger.

"It's himself is coming," says Finn. "It's Cucullin and doesn't he carry a thunderbolt with him that he flattened like a pancake with his fist?"

"Sure and you've beaten other giants, my fine husband," says Oonagh.

"Not one that shakes the entire country with one stamp of his foot. It's disgraced I'll be if I can't beat him," groaned Finn.

"Easy now. Go you and watch out over the mountains for this wee fellow," says Oonagh scornfully, "and by all the saints, I'll prepare a welcome for him. Indeed I will."

"You're a grand girl," declares Finn and out he went, leaving Oonagh to bake some very special loaves with iron griddles inside them. She was boiling a whole side of bacon when she heard a shout from Finn.

"He's coming and he's a terrible sight to see. It's a man-mountain he is. Glory be, I cannot fight him and him with that finger on him too." Everybody knew that all Cucullin's strength came from his forefinger and that without it he was just an ordinary man."

"Quiet, or you'll shame me," says Oonagh. "Now do as I tell you, my darling man, and put on this nightgown. And now this baby bonnet."

"Me! A baby. Never," screeched Finn.

"Stop fussing, man, or it's flattened you'll be! Now into the children's old cradle with you." Oonagh covered him with a quilt and pushed a baby's bottle into his mouth. "Lie there and trust me," Oonagh whispered. "He's coming."

She gave three long whistles, a sign that strangers are welcome and, sure enough, there came a knock on the door like thunder.

"Welcome stranger, come along in," called Oonagh, "and sad it is that my husband isn't at home to greet you."

"Would that be the great Finn McCoul?" and Cucullin himself walked in. "I'm sorry he isn't here for I'm told he is the strongest man in Ireland and I'd love to have the sight of him."

"Not just now you wouldn't," Oonagh said. "Some bastoon of a giant called Cucullin has been threatening him and Finn has rushed off to the Giant's Causeway to teach this boyo a lesson."

"I'm Cucullin," this giant roared, "and I'll be teaching him a lesson, I'm thinking."

Oonagh laughed. "Did you ever see Finn? You'd better hope that his temper has cooled before you meet him for he's much bigger and stronger than you. Sit you down and take a rest. You'll need all your strength if it's Finn you're after fighting."

She turned to the oven and pulled out the bread. "Ah now, if the wind isn't blowing right through the house. While you're waiting, would you just turn the house around for me," Oonagh asked. "That's one of the little things Finn does when he's at home."

Cucullin pulled on his forefinger then went outside, picked up the house and turned it away from the wind. Finn trembled in the cradle. What was his good wife thinking of, he wondered.

Oonagh didn't show her surprise at Cucullin's strength. "Thank you," she said. "Dinner is almost ready but not a drop of water can I give you. Finn was going to find a new spring right behind those rocks but he left in such a terrible temper that he forgot about it. Could you do that little thing for me?"

Cucullin heard water gurgling and knew his job was to crack open the mountain itself. He pulled his finger once, twice, nine times then he bent down and tore a huge hole right through the rocks. This hole is called Mumford's Glen even today.

Finn was terrified by Cucullin's strength but Oonagh calmly invited the giant to sit down and eat. She brought the side of bacon, fifty cabbages, a pile of her special flat loaves with iron griddles inside, and a barrel of butter.

Cucullin picked up a loaf and took a huge bite.

"Cinders and ashes," he thundered. "Here's two of my finest teeth gone. What's in this bread, woman?"

"Why, nothing," Oonagh said in surprise. "It's the very bread I make for Finn and doesn't he eat twelve loaves just for his tea! You'll not be beating Finn McCoul, I'm thinking."

Cucullin seized another loaf. "Thundering thunderbolts, that's another two teeth gone." He was now in a terrible temper but Oonagh smiled sweetly. "It's glad I am that Finn's away for he'd kill you for sure."

The giant roared and stamped round the room. Finn let out a yell as Cucullin bumped into the cradle.

"Now see what you've done," Oonagh scolded. "If you can't eat a decent loaf of bread then at least keep quiet and don't go bothering Finn's fine little son." She winked at Finn. "Is it hungry you are, my pet?" and she gave him an extra special loaf without an iron griddle inside it.

"Flashes of fury," Cucullin growled, nursing his sore jaw as he watched Finn tear off chunks of bread and chew them with happy little noises.

"Is this truly Finn McCoul's son?"

"Indeed it is," Oonagh said proudly. "He only eats a few loaves each day but he is growing strong like his Daddy."

Cucullin was astonished. "That baby must have strong teeth if he can chew that terrible bread." This was Oonagh's chance! "Powerful strong, they are," she agreed. "You can feel them if you wish. You must put your forefinger right in, though, to feel the back ones. Open your mouth wide, little man." And Oonagh pushed Cucullin's finger right inside Finn's mouth.

Snip, snap. Finn bit off the finger. "You've tricked me," Cucullin bellowed as Finn jumped out of the cradle. He hit out with his enormous fists but all his strength had gone with that finger. He turned and ran, down Knockmany Hill and away over the mountains.

Finn watched him go then he and his clever wife enjoyed a grand dinner in peace. After that Finn went on building the Giant's Causeway across to Scotland but maybe he should have asked Oonagh's advice for it never was finished even to this day.

THE CLEVER PEASANT GIRL

Czechoslovakian Traditional

Once upon a time there were two brothers, one of them a wealthy farmer without children and the other a poor peasant with a daughter called Manka. When the girl was twelve years old he sent her to his wealthy brother to work as a goose girl. For two years she worked for her keep and after that time her uncle employed her as a maid.

"Listen, Manka," he said to her one day. "Instead of your wages I'll give you a calf two weeks old. I'll bring it up for you and it'll be more use to you than money."

"Yes, let's do that," Manka replied. From that time on she worked harder than ever before and never cost her uncle a penny. But her uncle was a rogue. For three years Manka served him faithfully, but then her father fell ill and she had to return home. Before leaving she asked her uncle for the calf, which had grown into a good cow.

He made all sorts of excuses, saying that he had never promised anything, that he could not possibly give her something as valuable as a cow, and tried to palm the girl off with a paltry sum of money. But she was by no means satisfied with such a poor bargain. She returned home in tears and told her father what had happened.

As soon as her father was well again he went to the nearby town and brought the matter before the Judge. After asking many questions, the Judge sent for the wealthy brother, who knew that he would have to part with his cow, unless he succeeded in winning the Judge over to his side. The Judge did not quite know what to do for the best: the poor man was in the right, yet he did not want to make the rich man angry.

So the Judge solved the problem in a cunning way. He spoke to each of the brothers separately, and he gave each of them a riddle to solve: "What is sharpest, what is sweetest, what is richest?"

Whoever found the right answer first would have the cow.

The two brothers went on their way home, both of them in a pretty bad temper and puzzled about the riddle.

"Well, what happened?" asked the wife of the rich farmer when her husband returned home.

"I'm in a fine mess," he said, adding a few rude remarks about the Judge.

"What's the matter? You didn't lose your case, or did you?"

"Lose? No, I didn't lose it, and for all I know I may still win."

Then he repeated the riddle the Judge had asked him to solve.

"What a childish riddle! I know all the answers. What could be sharper than our black dog? What could be sweeter than our honey? What could be richer than our money box?"

"Wife, you are right. You've found the answers and the cow will be ours."

With these words the man sat down and enjoyed the good meal his wife had prepared for him.

The poor peasant was rather sad when he returned home to his wife and daughter.

"Well, Dad, how did it go?" Manka wanted to know.

He told her about the riddle.

"Nothing worse than that? Cheer up, Dad, I'll soon find the answers. Just wait till tomorrow. I'll tell you all about it in the morning."

All the same the poor farmer was so worried that he did not sleep a wink all night. In the morning Manka had her answers ready. "Tell the Judge that sleep is the sweetest thing, that the eye is the sharpest, and the earth the richest. But don't tell him who told you."

The father went back to the Judge, wondering if his answers would be the right ones.

The Judge first called the wealthy brother. "I believe I know the answers," the rich farmer said. "For what could be sharper than my dog who hears everything? What could be sweeter than my honey that has been lying in a cask for four years? And what could be richer than the box in which I keep all my money?"

"My dear friend," the Judge told him, shrugging his shoulders, "I do not think that your answers are correct. Let me hear now what your brother has to say."

"Sir, I believe that the sharpest thing is the eye that can see through everything. The sweetest thing is sleep, for sleep can make you forget your worries and give you happy dreams on top of it. And surely the richest thing must be the earth from which all wealth comes."

"You guessed correctly and you shall have the cow. But tell me who it was who told you the answers, for I do not believe that you could find out for yourself."

At first the peasant did not want to admit the truth, but, when the Judge insisted, he owned that his daughter had helped him.

"Well, if your daughter is as clever as that, tell her to come and see me tomorrow. But she must come neither dressed nor undressed, neither by day nor by night, neither on foot nor in a carriage."

Now the poor man was worried again.

"My dear girl," he said to Manka on entering the cottage, "you guessed right. But the Judge simply would not believe that the answers came out of my head, so I had to tell him that you helped me. Now he wants you to come to him yourself. But you must be neither dressed nor undressed, you must go neither by day nor by night, and you must travel neither on foot nor in a carriage."

"Don't worry, Dad. I'll manage all right."

Two hours after midnight Manka got up. She dressed quickly, putting on nothing but a thin sack. On one foot she was wearing a shoe but no stocking, on the other a stocking but no shoe. When the clock struck three – at the very moment when night is about to change into day – she rode to town on her goat.

The Judge was waiting for her. Looking out of his window, he could see for himself how cleverly the girl had solved the tricky problem. He went up to her, saying, "What a clever girl you are. If it suits you I will take you for my wife."

"Why not?" Manka replied casually. "It would suit me very well."

The bridegroom took the arm of his clever and pretty bride and led her into his house. Then he sent for her father and for the tailor who was to make new clothes for Manka, for she needed clothes that would be suitable for the wife of a Judge.

The day before the wedding the Judge asked his wife-to-be

never to meddle in his affairs. That was something he would never stand for. Should she try to interfere in what he considered to be his affairs, she would be sent back to her father.

"I'll do just as you wish," Manka promised.

The following day the wedding took place. Manka became a lady of importance. She soon got used to her new position, she was kind to everyone, and people liked her very much.

One day two young men came to the Judge. One of them was leading a foal. They wanted the Judge to decide which of them was to own the animal. The peasant who owned the mare claimed the foal and the man who owned the stallion also insisted it should be his.

The owner of the stallion was wealthy and important. After he had talked to the Judge alone, the latter decided in his favour.

But the wife of the Judge had overheard the conversation and disliked the unfair way in which her husband had acted. She decided to take matters into her own hands. She approached the farmer who had lost his foal as he was about to leave the house. "Why do you allow the Judge to cheat you like that? The foal should go to the man who owns the mare."

"I too think I've been cheated. But what can a simple man like myself do against the Judge?"

"Leave it to me. If you promise not to give me away I'll give you a sound piece of advice. Tomorrow about noon you must climb the top of Skarman Hill and pretend to be fishing. About that time my husband will be passing by with some of his friends. When he sees you he is sure to ask what you're doing. You must reply with these words: 'If a stallion can have a foal, fish can swim on top of a hill.' "

The man thanked Manka and promised to do as she suggested.

The following day towards noon he could be seen climbing Skarman Hill and throwing out fishing nets from the top of the hill. The Judge, hunting with his friends, soon passed by. He stopped and inquired what the peasant was doing.

"I'm fishing," was the reply.

"Are you mad?" cried the Judge. "Have you ever heard of fish swimming on top of a hill?"

"If a stallion can have a foal, fish can swim on top of a hill."

The Judge turned red as a peony. He beckoned to the peasant to step aside so that he could talk to him without being overheard by his friends.

"All right," he said, "that foal is yours. But you must tell me one thing – who gave you the idea to answer as you did?"

At first the peasant did not want to tell the truth, yet in the end the Judge found out that it was his own wife who had helped the man.

On his return home the Judge did not even look at his wife, let alone speak to her. She guessed what was wrong and waited to see what would happen.

After some time her husband, thoroughly angry, asked her, "Do you remember what you promised the day before we got married?"

"I do."

"Why then did you interfere in my affairs? Why did you side with the peasant against your husband? Why?"

"Because I hate injustice. The poor farmer had been cheated, and you know it."

"This is none of your business. Now go back where you came from. However, I do not want you to think that I am unfair to you, therefore you may take with you whatever you value most."

"Thank you for all your kindness. If you cannot forgive me I will do as you say and return to my father. But let's have one more meal together before we part. Let's be happy together and behave as if nothing had happened."

Quickly Manka went into the kitchen and ordered a good dinner and some of the best wine.

When dinner was served, husband and wife ate and drank a good deal. Manka encouraged the Judge to drink several glasses of the strong wine. When she noticed that he was getting sleepy, she beckoned to the servant to bring a special glass of wine. Then she begged the Judge to drink to her health.

Soon he was fast asleep. Without losing any time Manka ordered the servants to put her husband to bed. Then they picked him up – bed and all – and carried him out of the house to the cottage where Manka's father lived. They arrived at midnight and, after she had explained to her father what had happened, he made them welcome.

The sun stood high in the sky when at last the Judge woke up. He looked round and rubbed his eyes, for he was amazed to find himself in a room he did not know. After a while his wife entered the room. She was dressed in the wide red skirt and the little white bonnet Czech peasant women used to wear.

"Are you still here?" he asked.

"Why shouldn't I be here? I'm at home, after all."

"Why then am I here?"

"Didn't you allow me to take with me what I valued most? Well, it's you I value most. So I've taken you with me."

Laughing, the Judge said, "I forgive you, for I see that you are cleverer than I am. From now on you shall be Judge instead of me."

And so it was. Manka agreed, and ever since she took over the work of her husband all has been well with the people in their district.

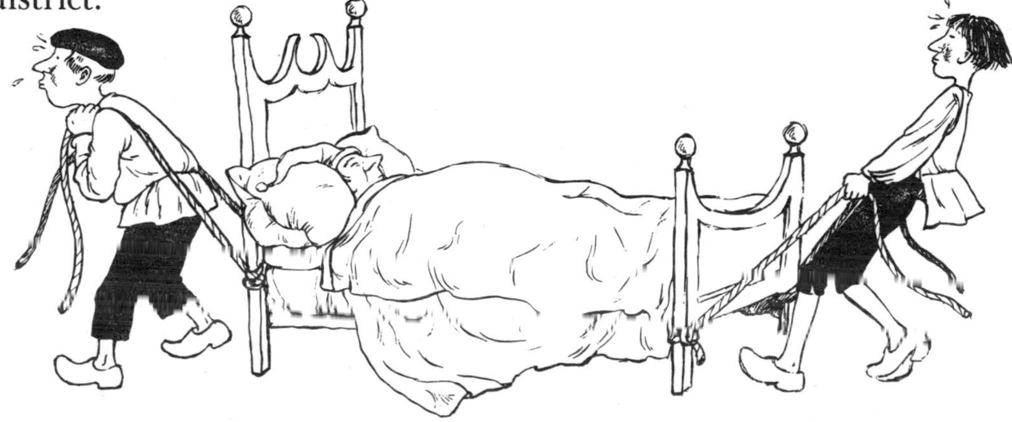

THE ELEPHANT'S PICNIC

Richard Hughes

Elephants are generally clever animals, but there was once an elephant who was very silly; and his great friend was a kangaroo. Now, kangaroos are not often clever animals, and this one certainly was not, so she and the elephant got on very well together.

One day they thought they would like to go off for a picnic by themselves. But they did not know anything about picnics, and had not the faintest idea of what to do to get ready.

"What do you do on a picnic?" the elephant asked a child he knew.

"Oh, we collect wood and make a fire, and then we boil the kettle," said the child.

"What do you boil the kettle for?" said the elephant in surprise.

"Why, for tea, of course," said the child in a snapping sort of way; so the elephant did not like to ask any more questions. But he went and told the kangaroo, and they collected together all the things they thought they would need.

When they got to the place where they were going to have their picnic, the kangaroo said that she would collect the wood because she had got a pouch to carry it back in. A kangaroo's pouch, of course, is very small; so the kangaroo carefully chose the smallest twigs she could find, and only about five or six of those. In fact, it took a lot of hopping to find any sticks small enough to go in her pouch at all; and it was a long time before she came back. But silly though the elephant was, he soon saw those sticks would not be enough for a fire.

"Now *I* will go off and get some wood," he said.

His ideas of getting wood were very different. Instead of taking little twigs he pushed down whole trees with his forehead, and staggered back to the picnic place with them rolled up in his trunk. Then the kangaroo struck a match, and they lit a bonfire made of whole trees. The blaze, of course, was enormous, and the fire was so hot that for a long time they could not get near it; and it was not until it began to die down a bit that they were able to get near enough to cook anything.

"Now, let's boil the kettle," said the elephant. Among the things he had brought was a brightly shining copper kettle and a very large black iron saucepan. The elephant filled the saucepan with water.

"What are you doing that for?" said the kangaroo.

"To boil the kettle in, you silly," said the elephant. So he popped the kettle in the saucepan of water, and put the saucepan on the fire; for he thought, the old juggins, that you boil a kettle in the same way you boil an egg, or boil a cabbage! And the kangaroo, of course, did not know any better.

So they boiled and boiled the kettle, and every now and then they prodded it with a stick.

"It doesn't seem to be getting tender," said the elephant sadly, "and I'm sure we can't eat it for tea until it does."

So then away he went and got more wood for the fire; and still the saucepan boiled and boiled, and still the kettle remained as hard as ever. It was getting late now, almost dark.

"I am afraid it won't be ready for tea," said the kangaroo. "I am afraid we shall have to spend the night here. I wish we had got something with us to sleep in."

"Haven't you?" said the elephant. "You mean to say you didn't pack before you came away?"

"No," said the kangaroo. "What should I have packed anyway?"

"Why, your trunk, of course," said the elephant. "That is what people pack."

"But I haven't got a trunk," said the kangaroo.

"Well, I have," said the elephant, "and I've packed it! Kindly pass the pepper; I want to unpack!"

So then the kangaroo passed the elephant the pepper, and the elephant took a good sniff. Then he gave a most tremendous sneeze, and everything he had packed in his trunk shot out of it – toothbrush, spare socks, gym shoes, a comb, a bag of bull's-eyes, his pyjamas, and his Sunday suit. So then the elephant put on his pyjamas and lay down to sleep; but the kangaroo had no pyjamas, and so, of course, she could not possibly sleep.

"All right," she said to the elephant; "you sleep and I will sit up and keep the fire going."

So all night the kangaroo kept the fire blazing brightly and the kettle boiling merrily in the saucepan. When the next morning came the elephant woke up.

"Now," he said, "let's have our breakfast."

So they took the kettle out of the saucepan; and what do you think? *It was boiled as tender as tender could be!* So they cut it fairly in half and shared it between them, and ate it for breakfast; and both agreed they had never had so good a breakfast in their lives.

KATE CRACKERNUTS

Joseph Jacobs

There was once a king and a queen, as in many lands have been. The king had a daughter called Anne, and the queen had a daughter called Kate. The two lasses loved each other like real sisters.

The queen was jealous of Anne, because she was so much prettier than her own daughter. She knew the henwife who lived in the glen had special powers and asked her how she could spoil the girl's beauty. "Let her fast for a while and then send her to me," the henwife said.

And so the queen did not let Anne eat a morsel all that day, and early the next morning she said to her: "Go, my dear, to the henwife in the glen and ask her for some eggs." On the way out Anne spied a crust in the kitchen and ate it.

When she came to the henwife's home she asked her for eggs. The henwife said: "Lift the lid off this pot here and see." The lassie did as she was bid, but nothing happened. "Go home to the queen and tell her to keep her larder door better locked," said the henwife. Anne did as she was bid.

The queen knew from this message that Anne had eaten something. This time she made sure she fasted properly and kept a close eye on the kitchen, then once again told her to go to the henwife's house.

The girl did as she was bid but on her journey she saw some country folk picking peas by the roadside and when she spoke to them they offered her a few ripe peas.

When she arrived at the glen, the henwife said: "Lift the lid off the pot and you will see." Again, nothing happened. This time the henwife was angry and said: "Tell the queen the pot won't boil if the fire's away." So Anne went home and told this to the queen.

This time, the queen went with Anne to visit the henwife. Anne lifted the lid off the pot and off fell her head and on jumped the head of a sheep. The queen went home happy.

The queen's daughter Kate took a fine linen cloth and wrapped it around her sister's head and took her by the hand and they went off together to seek their fortune.

They walked for many a mile until they came to a castle. Kate knocked and asked for shelter for the night for herself and her sick sister. In fact it was a king's castle, and they were made welcome at once.

This king had two sons and one of them had a strange sickness. No one could find out what was wrong with him. The strange thing was that whoever watched him at night was then never seen again. The king told the two girls this and then he said: "I am now offering a peck of silver to anyone who will sit through the night with him." Kate bravely said she would try.

All went well at first, then at midnight the sick prince rose, dressed, and slipped downstairs. Kate followed quietly behind. He went to the stable, saddled his horse, called his hound, jumped into the saddle, and Kate leapt lightly up behind him. Away rode the prince and Kate through the greenwood. Kate plucked nuts from the trees as they passed and filled her apron with them.

They rode on and on until they came to a green hill. The prince said: "Open, open, green hill and let the young prince in

with his horse and hound." And Kate added softly, "and his lady behind him."

Immediately the green hill opened and they rode in. They entered a magnificent hall, brightly lit and with many beautiful fairies dancing. The fairies surrounded the prince and led him away to dance. Kate quickly hid herself behind the door. She watched the prince dance all night until he fell exhausted on to a velvet couch. Then the fairies fanned him and he rose and danced once more.

Then the cock crew, and the prince jumped back on his horse. Kate jumped up behind him and away they rode.

The king came into his son's bedroom that morning to find his son sleeping softly and Kate cracking nuts by his bedside. Kate said the prince had had a good night and the king rewarded her with a peck of gold. She agreed to watch him the following night.

The second night, all happened as on the first. Away they rode into the greenwood. Kate gathered nuts as she went along and then they entered the green hill. But this time, as the prince danced, Kate saw a fairy-child playing with a wand and she heard one fairy say: "Three strokes of that wand would make Kate's sister as bonnie as she ever was." So Kate rolled nuts towards the fairy-child who toddled after the nuts and let fall the wand, which Kate quickly took and put in her apron. The cock then crew and they rode home as before.

As soon as Kate reached the castle, she rushed to Anne's bedroom and touched her three times with the wand. The sheep's head fell off and her own pretty head was there instead. The girls were overjoyed and hugged each other tightly.

Kate agreed to watch the sick prince a third time, but on one condition, that she should marry the prince after the night was over. All went as on the first two nights. Away they rode into the greenwood, Kate gathered nuts as she went along and then they entered the green hill. This time she saw the fairy-child playing with a birdie. "Three bites of that birdie would make the prince well again," she heard one fairy say. Kate rolled her nuts towards the fairy-child till she dropped the birdie and Kate put it in her apron. The cock crew and they rode home.

Kate cooked the birdie and a savoury smell arose.

"Oh," said the prince, "I wish I had a bite of that birdie." So Kate gave him a bite of the birdie, and he rose up on his elbow.

By and by he cried again. "Oh, to have another bite of that birdie." So Kate gave him another bite, and he sat up in bed.

He said again: "Oh, if I had but a third bite of that birdie." So Kate gave him a third bite and he rose strong and fit, dressed, kissed Kate and said they should marry at once.

When the king came in that morning he found Kate and the prince cracking nuts together by the fire.

His brother, meanwhile, has seen the bonnie Anne and they also agreed to marry: so, the sick son married the well sister, and the well son married the sick sister, and they all lived happy and died happy, and never drank out of a dry cappy.

THE QUEEN BEE

Grimm Brothers

Once there were two happy-go-lucky princes who went into the world to seek adventure. But they wasted all their money and they did not dare return home penniless. Their younger brother went out to find them and said he wanted to join them on their travels.

"How can you expect to make your fortune, Dumhead, when we, your clever brothers, have failed. Don't be stupid," they scoffed. However, Dumhead walked with them and presently they came to an anthill.

"We'll have some fun here," the elder brothers said. "Let's stir up the nest and make the ants rush about."

"Leave the poor little things in peace," said Dumhead, "they're harmless."

On they travelled until they reached a lake where many plump and fluffy ducks were swimming.

"Let's catch some," said the elder princes, "then we can roast them for dinner. What a feast we can have."

"Leave them in peace," said Dumhead, "they're too pretty to eat."

The three of them strolled on and soon they noticed a nest of bees in a tree. Hundreds of bees were buzzing busily around and honey was trickling all down the tree trunk.

"We'll build a fire," the elder brothers decided, "then the bees will be smoked out. They can't sting us and we can take all the honey we like." Dumhead cried out quickly: "Leave the busy bees in peace to make their sweet honey." So they did.

Next they came to a castle but there was something very wrong there. Servants, soldiers, horses, fish, birds, all were made of stone! The brothers walked around hoping to find something alive but there was only a stony silence. Then they noticed a door with a tiny shutter and three locks. The locks would not move so they lifted up the shutter and when each brother peeped inside, they saw a room and a little grey man sitting at a table. They called once, twice, and the third time the little fellow jumped up, unlocked the door and led the brothers to a table filled with good things to eat. He said not a word while the brothers enjoyed a splendid meal, then he silently showed them three comfortable bedrooms and they went straight to sleep.

Early next morning the little man showed the eldest prince a stone on which many words were carved. These described three tasks which if done properly could break the enchantment on the castle. The prince read the first task. "Easy," he thought to himself. "One thousand of the princess's pearls lie under the grass in the forest. Every pearl must be found by sunset or the searcher will be turned to stone."

The prince found the forest. He pulled away rocks and he scrabbled under the moss but by sunset he had only found one hundred pearls. Instantly he was turned into a stone statue.

The next day the little man let the second prince try his luck but he collected just two hundred pearls so he became a stone statue too.

On the third day Dumhead was given his chance. He went off and searched busily but it was hard work. Then he noticed the Ant King, followed by thousands of little ants. "You were kind to us," the Ant King said, "now we'll help you." And the ants crawled in the grass and pushed exactly one thousand pearls towards Dumhead. He thanked King Ant and rushed back to the castle to read what the next task was.

"The key to the princess's room lies at the bottom of a lake nearby. It must be found by sunset or the seeker will be turned into stone."

"How can I find a key in there?" said Dumhead when he had found the lake. "I can't even swim!" But the ducks on the water quacked cheerily: "You saved our lives. Now we'll save yours!" And one duck dived under the water and when it came up, it was holding the key in its beak. Dumhead thanked the ducks and returned to the castle to read about the last and hardest task.

"The king's three daughters lie asleep in this castle. The seeker must choose the youngest and sweetest or he will be turned to stone."

Dumhead soon found the bedroom but to his horror all three sleeping princesses were exactly alike, except for one thing. Before going to bed the eldest had eaten some sugar, the second some treacle and the youngest had licked the honey spoon. Dumhead was in despair. Which princess should he choose? He heard a buz-z-z and the Queen Bee flew into the room. "You saved my nest and my honey so now I'll save you," she hummed as she tasted the lips of each girl. "This is the sweetest and youngest," she said when she tasted the honey on one girl's lips.

Dumhead thanked the Queen Bee before she flew away and at that moment birds started singing, horses neighed and everybody in the castle laughed and cheered as they came alive again. The older princes hugged their brother, "We'll never call you Dumhead again because we were the foolish thoughtless ones." Joyfully then the oldest one fell in love with the oldest princess, the middle one loved the middle princess and kind gentle Dumhead married the sweetest and youngest princess. In time he became king because through his kind heart he had broken the enchantment of the castle.

SLEEPING BEAUTY

Charles Perrault

There once lived a king and queen who had no children, which made them very sad. Then one day, to the queen's delight, she found she was going to have a baby. She and the king looked forward with great excitement to the day of the baby's birth.

When the time came, a lovely daughter was born and they arranged a large party for her Christening. As well as lots of other guests, they invited twelve fairies, knowing they would make wishes for their little daughter, the princess.

At the Christening party, the guests and the fairies all agreed that the princess was a beautiful baby. One fairy wished on her the gift of Happiness, another Beauty, others Health, Contentment, Wisdom, Goodness . . . Eleven fairies had made their wishes when suddenly the doors of the castle flew open and in swept a thirteenth fairy. She was furious that she had not been invited to the Christening party, and as she looked around a shiver ran down everyone's spine. They could feel she was evil. She waved her wand over the baby's cradle and cast a spell, not a wish.

"On her sixteenth birthday," she hissed, "the princess will prick herself with a spindle. And she will die." With that a terrible hush fell over the crowd.

The twelfth fairy had still to make her wish and she hesitated. She had been going to wish the gift of Joy on the baby but now she wanted to stop the princess dying on her sixteenth birthday. Her magic was not strong enough to break the wicked spell but she tried to weaken the evil. She wished that the princess would fall asleep for a hundred years instead of dying.

Over the years the princess grew into the happiest, kindest and most beautiful child anyone had ever seen. It seemed as though all the wishes of the first eleven fairies had come true. The king and queen decided they could prevent the wicked fairy's spell from working by making sure that the princess never saw a spindle.

So they banned all spinning from the land. All the flax and wool in their country had to be sent elsewhere to be spun. On their daughter's sixteenth birthday they held a party for the princess in their castle. They felt sure this would protect her from the danger of finding a spindle on her sixteenth birthday.

People came from far and wide to the grand birthday ball for the princess and a magnificent feast was laid out. After all the guests had eaten and drunk and danced in the great hall, the princess asked if they could all play hide-and-seek, which was a favourite game from her childhood. It was agreed the princess should be the first to hide, and she quickly sped away.

The princess ran to a far corner of the castle and found herself climbing a spiral staircase in a turret she did not remember ever visiting before. "They will never find me here," she thought as she crept into a little room at the top. There to her surprise she found an old woman dressed in black, sitting on a chair spinning.

"What are you doing?" questioned the princess as she saw the spindle twirling, for she had never seen anything like it in her whole life.

"Come and see, pretty girl," replied the old lady. The princess watched fascinated as she pulled the strands of wool from the sheep's fleece on the floor, and twirling it deftly with her fingers fed it on to the spindle.

"Would you like to try?" she asked cunningly.

With all thoughts of hide-and-seek gone, the princess sat down and took the spindle. In a flash she pricked her thumb and even as she cried out, she fell down as though dead. The wicked fairy's spell had worked.

So did the twelfth good fairy's wish. The princess did not die, but fell into a deep deep sleep. The spell worked upon everyone else in the castle too. The king and queen slept in their chairs in the great hall. The guests dropped off to sleep as they went through the castle looking for the princess.

In the kitchen the cook fell asleep as she was about to box the pot boy's ears and the scullery maid nodded off as she was plucking a chicken. All over the castle a great silence descended.

As the years went by a thorn hedge grew up around the castle. Passers-by asked what was behind the hedge, but few people remembered the castle where the king and queen had lived with their lovely daughter. Sometimes curious travellers tried to force their way through, but the hedge grew so thickly that they soon gave up.

One day, many many years later, a prince came by. He asked,

like other travellers, what was behind the thorn hedge, which was very tall and thick by now. An old man told him a story he had heard about a castle behind the thorns, and the prince became curious. He decided to cut his way through the thorns. This time the hedge seemed to open out before his sword and in a short while the prince was inside the grounds. He ran across the gardens and through an open door into the lovely old castle.

Everywhere he looked – in the great hall, in the kitchens, in the corridors and on the staircases – he saw people asleep. He passed through many rooms until he found himself climbing a winding staircase in an old turret. There in a small room at the top he found himself staring in wonder at the most beautiful girl he had ever seen. She was so lovely that without thinking he leaned forward and gently kissed her.

As his lips touched her, the princess began to stir and she opened her eyes. The first thing she saw was a handsome young man. She thought she must be dreaming, but she looked again and saw he was really there. As she gazed at him she fell in love.

They came down the turret stairs together and found the

whole castle coming back to life. In the great hall the king and queen were stretching and yawning, puzzled over how they could have dropped off to sleep during their daughter's party. Their guests too were shaking their heads, rubbing their eyes, and wondering why they felt so sleepy. In the kitchen, the cook boxed the ears of the pot boy, and the scullery maid continued to pluck the chicken. Outside horses stamped and neighed in their stables, dogs barked in the yards, while in the trees birds who had stayed silent for so long burst into song. The hundred-year spell had been broken.

The princess told her parents how much she loved the handsome young man who had kissed her, and they were delighted to find he was a prince from a neighbouring country. The king gave them his blessing and a grand wedding was arranged.

At the wedding party the princess looked more beautiful than ever, and the prince loved her more every moment. The twelve good fairies who had come to her Christening were invited once again and were delighted to see the happiness of the prince and princess. Towards evening the newly married pair rode off together to their new home in the prince's country, where they lived happily ever after.

JORINDA AND JORINGEL

Grimm Brothers

In the middle of a deep forest there once stood a gloomy castle where an evil old woman lived. By day she flew around in the shape of an owl or she crept about as a cat. At night she turned into a witch who liked nothing better than playing cruel tricks on people. Around her castle she drew a magic circle and whenever a young man stepped inside he became rooted to the ground instantly, as if turned to stone. He could neither move nor speak until the witch set him free. If a young girl crossed this magic line she was changed into a bird, carried to the castle by the witch, then pushed into a basket. The witch had seven thousand baskets already in her hall, each holding a beautiful bird.

Not far away, a young shepherd called Joringel loved a sweet girl named Jorinda. One warm summer evening they went for a walk in the forest. Birds twittered cheerfully and the evening sun shone through the leafy branches overhead.

"How peaceful it is," said Joringel, "but we mustn't forget about the witch's castle and her magic circle."

"Don't worry," laughed Jorinda, "we're nowhere near it yet." And they wandered along a path, chattering happily.

Suddenly the birds fell silent. The sun was setting and in the half-light they could not see the proper path clearly.

"I'm frightened," Jorinda whispered, "there's something horrible around us, I can feel it," and she burst into tears.

Joringel stared about him. He glimpsed some grey stones through the bushes just as Jorinda began to sing mournfully:

"In yonder tree I see a dove that is crying, crying,
He is searching for his love, crying, cry . . . twee twee, jug jug,"

Joringel turned. While she was singing Jorinda had turned into a nightingale and an owl was swooping over her, screaching loudly:

"Tu who, tu who, look what has happened to you . . . u u u . . ."

To his horror, Joringel found he could not move and he

watched helplessly as the owl turned into the witch, seized the nightingale in her skinny claws and hobbled off, cackling loudly.

At last the witch came back, eyes gleaming and singing hoarsely:

"When the moonbeams fall on the basket in my hall,
Joringel goes free but the bird stays with me!"

When the faint moon peeped through the trees Joringel could move again. On his knees he begged the witch to bring Jorinda back.

"You'll never see her again," she cackled cruelly. "Never, never!"

He rushed blindly away from this horrible creature until he reached a faraway village where he found work as a shepherd. Every day he thought about Jorinda until one night he dreamt that he picked a blood-red flower with a heart of pearl. Everything he touched with this flower became disenchanted and Jorinda was returned to him. When he woke he set off and searched across valleys and mountains for eight weary days. On the ninth morning he found a beautiful bright-red flower with a sparkling dewdrop in its petals, more wonderful than the finest pearl. Carefully he picked this flower then he tramped day and night without rest until he reached the enchanted castle.

Boldly he strode through the magic circle. He was not held fast this time. He reached the castle door and touched it with the flower. The locks sprang open. Now he hastened to a hall where he saw seven thousand birds singing sweetly in seven thousand baskets. But which was Jorinda? As he looked desperately around, he spied the witch stealing away with a basket. Hurling himself forward, he touched her and the basket with the flower. Instantly Jorinda stood before him while the witch shrivelled away, all her magic power lost. He touched every basket and soon seven thousand grateful girls were laughing and cheering him, but Joringel and Jorinda danced home, where they married and lived happily together for many many years.

THE FROG PRINCESS

Russian Traditional

Long ago the Tsar of Russia had three handsome sons. One day when he thought they were old enough, he called them together.

"I long to have some grandchildren before I die," he said, "so it is time for you to marry, dear sons."

"We'll do as you ask, dear father," they replied, "but you must tell us who you want us to marry."

The Tsar smiled. "Take your bows and arrows into the fields beyond this palace. Loose one arrow and wherever it falls, there look for your bride."

The three princes bowed politely and went to the fields. There each one shot away one arrow from his bow.

The eldest son's arrow landed in a nobleman's courtyard and his daughter picked it up. The second son's arrow landed in a rich merchant's garden where his daughter picked it up. But the arrow of Prince Ivan, the youngest son, flew into the air and landed in a swamp. He chased after it until he found a frog sitting on a leaf, holding his arrow in her mouth.

"Frog, frog, give me back my arrow," he demanded.

"Certainly, if you will promise to marry me."

"Ugh, marry a slimy frog! Yet, I must obey my father." So Prince Ivan put the frog in his pocket and returned home.

Later the Tsar's eldest son married the nobleman's daughter, the middle son married the rich man's daughter and poor Prince Ivan married a frog!

Presently the Tsar called his sons together again and said: "I wish to see which wife can sew the best. Let them each make me a fine shirt by tomorrow."

The two elder princes went happily to their wives but Prince Ivan went sadly away and the frog hopped over to him.

"Why are you upset, my prince? What troubles you?" she croaked.

"My father wants you to sew him a shirt by tomorrow."

"Is that all? Go to bed, husband. Leave this to me."

The prince went to sleep and the frog hopped to the doorstep. She cast off her frog-skin and turned into Vassilisa the Wise, a beautiful and clever princess. She clapped her hands and cried: "Come, my trusted maids. Get to work and sew me a fine shirt fit for a king, just as my father was."

Prince Ivan woke at dawn. On the table he saw a shirt wrapped in a pretty cloth while the frog hopped about on the floor. Thankfully, he took the shirt to his father who was receiving the gifts from his other sons. The eldest one laid out his shirt.

"This shirt is not fit for a servant!" the Tsar said crossly. The middle son laid out his shirt and the Tsar grumbled again:

"This shirt is not fit for the poorest peasant!" Prince Ivan laid out his shirt, richly embroidered in gold and silver. The Tsar's eyes shone.

"This shirt is truly fit for a king!" he exclaimed.

The elder brothers went home muttering to each other. "What is Ivan's wife? She isn't a proper frog. She must be a witch!"

Later, the Tsar called his sons again. "Let your wives bake some bread," he said, "I wish to know who is the best baker now."

Prince Ivan went home, looking miserable again. The frog asked him, "Why are you so unhappy, husband?"

"My father wants you to bake bread by tomorrow morning," he replied.

"Is that all? Go to bed and leave this to me," she said.

The brothers' wives sent an old woman to find out how the frog was going to bake her bread. But the frog guessed what they were up to. She kneaded some dough then threw it into the stove and left it to burn. The old woman ran back and told the other wives what she had seen and they copied this exactly.

Meanwhile the frog took off her frog-skin and changed into Vassilisa. She clapped her hands and her servants appeared. "Come, my clever maids, get to work and bake me a loaf like the ones I used to eat in my father's palace."

When Prince Ivan woke next day, there on the table was a loaf covered with wonderful designs, castles, gardens and tiny people. He was delighted. He wrapped the loaf in a sparkling

white cloth and took it to the Tsar who was looking at the loaves the elder sons had brought. Their wives had tossed their dough into the stove as the old woman had said and their loaves were burnt black. The Tsar glared at the first son's loaf and threw it aside. He took the second son's loaf and threw that aside. But when Prince Ivan uncovered his loaf the Tsar exclaimed: "This bread is fit for the royal table. This very evening, I invite you all to a feast, sons and daughters-in-law."

Again Prince Ivan went home, very downcast. "My father has invited us to the palace," he said, "but how can I take a frog?"

"Don't worry," said the frog. "Go to the feast alone and I'll come later. When you hear thunder, tell everybody it is your frog-wife arriving in her carriage."

So Prince Ivan went alone. His family were dressed in fine clothes and they stood and jeered at him. "Why didn't you carry your wife in a matchbox? Or has she hopped back to the swamp?"

Suddenly, there was a crash of thunder which made the palace walls shake. The guests shrieked but Prince Ivan said: "Do not worry, it is only my dear wife arriving." He hoped that was the truth!

At that moment a golden carriage pulled by six magnificent horses drew up at the palace gates and out stepped Vassilisa. She wore a silvery blue gown and a sparkling diamond crescent in her hair. Ivan could scarcely believe his eyes. Was this really his frog-wife? The Tsar was enchanted with this beautiful princess and at once he led her to the table to begin the splendid feast.

When everyone had finished eating, the dancing began. "Let's see if a frog can dance," the wives whispered. "She'll hop all over the floor."

But they were wrong. Vassilisa glided lightly across the floor with her husband and soon everybody wanted to dance with the lovely princess.

Then secretly Prince Ivan slipped away. He wanted to be sure Vassilisa was his wife: so when he reached his house and saw a frog-skin lying there, he joyfully hurled it into the fire. "My beautiful wife can never turn into a frog again," he laughed, and he went back to the palace.

When the Tsar's wonderful party ended, Prince Ivan and Vassilisa went home. She searched everywhere for her frog-skin but when Ivan told her he had burned it, she burst into tears.

"Oh husband," she wept, "what have you done? I only had to be a frog for three more days then this cruel spell would be broken. Now Giant Koschei's magic powers will make me go back to his castle." And she vanished.

Prince Ivan wasted no time. He called for his horse and galloped off to find his wife. He searched far and wide but he did not find Giant Koschei's castle.

After many days, he was resting, tired and miserable, when an old man came into sight. "What troubles you, my son?" he asked. He spoke in such a kind way that Prince Ivan poured out the whole story. The old man smiled and pulled out a ball from his pocket. "Take this," he said, "roll it before you. Wheresoever it goes be sure you follow close behind. I wish you good fortune."

Prince Ivan thanked the old man and jumped on his horse. Quickly, he threw the ball and galloped away. The ball stopped at the feet of a huge bear. Ivan pulled out his bow but before he could aim his arrow, the bear shouted: "Do not kill me. You may need me one day." Meantime the ball went on rolling and bounced up to a drake which quacked loudly: "Do not kill me with your bow and arrow. You may need me one day." Ivan saw the ball rolling away so he followed until it stopped by a lake where a hare was resting and a pike was swimming. "Do not kill us," they said. "You may need us one day." So he spared their lives and dashed after the ball once more. This time it came to rest outside a broken-down hut where a witch called Baba-Yoga was crouched.

"So, you are the prince who married the frog," she cackled as Ivan galloped up. "Vassilisa the Frog is a prisoner in Giant Koschei's castle over the hill. You'll have to kill him before you can set her free. But you'll never overcome Koschei." She laughed horribly then she noticed the ball lying by her door. Instantly she stopped laughing. "Who gave you this?" she asked fearfully.

Prince Ivan told her about the kind old man and Baba-Yoga trembled. "That was a powerful wizard you spoke to. I'd better help you. This is what you must do. Koschei's death will be by a needle, the needle is in an egg, the egg in a duck, the duck in a hare, the hare in the chest at the top of the tallest tree outside Koschei's castle."

She pointed with her scrawny arm and Ivan hurried on but when he found the tallest tree, the chest was too high to reach. Then he saw the bear ambling along. To his astonishment, it seized the tree and threw it to the ground. The chest fell out and burst open. Out of the chest scampered a hare and another hare caught it and tore it to pieces! Out of the pieces flew a duck and in a twinkling, the drake struck it so hard that it dropped an egg deep into the lake. Ivan was desperate until he saw a pike swimming ashore carrying the egg! Quickly he cracked it open and snatched up the needle which was hidden inside. He turned it this way and that and suddenly he saw Giant Koschei standing by the castle gate. Prince Ivan twisted the needle and as he did so, Koschei groaned. At once Ivan bent and twisted the needle again and Koschei groaned even louder. At last the needle broke and at that moment, Giant Koschei fell down dead.

The prince jumped over him and ran inside. He unlocked door after door and set free many people captured by wicked Koschei. At last he found Vassilisa. The spell was now broken for ever and after they journeyed home they lived in happiness for many more years.